Also by Ambrose E. Korn, Jr.

Smelling Lilac

ISBN-10: 1453817638
EAN-13: 9781453817636

Library of Congress Control Number: 2010913874

Deutschtown's
PIGEON HILL

By
Ambrose E. Korn Jr

"No man is rich enough to buy back his past."

Oscar Wilde - Irish Writer

Acknowledgments

Special Thanks to:

William (Bill) Benzer for proofreading the manuscript and providing German-American background literature and sandlot football remembrances.

Donald Ford for proofreading the manuscript and along with my sister, Marlene, for a lifetime of favors.

Kathy Murphey who greatly assisted in the birth of my Pigeon Hill novel.

Jamie Wincovitch for proofreading the manuscript and doing those other computer geek necessities prior to publication.

My wife, Doris, for her unselfishness and for caring to my every need.

For My Brother

James Cornelius Korn

Born in the twilight of the Industrial Age - Died in the
dawning of the Information Age.

On a lumpy mattress, snuggling beneath a feathered blanket,
we kept warmer by the heat from our loyal dog, Pal, against
our toes. Somewhere on the outside of our bedroom's frosty
windowpane, and yet unbeknownst to you, awaited your future
bride, Sophia. Your smiling blue eyes and gentle ways are
missed by her, sons Jimmy and Danny, daughter-in-law Tina
and your Forever Valentine, Nicole. Rest in peace, brother.

"...And if I am dead, as dead I well may be
You'll come and find the place where I am lying
And kneel and say an "Ave" there for me..."
Danny Boy Lyrics

Prologue

It was a perfect hideaway for discreet couples. Off the main highway with dimmed lighting throughout the table and chair seating area. The waitress, older than most waitresses usually found in highway roadhouses, radiated a personality revealing she'd seen it all before, and whose lips were sealed should a jilted wife come snooping around. She expected big tips and got them.

Sitting at a table in the darkest corner of the roadhouse with Mrs. Bentley, Otto gave the waitress a quarter to drop in the juke box. He told her what records to play. When the *Tennessee Waltz* began playing, Otto coaxed Mrs. Bentley onto the dance floor and once she was in his arms, he felt confident that he was making headway with the beautiful, but reluctant housewife and mother of twins.

Normally, he'd have abandoned the chase for an adulterous affair if he'd not made progress after two dates, but he was unable to walk away from this woman in his arms. She was too beautiful to pass on. At the risk of getting caught and losing all he'd worked for in a divorce settlement, he nevertheless put that danger in the back of his mind as unlikely.

He was fixated on seducing Mrs. Bentley, and after months of picking her up once a week at a trolley stop and getting nowhere, tonight he felt he was making progress. He persuaded her to come to his favorite hideaway, got a highball into her, and now she was in his arms on a dim lit dance floor. It was looking good for success. Perhaps tonight.

"I've been longing to hold you like this since the first time I picked you up at the trolley stop," he whispered in her ear.

She laid her head on his wide shoulder. "I'm scared Otto. My husband will kill me if he catches me cheating. I like being with you. I enjoy talking with you, but it's not safe for me, going this far, out dancing while he's at work."

He put his hand under her chin and raised her face to his eyes. "You're too beautiful for such a fool; he should be showing you off, dressing you in clothes that enhance your looks. You're the most beautiful woman I've ever held and your idiot husband hides you in improper fitting clothes. When you walk by a man, the way you move, the way you smile, you might as well be naked to their eyes, that's how sexy you are. You can't hide what moves beneath those loose clothes from a man's hormones."

They were shuffling in a small area on the dance floor. One other couple was on the floor.

"What I see and imagine drives me crazy, and most other men, I'm certain." He kissed her lightly on the lips. She didn't protest, only laid her head back onto his chest. The song ended and he escorted her back to their table. Things were looking up and the goal of seducing the beautiful Mrs. Bentley was within reach.

"I must get home," she said and started putting on her coat.

"One more drink. You've got plenty of time before your husband comes home from work."

"I know Otto, but I'm scared and nervous. I can't rush into something that might get me murdered. I have children to think of."

"Okay." He reluctantly agreed. "We'll go."

They put their coats on and left the roadhouse.

Otto's thoughts were zooming wildly. So close and yet so far away from her Garden of Eden. He had to control himself, be patient. If he could do that, in time he'd be victorious. He had to control his yearnings which were screaming to be fulfilled. He'd kiss her again inside of the car and see how far that would get him. He was going to seduce Mrs. Bentley even if it killed him.

PART ONE

Christmastime 1949

"All things change - Nothing perishes"
-Ovid Roman Poet

CHAPTER ONE
The Incident

Walking at a measured pace toward the public steps, Jake felt something amiss when spotting the car nearby. He often climbed the steps after visiting Susan, but this cold night, with a car parked against the curb, its headlights off, engine running, yet empty of driver and passengers chilled the night air even more. Passing slowly by the dark sedan, he could see by the glow of the overhead street light that the car was very new. No one he knew owned a car near as new. He thought of skipping the steps and hiking a longer way home, up steep and twisting Brookhurst Roadway. A light snowfall had stopped earlier in the evening and the moon glowed bright. He could easily see far up the hillside steps as they made their way over brush, under snow covered tree branches, and at times straddled close to the edge of a cliff. He couldn't see anyone. He studied the footprints in the snow. Someone had walked around the front of the car leaving a set of prints, but the steps had many boot prints. The cold air and distress he was suffering over Susan hastened his longing to get home and into bed. There he could mope in warm darkness over his desire for her. He pulled his tousle cap further down over his ears, and grasping the cold wooden handrail began climbing the steps as fast as he could, taking them two at a time.

The further up he'd climb, the more of Brookhurst he saw over the handrail. The old row houses standing on each side of the road adorned with snow and Christmas lights were looking quaint and pleasing to him. He could see the red and cream-colored trolley worming its way up the roadway heading to the crest of Pigeon Hill and to the loop. After turning the loop, the trolley will head back down the roadway, off of Pigeon Hill, and travel through the remainder of Deutschtown before crossing the river to downtown Pittsburgh. Jake seldom had money, but if he did have coins handy, he would've never dropped them into a streetcar fare box just to keep from walking. Onward he climbed, leaning forward, climbing swiftly, his teenage leg muscles enduring the demanding climb with ease, his slim body moving with the agility of youth.

Suddenly he came upon the couple. They were standing on the landing ahead of him, arm in arm, kissing. The woman spotted Jake first and jerked free and away from the groping hands of the man. The startled man jumped backwards. Jake froze in place, legs separated as if still climbing. He was too stunned to reach out to the man slipping on the snow, crashing against the railing, and breaking through the wood. In seconds, the man was gone, falling from the landing, rolling and tumbling and yelling before falling over the cliff. The woman moaned loud creepy sounding utterances and somewhere a dog started barking. The back porch light of a row house below came on.

Jake looked at the woman, her hands swiftly rearranging clothing. Stepping up onto the landing, he kicked pieces of the splintered handrail over the side. "Are you okay Mrs. Bentley?"

"Yes," she blurted out while buttoning up her winter coat. "Mr. Wernher! That was Mr. Wernher!"

Jake, peering over the cliff could see the still body in the snow below. Pebbles continued falling from around where the big body bumped and brushed against the cliff wall on its downward plunge.

Mrs. Bentley spoke in a loud whisper. "Come! Hurry!" The dog kept barking.

Huddling together, they climbed the remaining steps to the street above; rushing along on the snowy cobblestone street, passing the Christmas decorated row houses until they reached her house. She turned to the lad and pulled at his arm. "Please come in," she pleaded. "I must talk with you."

He stood silent and alarmed, looking away from her and gazing further up the cobblestone street to where he lived.

"Don't tell anyone, please!" she begged in a mutter, her voice breaking with tears welling up in her eyes. "My husband will kill me!" She gripped his arm hard, and pulled on his winter coat sleeve uttering. "Please come inside, I must explain."

He didn't look at her.

Again she tugged at his coat sleeve. Then again, much harder. "Please." She pleaded.

He nodded his head reluctantly and followed her into the house.

Inside the hallway, she removed her coat and scarf and hung the winter wraps on a free standing pole hanger. She unfastened her fur lined boots leaving them on the hallway floor before guiding him by the arm into her living room. She switched on a floor lamp. A top front button of her gray dress was open and she quickly buttoned up while showing him a shy smile.

"Sit down," she said smiling with a wave of her arm toward the sofa.

He sat on the edge of the couch, bending forward, elbows planted on his knees. He was terribly afraid, ill at ease, and not looking at her. He stared at his cold hands.

Mrs. Bentley stood over him, and then touched his shoulder. She then sat down, slid close to him and asked softly. "How old are you?"

"Sixteen," he murmured.

She placed her hands over her face, slowly running her fingers up and down her forehead. "You're so young," she sighed, dropping her hands onto her lap. "But I must explain what happened tonight, and Jake, please try to understand." She paused and stared at his profile. He kept looking at his hands.

She started expressing her thoughts rapidly. "I'm thirty-three. I was only seventeen when I married Mr. Bentley sixteen years ago, that's as long as you are living, and almost half of my life. I love my husband, but things difficult to explain can happen in a marriage. I love my children." She abruptly stopped ranting and gazed at the youngster still bundled up in winter clothing. He was scared and bewildered.

She began realizing the need to control her thoughts, to choose her words carefully, and hoping that the words have the sound of believability on the teenager. Her future as well as her children's future depended on the boy being united with her in silence over the awful event on the city steps. She needed time to think.

She touched his hand. "Do you want some tea? It'll warm you."

He answered without taking his eyes from her smooth hand gently grasping his palm. "I gotta get home," he lied. "My parents will worry." Her hand felt warm, soft.

"What time is it?" He asked.

"Ten. You can stay. Can't you? It's Christmastime. School's out."

"I guess so." He mumbled.

"Good. I'll make tea. Take your clothes off, your coat and cap."

She stood and while walking toward the kitchen thought of what she'd just said, and knew that forevermore, in the presence of Jake Strussberger, she would need to pick and choose her words carefully. He did as he was told, removing his coat and

4

cap, bunching them up into a clump, and dropping both onto the overstuffed arm of the sofa.

"They're not home tonight," she called from the kitchen, "the twins and Mr. Bentley. Mr. Bentley works the graveyard shift at the mill and Carl and Cathy are at their grandparent's." She paused a few seconds then continued. "They visit them for a few days each year during their Christmas vacation."

He knew the twins were visiting grandparents, and Mr. Bentley worked the late night shift as long as he could remember.

"Use sugar?"

"Ahh, yeah."

She came back into the living room, went to the Christmas tree, and switched on the tree lights, thinking the colorful lights might make the lad more comfortable. "Are you hungry? I have powered donuts from this morning, still kinda fresh. Or a sandwich?"

"No, thank you," he answered without lifting his head to look at her.

As she returned to the kitchen, he glanced at the back of her tall figure before she disappeared into the bright kitchen. He stared at the tree lights. He heard the low noises coming from the kitchen as she prepared their tea. The interior of the house was like most other row houses in the neighborhood; large kitchen, high ceilings, a hall and stairway to the floors above. Her furniture was much more modern than at his home. The sofa was low and long, with Siamese figurine table lamps at each end, and the coffee table had a glass top. He couldn't spot protective embroidered doilies on tabletops like his mother loved to display.

He was anxious to leave her house. He'd experienced only playful dalliances with girls and had no firsthand knowledge of romancing a woman, but nevertheless, he knew enough to know that Mrs. Bentley and Mr. Wernher were sexually swept up with each other on the city steps. Fear of getting into trouble with the law was distressing him, and Mrs. Bentley, now appearing calm, acting as if nothing occurred, also confused his worrisome thoughts. He often didn't know how to act or react with adults while in their company, and now with Mrs. Bentley, he was more empty of ideas than ever before. He remained seated and scared, but wanted to go rushing out the front door.

She came to him with two steaming cups and placed his drink on the coffee table. Again she sat beside him. He picked up the tea, the heat felt soothing in his hands.

"Now where were we?" she said, uncertain about winning his loyalty. "They're good kids, Carl and Cathy. But, unless you help me, they'll be very hurt by what has happened, that terrible accident. You don't want to hurt Carl, do you, you're pals."

"No." He muttered.

She held her hot drink close to her lips with both hands, and began speaking to him in an untroubled voice over the steaming cup rim. "My husband hunts and bowls. If he's not working, he's playing or sleeping. He's a good provider," she paused. "But I have feelings too. I must seem old to a youngster like you, but I'm not. I like compliments, getting attention from both men and women, yet I'd never dream of deliberately seeking out a secret lover. Please believe that, Jake."

"I do," he whispered what he thought she wanted him to say.

She lowered the cup to her lap. "I go to Saint John's bingo games every Friday night."

She gave off a heavy sigh, not wanting to confess the details of her secret life. Yet, she had to risk opening up, spilling the beans, and hopefully saving her family from shame and untold troubles with the law.

Jake pretended to be sipping his tea. He had to pee.

"After bingo," she began looking into her teacup, "I take the trolley home. Several months ago I was waiting at the trolley stop when Mr. Wernher happened to drive by and offered me a ride. I let him drive me to the city steps. He wanted to drive me to my front door, but I was afraid my husband would find out. Mr. Bentley is very jealous. Mr. Wernher was very friendly. We talked about our families. He complimented me about my looks." She stopped talking, sipped tea and collected her thoughts.

Jake remained frozen in place, uncomfortable with what she was saying and with his full bladder.

"I guess," she perked up, put her cup on the coffee table and began confessing what she didn't want to reveal to anyone, yet alone to a friend of her twins. "I responded to Mr. Wernher's flattery more than I realized. Can you understand how nice words can make someone feel happy? His words made me feel good. I flirted with him. I only wanted it to be playful flirting, not develop into anything serious between us. Girls like to flirt, you understand. Don't you?" She looked at Jake, waiting for a reply. None came.

"Anyway," she continued, "Mr. Wernher kept picking me up at the trolley stop every Friday after bingo. In the beginning he only drove me to the steps and we'd exchange a playful goodnight, but after awhile we started stopping for coffee at a little place downtown. We just drank coffee and talked. It was nice to talk to someone interesting, about things other than kids and housework. Tonight we stopped at a bar." She stared at Jake.

"We danced." She put her hand on Jake's thigh. "Mr. Wernher kissed me."

Jake blushed.

She saw his red face, witnessing his bashfulness. He was too young. How could he possibly understand?

"Anyhow," she sighed while running her hand over the top of her head and red hair, tiring, but willing to persist rather than surrender. The stakes were too high to quit bidding to win his confidence. "We left the bar and he kissed me once again in the car, but I pushed him away. I really did. I told him. I can't be involved in an affair. I was very firm with him. He apologized and he drove to the steps. We hugged and said our goodbyes. I climbed the steps alone, but before long, he was on the steps behind me. He said he just wanted to walk along with me on the snowy steps to make sure I got up them safely."

She paused. Jake looked no different to her. Still, frightened. Still, uncomfortable. Still, quiet. "When we got to the landing where you surprised us, he started kissing me again, pleading with me to return to his car." She paused and turned fully toward Jake. "Now he's dead." she whispered with a long sigh. "If I tell the truth, my husband will leave me, my children will be embarrassed, and God knows what will happen to me. What am I going to do, Jake?"

Without looking at her, Jake swallowed some tea and asked. "Can I use your bathroom?"

By deliberately ignoring her question, he didn't give her the assurance she was seeking. "Sure," she said. "Top of the stairs."

He gently placed the teacup on the coffee table and walked to the stairs. She watched him walk away and wondered if he ever experienced a girl. Sex was new, mysterious at sixteen. She doubted he had any sexual experience beyond kissing. She began having different thoughts about her approach to the tense lad. Maybe a slight flirtation could seal them together into a bond of secrecy. She sat staring at the tree lights trying to slow down her racing thoughts over what to do to escape from the events of the night and return her life back to some sort of normalcy.

Jake returned, awkwardly sat near her, yet further away than before.

Her tea was lukewarm now as she lifted the cup to her lips and spilled some tea on the front of her grey dress. "Ohh!" she cried out. "How clumsy of me. I didn't splash any on you, did I?"

"No."

Before standing she patted his knee. "Excuse me. I'll be right back." She left the living room, went into the hallway and up the stairs.

In her bedroom she quickly took off her loose-fitting dress and let it fall to the floor. In the dresser mirror she studied her image. The outline of a tall slender body showed underneath the pink slip. She let her slip fall to the floor and removed some hairpins. Her red hair fell to her shoulders. She tossed it some-what gently and it became fuller. She was healthy looking, her skin clear and bright. Her green eyes wide-eyed and revealing. She was frightened over all that was happening to her, but not confused about what she had to do to survive. Her breasts fell slightly when she removed her brassiere, remaining well spaced and shapely.

Digging down beneath her everyday clothes, down to the secret place of her deep dresser drawer, she pulled out from under the stack of winter clothing a white summer pullover. She quickly put in on over her naked breasts. After stepping out of her panties, she reached back into the bottom of the drawer, took out pink slacks and pulled them up over her attractive legs. She examined herself in the mirror. These were the only sexy cloth-ing she owned and she kept them hidden from her jealous mate. "What do I have to lose?" she murmured toward a framed picture of her handsome husband holding his rifle and kneeling beside a deer carcass. She checked her makeup, applied more red lipstick to her full lips, gathered the discarded clothing and pushed them under the bed and then went back downstairs to Jake. "I'm back!" She called out cheerfully upon entering the room.

He was startled and dazed by her appearance and joyful entrance. She was beautiful. He'd never seen a woman as sexy in person, only in magazines and at the movies. He'd never looked at her before as a symbol of arousal for maturing boys or heard any of the other teenage boys in the neighborhood talk about her as if she was a sensual knockout. Before this moment she was only Carl and Cathy's mother and she always looked as plain as his own mother, as all of the mothers he knew on Pigeon Hill.

"You like my slacks?" she asked while spinning around in front of his fixed stare and half opened mouth. "He's stunned," she thought to herself while smiling at his dead fish look. She wiggled somewhat, enough to make her bare breasts move freely beneath the thin pullover.

"Huh," he answered with difficulty. "Yeah."

"Only the two of us must know the truth," she paused and sat next to him, gently placing her hand on his thigh and leaving it there. "You do understand the enormous troubles that incident on the steps could cause me. And what purpose would it serve? Mr. Wernher would still be dead. His family would be in disgrace, and my husband's response would probably be to kill me at most, or kick me out into the street at the least. It would be ugly for both families. He's so jealous. On our honeymoon, he got sore at me for wearing a low cut bathing suit that he felt showed too much of my breasts. It had green and yellow polka dots. I can't wear these slacks and top outside. He'd be furious. He never even saw these clothes. Honest, he hasn't. I keep them hidden from him, or he'd destroy them in a rage if he thought I had ideas of wearing them outside to be viewed by other men. Will you share this tragedy with me in silence, Jake?"

He nodded. "Yeah. It wasn't your fault. It was an accident because I frightened you."

She took his hand into hers. "Oh, thank you so much Jake," she whispered into his ear.

A wave of excitement passed over his body. "I want to help Mrs. Bentley. I really do."

Lightly squeezing his hand, she started giving him his instructions for their mutual cover-up of the night's dreadful events. "Then listen to me and do exactly as I say. No one knows I was with Mr. Wernher tonight or any other night. The people at the bar across town don't know me. I don't believe anyone saw the two of us walking together tonight. It's a cold night. I doubt if any neighbors looking out of their frosty windows would see anyone or anything very clear." She rubbed his hand softly, smiled, and continued with questions and instructions. "Where were you tonight? Where were you coming from?"

"Susan Mallhauser's house."

"What were you doing there?"

"I went with Henry Schneider."

"Did Henry leave with you?"

"No."

"Why?"

"He goes steady with Susan. We always go to her house together and watch television until her parents go to bed. Then they start kissing and I leave so that they can be alone. I'm just a decoy. Her parents think nothing will happen between them if I am there, but soon after her parents go to bed, I sneak out the door."

Lifting his hand to her chest, she asked, "then, no one knows the exact time you left Susan's home?"

"I don't think so."

"If anyone questions you, tell them you walked up the steps tonight just as you do any other time after leaving Susan's, but saw nothing unusual. Okay?"

He nodded, but could hardy understand what she had said and only wanting to open his hand and caress the warm breast he could feel against the back of his hand.

"Good." she said firmly, "Now you better get along home."

Now, not wanting to leave her, he blurted, "What about our tracks?"

She smiled into his bright brown eyes. "Everyone on this side of Pigeon Hill uses those old steps. Don't deny using them tonight should you be asked, but don't volunteer any information to anyone either. Anyway, it might snow before daybreak. And who's going to think we know anything? Why should anyone?" She let go of his hand. "Now, you better get along home. Your parents might worry."

"They're probably asleep. When I don't have school, I stay out late."

"Tonight, you need to go home, just in case they're awake."

Slowly, he stood up and put on his coat and cap. By his arm, she walked him to the dark hallway and front door. He was as tall as she was, perhaps a bit taller. Facing him and cupping his hands in hers, she whispered, "Thank you."

"I want to help you," he whispered back. "I really do."

She kissed him lightly on the lips, allowing her cheek to slide against his, and murmuring into his ear, "I'm frightened. Very afraid."

He'd never been so sexually excited in all of his short life, but his mind was racing so fast about all that had occurred to him on this night that he could not relax enough to get an erection. He was so full of overflowing feelings of fear, terror, and sensual sexual thoughts that he stood against her like a harmless mannequin.

She took his hands, cupping them in hers, and lifting them up between her breasts. "I trust you, Jake. My life is in your hands."

"I won't let you down, I promise," he managed to whisper.

Slowly releasing his hands, she slipped her arms around his neck, and pressed her body against his, kissed him lightly on the lips. "You're my hero."

He left his hands folded as in prayer between her breasts, the soft warmth of her flesh thrilling his entire being.

She gave him another soft kiss on the cheek and released him slowly. His hands dropped to his sides after being close to heaven.

"Goodnight," she said while opening wide the door and prodding him into the night.

He stepped outside. She rapidly shut the door behind him and against the cold winter air.

CHAPTER TWO
Kaffecklatsching

Jake heard his father bellowing from the kitchen. "Jake! Get up!"

"Huh?"

"Get up and come down here! You have company! Teddy Vonovich is here!"

Rolling out from under the covers, he sat on the edge of the bed, first yawning, and then rubbing his face hard before yelling back. "I'm coming!" Late morning snowflakes were drifting past his window pane. He thought about Mrs. Bentley. How could he have missed noticing how pretty she is before? His mother was right, clothes do make a difference.

Sensuous thoughts began stirring his hormones. He urgently stood up. Dressing in khaki pants and white sweatshirt, he studied his reflection with a hand-held mirror. Even by vigorously brushing his hair, he wasn't able to groom his crew cut as he desired. His brown uneven hair needed a trim. That meant money, he had none.

He was feeling good about helping Mrs. Bentley. She was right. What good would it do to tell the police about how or what happened to Mr. Wernher? Noticing a tiny mark on his cheek, he brought the mirror closer to his face. "Oh, my God!" he gasped. "It's her lipstick." He rubbed the speck away while remembering how it got there. Closing his dark brown eyes, he dwelled on the warmth of his friend's mother, and wanted to be with her at that very moment. Opening his eyes and sighing loudly, he went downstairs to the kitchen.

"Morning, Jake," Teddy greeted him.

"Did it snow much over night?" were Jake's first words to his lanky pal, imagining a snowy path of footprints leading from the city steps to Mrs. Bentley's front door.

Teddy nodded.

"Four inches," Jake's father spoke from the kitchen sink, his back to the boys, busy washing dishes. "And it's still coming down."

"Want coffee?" Jake asked.

"Sure," Teddy smiled, pleased by the offer for something hot. He had a head cold.

"You'll have to make a fresh pot and clean up after yourselves!" Mr. Strussberger firmly reminded the lads without turning away from the dishwater. The teens looked at the back of the old man's baggy pants, held up by wide suspenders over red faded long johns, and grimaced at each other.

The overhead light fixture hadn't a shade covering its glaring bulb. Mr. Strussberger kept the unshaded bulb burning even when sunlight through the windows was adequate. He spent most of his time in the kitchen and liked it bright. He only liked the modern oven with four burners, but he loved the icebox and oak table he inherited from his parents. He refused to replace the icebox with an electric refrigerator, often arguing with his wife when she made suggestions that they do to become more up to date with the times. As long as the iceman made his rounds selling blocks of ice, he'd keep his icebox. There was a weak knock at the door.

"Get the door, Teddy," Jake called out, busy at the stove brewing coffee.

Through the window Teddy could see the old lady standing on the covered stoop. Opening the door to a chilly breeze, and then stepping aside, Teddy felt her cold coat brushing against his hand when she carelessly rushed by without a nod or greeting to anyone. She went to Mr. Strussberger. She was excited, blue eyes intense, wide-eyed and glowing. "Struss," saying his nickname and grabbing his forearm, "Sumvun uff cliff! Vus man!" She paused to catch her laboring breath while shaking her babushka-covered head to and fro. "Vood step's kaputt dem say. Vot a luff. Vot a luff."

"Is he dead?" Struss asked, shaking water and soap suds from his hands.

"Ve 'll for sore!" she answered, waving her arms about her face, speaking just as his German parents and elderly neighbors spoke when he was growing up. He understood her speech perfectly. "Mash noggin, dey say. I vus up steps. Dey chust tok him, dey vork'ink hard, moof 'ink him in der snow, all stiff uf corse."

"Who was he?" Struss asked. "Did the police say?"

"Not'tink yet." she answered. "Vun tings iss sure, dem say, somevun vuz mit him, somevun know some'tink."

"I was wondering what happened," Teddy commented in a matter of fact tone. "Walking here I saw the police by the steps. They were talking with Mrs. Bentley and others." He sneezed into his cupped hands.

"Gesundheit!" Struss and Mrs. Krombach called out in unison, loud enough for heaven to hear.

Jake's heart jumped and he mumbled under his breath, "She went and looked!" He began picturing her in a calm state, wearing the pink slacks and white top, standing erect, watching the corpse being carted away. The coffee started percolating, awakening him from his Mrs. Bentley hallucinations. Her strange unpredictable behavior puzzled him, causing him nervous anxiety, yet his fascination over her was growing mightily. He offered Mrs. Krombach a cup of coffee.

"Ve'll for sore," she said. "Der heck mit diss ice und snow," and took off her babushka and unbuttoned her coat. "Diss time year I miss der garden'ink, der fresh crops." Teddy took the coat and babushka from her, and into the hallway. Before sitting at the table she ran her wrinkled hands over her white hair, and drew it together into a tight bun at the back of her head.

Struss joined her at the table. "Politicians," he complained. "Every election year they'll promise to replace that rotten splintering wood with concrete steps. They already have on the other side of the hill years ago. I can't understand why our side of Pigeon Hill is last on the list when it comes to services. I don't get it, we're all Democrats, and our ward boss knows that. The Democrats run this city, yet time after time, I hear about those wealthy Republicans on the other side of the hill getting the better services."

Jake poured everyone coffee, then both boys joined the adults at the table.

Struss kept talking. "Politicians, boys, never trust them, they always run to the money! Better yet, beware of anyone living off their yakking mouths. Politicians, salesmen, traveling preachers, even beggars, they all want your money. You're only a feedbag to them."

"'Dem no gout!" The old lady cried out to the boys, giving her support wholeheartedly for what Struss was preaching. "Ve der dumpkoffs! Dot's iss sore ting."

"That is for sure," Struss chuckled.

Struss and Mrs. Krombach continued talking about the neighborhood, its problems and people, while the boys sat and listened. The old lady was calm now after unloading the news about the dead man and was enjoying her coffee and gossip with a faithful friend. Jake knew from what his father had said that she was a strong woman, outliving her husband by many years, and raising her children alone. Her grown children moved to the suburbs like many others that grew up on Pigeon Hill before World War Two.

She was somewhat regarded by new or younger neighbors as a meddlesome nuisance, spending most warm weather days walking around the neighborhood seeking someone else out and about to talk to. The citizens she was fond of gossiping with, or about, often dreaded seeing her walking their way. She dressed the same way at all times, in black from head to toe, as if staying in perpetual mourning over someone or something. In the colder months, she'd linger at the local delicatessen, and like an excitable teenager at a drugstore soda fountain, she'd hope to find someone sweet enough to listen to her tales for a short span of time.

The delicatessen, specializing in German meats, bratwurst, sauerbraten, knockwurst, and other hearty Deutsche dishes, became a delightful place for her to meet and greet others. Long time residents thought kindly of her, speaking of her generous ways, when from her large backyard garden she'd give away many varieties of vegetables. Free fresh vegetables for the low cost of an invite to sit for a time in their kitchen and kaffecklatsch.

"They'll perform an autopsy." Struss said. "He could've died of exposure, not the fall."

Jake perked up. The thought of Mr. Wernher still alive at the bottom of the cliff hadn't occurred to him. His mood turned blue. He felt guilty of something, yet not certain just what he should be blameworthy about. He lost all interest in the table talk, sat dumbfounded, feeling cold despite swallowing the hot coffee.

* * *

After Mrs. Krombach departed, Struss had the boys bring the evergreen into the living room before they too left the house. He'd gotten the tree over a week ago and it lay in the snowy backyard ever since. He couldn't ignore his wife's nagging comments any longer to bring it inside before more snowfall completely covered it up. The boys cleaned the watery aftermath made while dragging the snow laden pine through the house, but now that it was upright in its stand, he needed to decorate its branches before she came home, or else he'd be in for more nagging.

He loved his wife, but he wasn't able to come out on top in any of their disputes, not having mastered the snappy sarcastic quips she inherited by growing up in a large Irish family. Long ago he learned he'd be verbally outgunned by her in any of their disagreements. Remaining silent and giving off no limp responses, proved to be the best way to handle her mocking wit until she'd settle down and again become his sweet Irish Rose.

When he was satisfied with the way the tree looked and thought that his wife would be pleased with his effort, he picked a wreath from the storage box. Going to the one living room window, he looked out from his high on the hill row house at the city he loved.

Struss' Pittsburgh was a dirty place. A tough city where workers carried lunch buckets stuffed with meaty sandwiches to be consumed near scrap metal piles, on coal barges, in sweaty mills or in filthy foundries. Where open hearth furnaces illuminated the nighttime sky with flickering reddish-orange colors and starlight is seldom seen. Where city daylight gives way early to mill smoke and grime and watching soot settle on everything outside of a sheltered place is common.

He could never live elsewhere and he detested the new suburbs being built in the hinterlands where his younger brothers built homes using the government GI bill to finance their way into debt. The program was destroying his neighborhood and spreading families away from each other. Cousins were growing up barely knowing each other because they lived so far apart. Row homes, corner stores and neighborhood saloons were all that he wanted to live around. And German biergartens where he could sit, sing, and dance, while munching pretzels and guzzling beer.

After hanging the wreath, Struss got the beer he'd been chilling inside the icebox, sat down, and admired the Christmas tree. He shook his head from side to side. How could his brothers walk away from cobblestone road memories without showing any regret? How could they not miss the loving neighborhood that filled his heart? He shook his head again and gulped some beer. "Suburbanites!" He growled, hating the sound of the word and mumbling "Verdammter mist!" A German quote his father would grumble when disturbed. He thought it meant goddamn it.

CHAPTER THREE
An Opportune

At the casket closing, Mrs. Wernher wept mildly by giving off a damp sniffle. Yet even then as she'd done throughout her bereavement, she'd gotten a quick grip on herself and kept her emotions and tear ducts buttoned up. She was tall and thin, used little makeup, and kept her dyed black hair short. Except for her engagement and wedding rings, she avoided wearing jewelry. Attaching jewels with no purpose, for no reason other than to adorn oneself, was impractical and for only the silliest of fools. She thought of herself as regal in appearance rather than beautiful. She was discreet, and standoffish with neighbors, reinforcing their opinions of her as an egotist who placed herself a step up socially on them. She herself thought many steps up.

She had known her husband many years as only another boy of many boys in her Pigeon Hill neighborhood, never noticing any special characteristics about him that drew her attention. His only noticeable difference to her as a teenager was that he'd been a star athlete in high school, but that attribute alone wasn't enough for her reserved personality to be drawn to him romantically. It was only after they'd both graduated from State University and came back home that she'd began seeing him as more than her friend. Her decision to accept his marriage proposal came only after he'd pleaded to her many times. She'd have preferred to have married a more intelligent man, had one asked for her hand. From the few men that wooed her, she liked him the most, and by that reasoning, she accepted his proposal one summer evening. That rare starry night was the only special thing a silly romantic could, or might, see in his request for her hand. And for her part, it was a matter-of-fact event. She didn't lean toward male superiority or playing by the social rules. She missed discussing equality matters with like-minded females during her college days.

His parents were wealthier than her family and before their wedding, she'd already persuaded him to enter into business for himself. They opened their small used car lot soon after exchanging rings and she assisted him in achieving moderate success. "He was such a simple man," she mumbled, opening the morning newspaper, spreading the open pages over rich bedding and reading the article again.

Pigeon Hill Death Remains Mysterious

Police report no additional clues in the death of Mr. Otto Wernher. It still isn't known if Wernher fell accidentally or foul play caused his fall from the Pigeon Hill city steps. People living nearby report loud hollering the night when the police say Wernher fell. From her bedroom window, one resident reported seeing a couple walking beneath a streetlight bordering the steps. Other baffling circumstances in the case has left investigators puzzled. Wernher parked his car haphazardly with its engine running. At discovery, the car was out of gas. Police hint Wernher left his car suddenly, possibly to help someone in need. Authorities are continuing their investigation and seeking the couple seen by the eyewitness.

She folded the paper and stretched out over the king-size bed. Bunching up a satin-covered pillow and pressing it against her small breasts, she lie on her back staring up at the ceiling.

Lifting her right leg out from under her white nightgown, she raised it straight into the air and inspected the lean smooth limb for imperfections. At forty, she was concerned about growing old. She exercised often, practiced healthy habits, never smoked, limited alcohol, and ate wisely. Her leg was firm and without any blemishes. She dropped it and inspected the other. It had a small varicose vein and the blue spot upset her. She lowered her leg and tossed the pillow aside.

Why her husband was on the steps was as mysterious to her as it was to the police. The homicide detectives had questioned her about the possibility of her husband seeing another woman, of having an affair. She assured them that he'd never given her any reason to suspect he would enter into unfaithfulness, and that they were happily married. Attempts to conjure up thoughts of him having sex outside of their marriage failed her completely. She'd never been that excited over sex, neither actual nor in imaginary ways. She much more enjoyed reading, or participating in a smart and rewarding conversation with the right people. Having sex before falling off to sleep wasn't thrilling for her, yet when he bothered her for his own relief, she never withheld her body from him.

She left her bed and went to the living room where her two children waited. Jean, the eldest, eighteen, was taking her father's death the hardest and cried often. Sixteen-year-old Otto Junior, nicknamed Junior, was adjusting toward the neighborhood thought that his father rushed to someone in distress and might indeed be a hero. She didn't discourage those consoling thoughts for him and hoped that's what really happened. Otherwise his death might be embarrassing to them all.

Both children sat on the sofa in pajamas. She stood by the glowing fireplace. "Children, I don't want you to lose your sadness, but I do want us to overcome our loss and go ahead with our life as your Dad would want us to do." Jean started sobbing.

She waited until Jean dried her eyes.

She spoke softly. "We are still a family. Jean, I want you to finish decorating the house for the coming holidays, not as much as past years, but complete the Christmas tree and hang the wreaths in the windows. And Junior, get dressed, I have a list of things I need from the store. We've always enjoyed certain Christmas customs in this family and I intend to keep those traditions as your father would wish and you should also. Now, let's get on with our lives."

Jean was crying again and she walked to the tree, which stood thinly decorated since the accident, and she started hanging ornaments. Junior lumbered from the room, hanging his head, making his overweight body seem more rotund.

Mrs. Wernher believed activity eased the mind, allowing one to think more clearly. Nineteen-fifty would indeed be a new year. Otto carried more than enough life insurance. She would continue operating the used car lot. It was a small business, but now, given opportune by the hand of fate, she lusted to expand both the business, and her prestige. She would enjoy her sudden independence as a lone businesswoman.

CHAPTER FOUR
Heart Mending

Packing her husband's lunch bucket, Mrs. Bentley wished to feel remorseful over her wantonness with Otto Wernher, but couldn't find that shame-on-me feelings that she desired. She liked the arousal Otto stimulated in her that evening and had Jake not shocked them, she would've returned with Otto back to his car. She lied to Jake about loving her husband. Now, she was wondering if she'd ever loved him.

He wasn't from Pigeon Hill. They'd met at an Oktoberfest dance at the local German Club that was held for teenagers each year. He'd come with a friend from the neighborhood and most of the girls went gaga over him. She too was taken in by his good looks and bold character. He was four years older than her, and at the time, she'd believed him to be the lover every schoolgirl dreamed of in their girly longings. She'd quit school and they'd wed four months later, lying to her parents that she was pregnant to get their quick permission. Soon after exchanging rings, she did become pregnant with the twins. How young and foolish she'd been. Exchanging teenage carefree years for the responsibilities of a wife and a mother. Yet, in spite of the distaste for her mate and his possessive tendencies, she couldn't boldly seek romance outside of her marriage.

The incidents with Otto before the accident were just as she'd told Jake. Perhaps out of fear of her husband's temper. Or morally bothered by wrongdoing. Or for the love of her children and the shame it would set upon them, she couldn't willingly search for a man to comfort her secret longings. However, if opportunity came as it did with a man as charming as Otto, her suppressed desires for affectionate kisses and flattering words would drive her on, losing all resistance, and into an adulterous affair.

She thought about Otto's wife and children and stayed suffering over the ordeal they were experiencing. She knew Otto's son, Junior, who hung out with her Carl, but never met Mrs. Wernher, or Otto's daughter. They lived on the other side of Pigeon Hill. She was relieved to read the coroner's report in the newspaper that he'd died instantly. A broken neck along with multiple lacerations. How awful she thought of herself. To be so terrified of her husband's outrage, she'd taken a chance by not seeking help, thinking that Otto was already dead and would not die alone in the cold. Tears ran down her cheek, for both Otto and for what her character had become. She was finding it hard to discover that she'd become a self-serving liar and coward this late in her life.

She shut the food stuffed lunch bucket and a thermos of hot black coffee, and put them near her husband's winter coat hanging on the back of a kitchen chair. She'd always had everything he needed for work near at hand, wishing him quickly out the front door. Only then could she relax, knowing he was at the mill for eight solid hours. Often, while her mate was at the mill and the children slept, she went braless around the house, dressed in her secret slacks and tight sweater that she'd worn for Jake. She knew she could be appealing to men, even sexy in the right clothes. She enjoyed the looks that some men gave her, the men that took the time to peer beyond the good but formless clothes her husband insisted she wear.

She didn't want to be like Mrs. Vonovich across the street, who drunkenly came and went as she pleased, virtually abandoning her husband and son, Teddy. She just wanted to love and be loved by a caring witty man with interests outside of himself. She heard the boys entering the house.

"Hey Mom!" Carl called from the front door. "I brought Jake and Teddy home with me to show them the rifle I got for Christmas."

"Fine." she answered. "Wipe your shoes off, all of you!" I don't need snow and slush tracked throughout the house."

The boys stumbled into the kitchen and sat around the table. Mrs. Bentley spoke with her back to them. "Did you boys have a nice Christmas?"

"Yeah," Teddy lied, he'd received nothing. There wasn't a Christmas tree in his home. Jake mumbled something that was unclear to her. His head was hanging, too afraid to look at her in the bright kitchen.

She turned abruptly. "Jake, did you?" she asked him with a stern voice, almost demanding that he answer.

He looked at her. "Yeah," then quickly turned away. He couldn't believe it. There she was, all motherly looking, bunched up hair in the back of her head, bulky clothes, with shapeless breasts. He heard her speaking to Carl.

"Get the gun quietly. Your Dad's still sleeping." Carl rushed to get his present.

She sensed Jake's uncomfortableness. "How are your parents Jake?" He mumbled something. She raised her voice. "It's okay to look at me."

Jake looked at her as if she'd dared him too, and in that moment of eye contact, he'd felt the same crushing weakness conquer his body as when she'd hugged and kissed him on the night of the incident.

"Jake, are they okay?"

"They're fine." he spoke up.

"What did Santa bring you, Teddy?" she asked the boy in his old winter coat with frayed cuffs.

"Uhh, uhh," he stammered, surprised by her question.

"Well, an 'uhh' is a wonderful gift," she teased, realizing her blunder. She guessed he'd gotten nothing. Her motherly feelings went out to him. She went to him, gently stroking the back of his neck. "Boys," she smiled. "Take off your coats and caps."

She helped Teddy with his coat. "I'll make some tea."

"There she goes with the tea again." Jake mumbled under his breath.

"Did you say something Jake?" she asked.

"I'm not staying long! No tea for me."

"Me either." Teddy said.

Sensing Jake's sudden hostility, she looked at his drooping head over the tabletop. He was jealous because she'd rubbed the back of Teddy's neck.

"And what did you get for Christmas?" she demanded.

Her commanding voice caught him by surprise. "Uhh."

"Oh," she quickly thrust at him. "You got an 'uhh' too! Boy o' boy, Santa must've had a bagful of them."

"I got clothes and a wristwatch."

"So nice to get presents, isn't it? Believe it or not, some people don't get presents at Christmas."

Jake lost his bit of jealousy and took off his coat.

Carl entered the room, proudly carrying his rifle and laid it across the table for the boys to admire. They did, full of awe, examining it with both hands, from stock to barrel, from chamber to sights.

"Where's Cathy?" Carl asked.

"She went to the movie with some friends." she answered, then added, "I have a job for you young man."

"What now?" Carl asked annoyed.

"Take the trash out." She handed him one of two big paper bags full of Christmas wrappings. "And Teddy, would you take this other one out for me? Thank you."

"I can carry them both," Carl said. "What, you think I can't carry bags of paper?"

"No," she said. "It's slippy outside, do as I say."

The boys left with their garbage into the snowy sloping backyard.

She turned to Jake. "You were jealous over me touching Teddy? Weren't you?" she whispered, standing across from where he sat.

"I don't know why I got mad."

"Well, I do!" she said, keeping her voice soft, pointing to the ceiling. "You're acting just like that one upstairs. You alone in this whole world know how I feel about controlling men."

"Sorry." he muttered.

"You'd better be. I confided in you, trusted you. I don't want you to grow up into a jellybean."

"I'm not. I won't." Then wanting to be on her good side added. "I promise."

She went to him and laid her hand on his shoulder, touching the side of his neck. "Good." She stroked his crew cut. "Did anyone question you?"

"No."

"Me neither. Only if I'd heard anything suspicious or saw any strangers around the neighborhood that night."

"Did you see him?" he asked.

"Who?"

"Mr. Wernher?'

"What are you talking about?' she asked.

"His body. Did you see his body? You went to the steps, didn't you?"

"Yes, I did, like most of the neighborhood women. Why should I not be curious like every other housewife living near the steps?"

His respect for her cleverness was still growing.

"Ooh, Jake," she murmured, letting her hand slide from his hair to his neck. "What's going to help us to forget?"

He wasn't thinking about Mr. Wernher's death, only imagining her warm body beneath the loose sagging clothes.

She could hear Carl and Teddy returning. She walked to the stairs. It wasn't time to awaken her husband for work, but she needed to avoid small talk with teenagers, to get away and be alone. Her flirting with Jake had won not only his silence, but also his heart. She'd hoped to excite him somewhat, awaken his blossoming manhood. Using her body as a signpost, showing him the way from adolescence to manhood, and sealing the secret of Otto's death forever entwined with an unforgettable fond memory. She'd only thought to be a signpost for the boy, showing him what warm and exciting discoveries await him in his future, but not actually taking him there herself. It wasn't going to work out that way she feared, he was infatuated with her. How to discourage him? She closed the bathroom door, sat on the commode and pondered her problem.

Shunning might upset him. He might reveal her amorous secrets with both Otto and himself on that horrible night. She would be accused of being a child molester on top of a jezebel. That would be prison for certain. After all, she didn't know Jake any better than she knew any of the other boys that associated with her son from time to time. She would have to handle him carefully, walk a tightrope, but at the same time, let any expectation he may desire for more caresses die a soft death. She'd become closer to him in a friendly way.

"God help me." she pleaded softly. She'd been raised up by Christian parents, belonged to a German Evangelical Lutheran Church, and attended Bible studies. The passages referring that everything done in darkness will be brought into the light haunted her mind. Sins, she was taught, cast long shadows into the future and don't fade away with time. Time does not heal all things. She could only plead her case to God. She felt all alone. Her parents were gone. Her brothers, all World War Two veterans had married and moved to the suburbs. Anyhow, her brothers seldom visited even when they still lived on Pigeon Hill. They didn't like her mate from the first day she brought him home. He was too much of a talker and braggart for them to stomach.

She stood and studied herself in the mirror. She would need confidence to guide Jake through the nightmare she caused and pray they'd both come through the mess unharmed. She left the bathroom, crept past her bedroom door and down the steps to the first floor. She could hear Carl talking. Bragging a bit like his father.

"I can't wait to go hunting. I know I'll bag one. Maybe a six-pointer."

Jake and Teddy sat quietly fingering the rifle, letting Carl talk.

"You guys ought to get your hunting license. My Dad would take you along. It's fun."

She'd nothing against hunting and her German mother made wild rabbit as tasteful as any meat can be made, but guns in the house with an easily angered husband made her mentally ill at ease. She changed the subject. "Well, tomorrow is New Year's Eve. What are you boys planning?"

"Nothing," Carl answered. "Just hanging out at the Owl's, like we do every night. Are you gonna let me stay out later than usual?"

"No way!" she snapped. "Home before midnight. Your Dad is off; we'll bring in the New Year together as a family. What you boys see in the backroom of that old store is beyond me."

"Girls! Girls! Girls!" Carl answered.

"Oh, I see." she smiled. "A girl goes to the store and from out of the backroom a pack of lusty wolves eyeball her up and down."

"Up and down and all around," Carl sang. "Anyway and every way, they really come to see me."

"Boy! Bring those girls here, I'll tell them what you're really like. Show them your messy bedroom."

Jake and Teddy giggled.

"Ha-ha-ha." Carl mocked their giggles, upset at both his mother and his friends.

"Do you have a girlfriend, Teddy?" she asked.

"Him!" Carl shouted, pointing his finger across the table at Teddy. "Who would go with him?"

"Shhh!" she warned her son. You'll wake your Dad! And Teddy's cute, you wisenheimer. And he has manners, something you could and should learn."

"Well, you need glasses," Carl snapped back quickly.

Teddy sat stone face, making no attempt to defend himself against Carl's rude remarks.

"What about you Jake?" she probed. "Anyone special?"

"No." Jake shook his head.

"But he likes someone," Carl teased, speaking each word slowly.

"I do?" Jake asked. "News to me."

"Come on, you like Susan. Doesn't he, Teddy?"

"I don't know." Teddy stammered. "Keep me out of this."

"I heard she went with Henry Schneider?" Mrs. Bentley interrupted them, searching for a sensitive spot in Jake's life. Maybe by getting him to unlock his feelings about Susan, in trusted confidentiality, she could find a way to mend the hurtful feeling that she'd put upon him.

"She does go with Henry." Jake answered.

"But you love her." Carl teased. "Everyone knows it. Even Susan."

"Now I love her. A second ago I liked her. Suddenly I love her?"

"Susan and Henry are probably at the Owl's now." Carl teased, continuing to ride Jake. "Let's go see her." Grinning and patting his chest, "Hear your heart make pitter-patters."

Jake hid his growing anger and tried to answer his tormenter maturely in front of Mrs. Bentley. "Okay, okay, knock it off. I used to like her, but I don't anymore. Okay?"

"Let's go! See if Susan is there." Carl said cheering up. "The Owl has a new pinball machine I want to beat."

"You can tell him if Susan's there when you return." His mother said, and then lied. "I need some bread for your Father's lunch."

"Oh crap." Carl moaned. "Let's go guys."

"You and Teddy go. You got Jake upset with your harassing; he might say something out of turn to Henry or Susan. He can wait here till you return and keep me company."

"He's fine." Carl laughed. "He's a big boy, he'll get over it."

"Just do as I say. Mothers know best."

"Come on Teddy."

"Here's some money, buy a snack for the two of you. And put the rifle away before you leave."

Jake sat sulking until he heard them leaving the house. Sometimes he hated Carl. Mrs. Bentley sat across from him at the table. She spoke softly. "Do you like Susan?"

"Not really."

"What sort of answer is that? Either you do or you don't."

"I did."

"How long ago was that?"

He didn't answer her, just hung his head.

"Jake, answer me."

"I like you," he mumbled.

"Oh Jake, how sweet." She paused and took his hands into hers across the table. "I know I owe you a great deal, more then I can ever repay. You saved my marriage, probably my life. I'll be forever grateful, but when I kissed you the other night, and let you..." she paused again, casting her eyes downward. "Well, I was reacting to a man, a man that saved my life, the twin's happiness, and my marriage. I was showing my appreciation to you by giving you a part of myself, a part, being a man, I thought you would like. Nevertheless Jake, it doesn't mean anything else. You cannot look at me as you do Susan. I'm not a girl. I'm a woman. I have a mate whom I sleep with day in and day out.

"I know," he whispered.

She continued discouraging any dreamy expectations he may have of ever feeling her up again. "What happened between Mr. Wernher and I will never happen again with any other man. I didn't even know him that well and it was improper of me to let him drive me home the first time. My friendly behavior only encouraged him into thinking I was seeking an affair. Everyone makes mistakes and I did make a mistake."

She let go of his hands, but continued lecturing the lad.

"I fight with my husband, we have our troubles from time to time, but so do other husbands and wives. Do your Mom and Dad fight sometime?"

"Yeah."

"Sure they do. But then they kiss and make-up, just like me and Mr. Bentley." She reached across the table and lifted his chin. "Look at me, Jake. What happened between us will never happen again. I belong to Mr. Bentley."

No motion or emotion came from the teen, only stillness and silence. She changed the subject. "How did you let a jerk like Henry get Susan? You're much better looking."

"I don't know, he just did. I'm too bashful, I guess."

"You're not bashful, only nice. Sometimes teenage girls get carried away with boys that are bold. They seem exciting to them. Being nice and polite is thought of as a handicap to those type guys, but with age, girls begin to see that nice guys are just as exciting in matters that count and they make much better husbands and fathers. I think many exciting times await you with some lucky gal."

He began feeling comfortable with her. "I don't know what to say to girls. Every time I talk to Susan, I say something dumb."

"Like what?" she quizzed him.

He gave off a wide grin. "Once at the Owl's, she complained of stomach cramps. And dumbbell me said, 'Maybe it's something you ate.' The gang had a good laugh on me. She was having her monthly. I didn't know what everyone else knew. I don't have a sister, wish I did." he chuckled. "I wasn't the same for a week. So stupid, it was embarrassing."

His elated voice pleased her. "Don't worry; anyone that can laugh at their blunders in life will always come out on top. You can take that advice to the bank, young man." She heard the front door open. Carl was noisy. She rushed into the hallway. "Shhhh," she hissed. "Your Dad is sleeping. Remember?"

Carl dropped the loaf of bread onto the table. "Come on, Jake. Get your coat on. The whole gang is at the Owl's. Cathy too, Mom."

"Bye." Jake said.

"Bye Jake, keep your chin high."

He nodded and along with Carl rushed out of the house.

She walked to the stairs; it was time to awaken her ruler. "Maybe I'll dress myself up tonight," she thought. She needed to look beautiful and cheer herself up.

CHAPTER FIVE
The Peddler

Struss often hurried his household chores, and at times, some chores he'd put off cleaning for another day to the dismay of his factory working wife. Cleaning the living room window, he'd never put off very long. Through his living room window a panoramic view of his beloved Pittsburgh greeted him each morning, along with his stein of hot black coffee. He often bragged at the local Biergarten about his unrestricted sight of the city. Few homes on Pigeon Hill could claim such a sight. Most of the aging row homes had obstacles; houses or trees blocking out a good view of downtown. Pittsburgh, a city in a forest, was constantly trimming trees along its streets and power lines in its never-ending battle to beat back the foliage from reclaiming neighborhoods. The living room was the one room in the old house that was remodeled and only to install the wide bay window Struss and his wife longed after.

Struss stepped back from the window and looked it over for streaks. In his hands he held pages from yesterdays' newspaper. His mother had often said in broken English, "das newspaper vork best," and she was right, wiping the glass dry with newspaper left the panes streak free. He moved closer to the window and spotted Jake and his pals leaving the Bentley home, heading to Millers Store, he guessed. He watched his son until he passed out of sight and then lifted his eyes toward downtown. He could see bits of the Gulf Building through the haze. When the mills were running at a high capacity, his view was blocked by the soot and smoke in the air and today was one of those days. On good viewing days, when steel output dropped off or furnaces were idle, he'd get a good view of the city buildings and some bridges crossing the Allegheny and Monongahela Rivers. He cherished viewing the historical Point, seeing the rivers joining together and watching the mighty Ohio flow start its journey to the Gulf of Mexico. Inside the crinkled newspaper he was gripping, he'd read an article about the famous Point. It mentioned about the cleaning up of the Point and making a walking park where factories now operated. It was calling the idea a rebirth, a Renaissance. He hated the idea. He liked smokestacks and the belching soot and grime they deposited over the city from time to time when the mills were producing around the clock. Belching smokestacks meant bread on the table and many other monetary pleasures for working Democratic Party families.

It was all beautiful to him as it stood the same as when his immigrant father, dressed in his Sunday best, took him after Mass to the Biergardens throughout Deutschtown. Inside those Beer Gardens his father enjoyed his heritage: drinking beer, munching pretzels, singing drinking songs, and celebrating his German work ethic with other hardworking men. The newspaper also printed a layout of the proposed Point Park. At the site where the rivers merge, and Fort Pitt once stood, a jet stream of water would be blown into the air. "A fountain." he grumbled under his breath, shaking his head in disbelief.

He spotted a flock of pigeons swooping and lifting and circling above the hillside homes below his house. It was a wondrous site. Fewer neighbors flew pigeon flocks any longer and racing clubs fell out of favor since World War Two. Struss remembered many coops built on hilly backyards while growing up. Pigeon racing clubs flourished then; a hobby brought from Europe by the immigrants. Most coops stood empty now, younger men showing no interest in the hobby and being more interested in moving to the suburbs and mowing grass. Pigeons weren't following people to the manicured lawns in the hinterland. Struss imagined pigeon shit raining down upon his younger brothers' suburban homes and causing frowning panic in their everything-up-to-date thinking wives.

Struss wondered if his only child, Jake, would stay in the city and live on Pigeon Hill after he married and raised a family. He wanted to see his grandchildren live nearby to celebrate their birthdays and first communions and tell them stories about their roots. He loathed the differences in Pigeon Hill and the surrounding communities since the end of the World War. Families moving away and bakeries, general stores, butcher and barber shops were closing. The changes made him uneasy. He could see the changing ways happening through his cherished window, where his community burdened with small roads and big cars struggled to adapt to the increasingly mobile society.

Struss had no driver's license, never thought to get one, and didn't want a car. Trolleys were all he needed to get around town just like the Jew he spotted walking up the road carrying his cardboard boxes, tied together with a cord. He was glad the Jew kept coming around. The horse and wagon huckster peddling fresh produce and the roving knife sharpener, carrying his grinding stone wheel on his back, were vanishing from the streets. Now, only the iceman, coal delivery man, and the Jew still came door to door. He missed the ways that weren't any more, and the hard-working people that had passed onto their eternal reward. He believed in hard work, but not for himself. His last job was during the war years, in an iron casting foundry, melting and pouring, a cast part maker. It was filthy, sweaty, tough labor and he was happy to be laid off after the war ended and demand from a victorious military diminished.

With the need for factory workers so great during the war, Struss' wife easily found work paying high hourly wages. Steel mills and factories, producing immense outputs of steel and machined parts for the war department offered full employment to any man or woman willing to present themselves for the grinding labor. His wife got work manufacturing nuts and bolts and stayed working at that plant ever since. After he was laid off, by mutual agreement, they settled on their present system. She would be the bread winner and he would tend to Jake and the household. He did the house cleaning, the cooking, and the washing and ironing clothes as best he could, not that he wanted to do such work. But compared to the foundry, it was like playing in a sandbox. And he could work at his own speed and now and then, stop and enjoy a cold beer.

He liked to read true crime magazines in his spare time and thought he'd have been a lawyer if given a chance at a higher education. He thought about the affairs of the world, read the newspaper editorial page daily, and believed he had many great ideas on many subjects. He shared a similar past with the Jew. Each the oldest of a large family, their parents immigrated from Germany toward the end of the last century, but the Jew spoke German and Struss wished he'd learned more Deutsche as a child. Both were approaching fifty years old.

Struss left his streak free window, and after tossing the wads of damp news in the kitchen trash, washed his hands thoroughly, and waited by the kitchen door. Before the Jew could knock with cold knuckles, Struss opened the door.

"Hello Strussberg!" the tall man on the stoop called out, starting a friendly battle of wits with his customer.

"Strussberger," he corrected as he entered the house. "What the hell do you want?" Struss pushed the door shut against the cold windy air,

"Beeziness, I want your beeziness." the Jew said while pulling up a chair to the kitchen table, making himself at home.

"My money, you mean?" Struss snapped, sitting across from him, wishing he had the thick silver white hair of the Jew.

The Jew laid his black homburg and ear muffs on the table. "That too." he chuckled. "Time for Jake to get a new coat? Maybe summer clothes? Low prices on summer clothes in the cold months. Your bill is low now, almost paid off."

"Afraid I'll drop you, quit buying?"

"I like customers that pay steady, like you Strussberg. I got expenses too."

"Nothing today. Before Easter, Jake will need some outfitting."

"Brrr! I feel like a two stick Popsicle." He was shivering.

"I can hear your teeth rattling, or is that your money?" Struss said laughing hard.

"Ha ha," The Jew mocked. "Not bad from a kibitzer."

From his dark overcoat pocket, the Jew got his customer book and opened it to Struss' account. "Paying on your account today?"

"You'll fine comb Pigeon Hill till you get its last dime. Won't you?"

"Only a few customers lately on this side of Pigeon Shit Hill. On the other side, I do well, people are better off over there." the Jew teased, well aware of Struss' unproven assumptions that wealthy Republicans live in clusters on the opposite side of his community.

Struss stood. "You know why, don't you? They're Republican outsiders. Living off the sweat of workingmen."

"Outsiders!" the Jew howled, while laughing hard. "They're you, offspring of German immigrants." The Peddler kept chuckling as Struss, ignoring the Jew's remark, walked across the floor.

"I'll see what I can find," Struss said, fumbling around in the cubbyhole above the icebox for the two dollars he put aside.

The Jew came around the neighborhoods weekly and if customers needed a shirt, pants, dress, or any type of cloth clothing, he'd take their measurements and bring the items on his next visit. Before the war and numerous automobiles, the Jew had many customers. Prosperity was creating a mobile society and the Jew could only hope for a few more years of peddling before the ownership of automobiles became a common occurrence and killed his business. He thought of his trade as a convenience for housewives. Mothers trapped with cooking, cleaning, caring after little Brats, and husbands grinding away at the factories. Who had time for riding a trolley downtown to shop for children's clothing which they outgrew soon after putting them on? Factory workers, ending their shift of labor, dirtied and exhausted never stopped to shop. He kept his own books and gave no receipts. Asking for a receipt was being suspicious of his bookkeeping, and that sometime innocent request gave the big man a noticeable frown.

"This will make you happy," Struss said, waving two dollars above his head.

"As I said, you're a good customer."

"Want a beer? Schnapps?" Struss offered, opening the icebox and taking out a beer and a small brick of Limburger cheese tightly wrapped in foil.

"What sort of Schnapps?"

"Peach and peppermint, down in my Rathskeller."

"One of these days, when I have time, I'll check out your Rathskeller. I could go for Schnapps. It's cold walking the streets, but no, thanks." He opened his logbook. "Strussberger; two bucks." and he went on. "And those cobblestone streets are slippery. Why aren't there any sidewalks around here? The Outsiders, as you call them over on the North Slope have wide sidewalks, but not this side? I'd call the Ward Boss if I were you. Complain, tell him you're going to join the Outsiders, become a Republican if the city doesn't put some sidewalks in place."

"Scher dich!" Struss uttered. "I do complain. Because our neighborhood developed sixty years before the other side, we're told to wait, improvements are coming. Yeah, and it's chilly in hell."

"I'm impressed! Cussing me in Deutsche, wishing me to hell. My good student."

The Jew buttoned his overcoat and looked at his friend unwrapping the foil. He was a short man with broad shoulders. Bald, except for a thin outline of brown and gray on the sides and back of his head. His light blue eyes were penetrating.

"That cheese caused you to go bald."

Struss ignored him and dipped a stinking chunk into a dish of dark mustard and pushed it into his mouth, followed by a gulp of beer.

"Whew!" the Jew said, waving his hand in front of his nose. "You know, that comes in a jar now. A lot less smelly."

"Really?" Struss questioned. "Christ Almighty, the world is coming to its end."

The Jew gathered up his hat, muffs, and log and started for the door. "How is Jake?"

"Fine. Your sons?"

"Still in medical School. You know Jewish mothers, have ten sons, and expect ten doctors."

"Before you go, How do you say; 'Happy New Year' in German?" Struss grinned. "It'll come in handy tomorrow at the biergarten New Year's Eve party."

The Jew's dark eyes widened. "Maybe I'll give you a translation of something else, like, Happy New Year, smart ass."

"And lose a good customer like me?"

"Frohes Neues Jahr." The Jew spoke slowly. "Frohes Neues Jahr."

"Thanks see you next week."

"Auf wiedersehen." The Peddler left the house with his boxes.

"Auf wiedersehen." Struss murmured, and started repeating, "Frohes Neues Jahr, Frohes Neues Jahr," over and over for most of the remaining day.

CHAPTER SIX
The Owl's

Miller's Corner Store, a three-story structure built before the turn of the century, was located in a unique spot, close enough to the summit of Pigeon Hill to attract customers from each side of the hill. Only Resurrection Cemetery held a higher elevation. That fenced in land of grave stones forever sealed off the crown of Pigeon Hill from any future use by the living. Each generation of teenagers used the store as a common gathering place. It was called "Miller's" by some, "The Corner Store" by others, but the current group of teens tagged it "The Owl's" after the grandson of the store's founder. He looked like an owl, they said, small and squatty, a nose like a beak and wore horn-rimmed glasses.

The Owl lived above the store, on the third floor, fondly called "the nest" by the youth. His grandmother lived on the second floor. His grandparents raised him after his parents met an untimely death. After school, he'd work at the store learning its methods well. After his grandfather died, his aging grandmother turned the management of the store over to him. He was ambitious and soon to marry and he quickly made modern changes to the roomy, olden-day appearing store. He removed the barrels of nails, trays of flower and vegetable seeds, and the jars of rock candy and other unwrapped homemade candies that his grandma made. The wide lidded penny candy jars were bulky compared to commercially wrapped candy, which could be stocked in less space. He removed the long counter and installed a checkout stand, establishing a self-service system similar to the newer suburban supermarkets. He also converted a backroom into a soda bar. If the neighborhood teenagers insisted on using the store for a hangout, he'd make it convenient for them to spend their money. The soda bar was his fiancée's idea and she managed it and the teenagers, if they got out of line by being too loud or cursing. The teens nicknamed her "Feathers." The Owl and Feathers planned a July wedding.

The Owl's grandma, upset over the changes, allowed him to make them. She reasoned she'd be dead soon and would no longer suffer the agony of sleeping above a Showcase, as she now called the general store. She forcefully insisted on having her homemade soft pretzels sold, and conveniently displayed on open trays near the cash register for the older customers. She wouldn't give in to his pleading that they ruined the orderliness of Miller's Mart as he now referred to his business. She scolded him often in German. The Owl's business plan was someday to stock only commercially wrapped products and to get away from weighing and selling items like nails by the pound. Besides, companies that delivered commercially wrapped and boxed foods, general items, and other household needs gave credit for returns.

Inside the soda bar with the rest of the gang, Teddy was content listening to Mr. Bentley and watching Cathy's every move. She stood next to her father and twin brother. Her golden hair, pulled into a short ponytail, wagged slightly whenever she nervously darted her blue eyes around the room searching for a place to fix them, other than on a boy. She was aware of them eyeballing her up and down, especially Junior Wernher and Teddy Vonovich. Wearing red corduroy slacks, a short feathery-looking white coat and brown fur-lined boots, she stood tall and lean, emitting a pulsating beauty that had specific affects on the unrelated male hormones in the room. Lately, as did other girls her age and while on parental shopping errands, she'd linger at the Owl's longer then she had to.

Mr. Bentley, a powerful looking man without a protruding stomach as many men his age, stood in the middle of the room dressed in blue jeans and a sweater similar to the lounging boys surrounding him. He was talking to Junior. "Someday they'll nab the creep that killed your Dad."

"What I can't understand," Junior answered. "Where is the woman my Dad went to help?" He leaned his heavy body against the pinball machine. "Why doesn't she help the police?"

"Well," Mr. Bentley answered while looking at his daughter, "Women aren't like men, they can be ashamed easier. And a trial would bring her a lot of publicity."

"It wasn't her fault."

"People will say it was," he warned, "If she flirts a lot or is a dresser, the tight clothes type."

"My Dad tried to help her, she owes it to him!"

"I wish I'd got my hands on that rat," Mr. Bentley said, shaking his clenched fist. "Cops wouldn't have much left of him to put behind bars." He laughed loud. The boys joined in the laughter. Feathers hushed them quickly and they quieted down.

"He would kill him!" Carl was excited by his father's machismo. "He really would."

"Your Dad deserves a medal, Junior." Mr. Bentley continued. "Someday they'll nab the killer, give him the electric chair. Juice his butt!" he chuckled.

The Owl called from the checkout stand. "Teddy, your mother's outside!"

"Teddy," Henry giggled. "Your ma-ma wants you."

Teddy went quickly through the store, but not fast enough to outrun the snickers coming from Henry and Junior. Outside, he stood under the Mart's overhead entrance light. His mother turned down the car window and called out to him from across the street. Her face, framed in the open car window, excessively rouged and powdered, reflected the bright store light. She sat bundled in a moss green coat and wore a small yellow hat. "Teddy, come here honey. I wanta wish you Happy New Year."

Teddy went to the open window and leaned to his mother's face."

"Hi, kid," the strange man winked.

She touched her son's face. "He's not my little Teddy Bear anymore. He's my big man now." She rubbed his cheek. "Isn't that right, honey?"

"Yeah, Mom." He could smell whiskey on her breath.

"Let's go, Baby," the stranger pleaded. "It's cold."

"Okay, okay, I just wanted to see my big man."

"I'll see you at home, Mom."

"Okay honey; don't forget to get up for school."

"I won't," he said, not bothering to tell her he was still on Christmas vacation.

"Ready?" the stranger asked. "Close the window."

"Gimme a dollar for my big man," she slurred, opening her hand to her newest friend.

The man fumbled in his wallet. "Here kid." he said, thrusting a greenback at Teddy.

Teddy pocketed it. "Thanks."

"Gimme a big hug." Teddy leaned through the window. She hugged him hard. "Be a good Teddy Bear. I love you."

"I love you too, Mom."

She released her son.

The man saw his chance and drove away, calling out. "Happy New Year, kid."

Teddy took the greenback from his pocket. He was shocked. Five dollars! He entered Miller's Mart elated. Cathy's Dad was still talking.

"These two," he pointed to the twins. "Know the outdoors. I've been taking them camping and fishing since they were tots. I got a swell spot near a lake, all the fish you can eat. And I take Carl hunting every season."

"And we hook a lot." Carl added.

"Speaking of fish," Mr. Bentley said pointing at Cathy. "This one swims like a fish."

Cathy blushed.

Her father went on bragging about her skill. "She's been taking swimming instructions at the Y since she was small. She's a natural. Won many trophies."

Cathy turned her red face away from everyone. "They know I swim Dad, don't embarrass me. Change the subject. Please."

Junior did. "Seen my new car, Cathy?"

"You got a new car?" Mr. Bentley asked. Surprised.

"A used one. My mother let me pick it myself from her quality used car lot. My Christmas present."

"Well, I better march myself home," Mr. Bentley gently said to his son, then turned to Cathy, and raised his voice. "Remember, home by nine o'clock."

She didn't answer him. Her Dad left the Mart.

Soon after Mr. Bentley was out the door, Henry and Susan held hands and cuddled. Henry was the oldest and tallest in the gang. He had a long face, big blue eyes and could be very charming when he wanted to be thought of as nice. Before going steady with Susan, he'd claimed to have had several sexual triumphs and often told the others boys about his successes. His victories all seem to occur off of Pigeon Hill when he was away visiting relatives. He couldn't claim Susan. She was strong-willed and able to halt his advances even when she was aroused. Henry loved her and knew that Jake had strong feeling for her also, but he never felt threatened by him or ever thought that Susan would cast him aside for any other fellow.

Susan was always upbeat, cheerful, friendly, pert, and easily made to laugh. She was pleasingly plump and had the largest breasts of any other girl that hung out at the Owl's. She also dressed to show off her two trophies. Tonight she wore a snug maroon sweater with a vee neckline and black slacks with the leg ends tucked into white boots. She was practical, always expecting her Henry to be interested in other girls. She didn't trust him when he was out of her sight. She was smart enough never to give in to his sexual advances. The longer she denied him, the more he desired her. His longing for her was stronger than a chain around his neck. His inability to sexually overtake her stopped him from running away. And if he did, she felt for sure that her awaiting virgin prize would bring him running back to her.

"Feathers," Carl asked. "How about a treat? On the house?"

"Christmas is over, sweetheart."

"I got money," Teddy said. "Five dollars."

"Let's eat!" Henry gave his order to Feathers. "Two scoop chocolate for me."

Feathers looked at Teddy for approval. He nodded. The treats were on him. The rest of the teens placed their sweet treat orders then sat calmly along the counter stools watching Feathers preparing their orders in anticipation of licking ice cream. Feathers handed Teddy his cone first, and then to the others in no particular order. Junior glanced longingly at Cathy licking her ice cream. Susan sat between Jake and Henry, close enough for Jake to breathe in her scent and know that he loved only her after all, and not Mrs. Bentley. Henry said something that made Susan giggle but Jake didn't hear it. He tried to think of something to say to her, something funny to make her laugh and lean into him as she'd just did to Henry's remark. He couldn't think of anything funny to say to her. It was hard to talk to a girl that you secretly loved. Soon the night would be over and he hadn't uttered a meaningful word to her all night. His heart coaxed him to say something to her, but his mind warned caution. His heart won the struggle and he spoke. "How's your ice cream, Susan?"

"Cold!" she snapped.

He felt stupid, once again, in her company. He hardly licked his ice cream, alternating his thoughts between Susan and Mrs. Bentley, while the others ate lavishly. They were a splintered group, a lamb and lion mix, with Henry, the cohesive know-it-all, leading them away from childish games and into adult fun.

"Last call," Feathers said.

"It's not nine o'clock yet," Junior said.

"It's New Years Eve, got a reservation to bring in the New Year dancing." Feathers said shaking her skinny hips.

"Yeah." Henry stood and looked at Teddy. "We gotta get something going for tonight. How much money you got left?"

Teddy counted his money. "Two dollars and ..."

Henry cut him off. "Not enough. Shit, we blew it, on ice cream instead of beer."

"Watch the mouth, Henry. Swearing is out in the store." Feathers warned. "And you're too young for alcohol!"

"What's up?" Junior asked.

"Brew." Henry explained. "We need some beer to ring out the old and bring in the new. I know a bar where I can buy it to go."

"Hey," Susan slapped him on the shoulder. "You're going home with me."

"Not tonight, Honey. Your folks will be awake till midnight watching television."

"So?" Susan stomped her foot. "I want to be with you at midnight."

Henry laughed. "I ain't gonna sit all night with your Mom and Dad in the room."

"Shooo, I won't have anyone to talk to."

"Talk to your parents," he teased.

"Shooo." She slapped his chest.

"I'll drive home and get some money," Junior said, lifting his hefty frame off of the counter stool. "Want a ride home, Cathy?"

"No, thanks." she answered without looking at him.

Junior hid his disappointment over her refusal. "Carl, wanta drive along?"

"Sure," he answered and turned to Cathy. "You better get home, it's almost nine."

She didn't answer her twin, upset with her father's unfairness. Rules for her, but not for Carl. He could stay out later because he was a boy. Her mother spoke to her father once about his different rules, but his displeasure at being questioned about how he controlled his children turned into anger and the subject was never brought up again by anyone in the family.

"Let's go." Henry said while handing Susan her coat.

"You're cruel, Henry Schneider!" Susan said and walked to Cathy's side.

The boys left the store together, except for Teddy who stayed behind with Cathy and Susan. "Want some chewing gum or something else?" he asked the girls showing them his money.

"No thanks." Susan said. Cathy declined his offer by shaking her head.

"Sure?" Teddy questioned.

Neither girl answered him and continued chatting as they walked outside.

"I'll meet you guys here in thirty minutes." Henry said

"Brrr." Susan said while tightening her coat. "Happy New Year, everyone." She left arm in arm with Henry.

Junior and Carl drove off to get the cash.

Jake looked down the road. He could see Henry and Susan kissing under a streetlight. He felt blue. "I ain't feeling well," he said to Teddy.

Cathy was also watching the kissing couple.

"Don't go home," Teddy pleaded. Jake was his best friend, sometimes his only friend. "Stay out awhile. Drink a beer."

"Naw, I'm not feeling good. Upset stomach." It was true. He was sick, but with himself, not his belly. He decided to head home, take another flop into his lonely bed and wish he'd the charm of a Henry. "Call me tomorrow, Teddy. I'm heading home. Goodnight, Cathy."

"Bye," they both said and then Teddy added. "Happy New Year, buddy."

"Same to you, pal." Jake walked away.

The Owl bolted the Mart's door and switched off the outside entrance light.

The pair stood in the dark. Teddy was trying to think of something clever to say to Cathy, but she spoke first. "Does he ever talk about other girls?"

"Who? Jake?"

"No silly, Henry."

"Henry? I don't know. He likes Susan."

"But does he ever talk about other girls?"

A gust of wind blew and tossed her ponytail a bit. Henry talked dirty about girls most of the time when he wasn't with Susan; including Cathy when Carl wasn't close enough to hear. She was confusing him with her questioning. "I don't know," he lied.

"I better get home." She walked away.

Seconds later he called out and began walking after her. Excited about being alone with her and having a conversation. Not just the normal routine salutations that usually passed between them. He was thinking Susan had put her up to checking on Henry. "You'll tell Susan, won't you?"

"No, I won't," she answered over her shoulder, slowing, allowing him to catch up to her.

"Why do you want to know?"

"I'm just curious, that's all."

Teddy didn't answer her. She walked faster. Teddy walked a bit behind her, watching her ponytail bounce around and loving the sight. He was joyous. They were nearing her house. His happiness would soon end. "Sometimes he does."

She stopped and faced him, showing a smile like a crescent moon. "Does he ever talk about me?" Teddy was crushed.

She waited for his reply. Streetlight shine showed her sparkling blue eyes fixed on his quizzical face features.

"No," he lied.

"Never, not even once?"

"Never."

She turned and ran to her house.

* * *

Junior steered his car under the arched steel gate. Pigeon Hill residents, when traveling from one slope to the other, often took the shorter route through Resurrection Cemetery. The narrow dirt road, frozen and snow covered from a recent storm, zigged and zagged throughout the cemetery hilltop. But those hazardous conditions didn't slow Junior down. He flicked on his high beams. The light passing over the snowy graves and tombstones looked spooky.

Earlier in the year, before Armistice Day, the Cemetery Committee directed the caretaker to place a bronze plaque on the cemetery grounds to commemorate the men from the parish who served in World War Two. He fastened the plaque onto a cut granite rock and on his own initiative decided to erect a flagpole alongside of the stone. After fastening pipes together and painting the pole grey, it still lacked the authenticity of a flagpole. Recently, he'd replaced a tin float on the cemetery toilet flushing mechanism. The metal shaped ball with a small hole was filling with water, sinking instead of floating. He painted the ball and attached it to the pole. On strong windy days, the air swirled inside the ball, making a shrill whistling sound all around.

On this strong windy night, the Caretaker, drunk because of his beer guzzling ways at the local America Legion, went amongst the graves staggering to his home on the cemetery grounds. He helped his wobbly body from falling by reaching out to the bigger grave markers as he passed them. He heard the speeding car coming his way. Young minors, using the solitude of the graveyard to drink their ill-gotten beer and then breaking the empty bottles against tombstones and tossing other trash about for him to clean up, greatly annoyed him. He made a stack of snowballs, and then hid behind a monument, waiting in ambush for, "the varmints," as he referred to the teenage intruders in his sacred territory. The car came into his sight.

"Zap!"

"What in the hell was that?" Junior asked, hitting his brake pedal hard. The car slid to a stop. The engine stalled.

"Zap-zap-zap!"

"Someone's out there," Carl yelled. "Throwing snowballs at us. Get outta here!"

Junior turned the ignition key. The engine turned over but didn't start.

"Zap, zap."

Carl opened the car door, got out and scanned the surroundings.

"There he is," Carl said, while pointing. "By that big gravestone."

Junior turned down the car window just as another volley of balls smashed against his car.

"Zap, zap, zap."

"You crazy goon!" Carl shouted out at the thrower. Junior turned the ignition key. No engine start up and he became frustrated, cursing the car from his mother's lot. "Start, you piece of shit!" he screamed.

A gust of wind blew as the Caretaker stood and threw his last snowball. "Zap." The flagpole ball began shrilling.

The car started and Carl jumped into the passenger seat and slammed the door shut. "You see that? Whatever!" he cried out. "He's whistling! Go! Go! Go!"

Junior sped away.

CHAPTER SEVEN
Rathskeller

From his perch at the bay window, Struss spotted the Jew coming his way. The Peddler was stepping carefully on the wet cobblestones. After decades of walking roads, he learned the hard way how slippery cobblestones are when wet. As a younger man, he'd rush from customer to customer over the streets until the time he slipped, fell and broke his leg.

His family suffered economically and it took an extended time before he could pay back his relatives for supporting him until he recovered. With the last piles of winter snows melting and April showers approaching, the cobblestones would be wet often until May.

Struss opened the door and greeted his friend. "What, only one package? Business that bad?"

The Jew walked past him and took his regular seat at the kitchen table. He put his homburg and customer record book on the table and loosened his tie. "This package is for you," the Jew smiled. "A gift for your Rathskeller, that cellar sanctuary where the Strussberg coven celebrates their heritage."

Struss sat across from him. "Really?"

"I've been coming here for Jake's lifetime, you've been a good, no, a great customer so I said to myself, a gift would be nice for Strussberg."

"Strussberger." Struss growled. "I won't take it. For just as many years, I've been inviting you to check out my Rathskeller, but you never do, even when I offer schnapps. Come downstairs, have a drink and I'll accept your gift."

The Jew shrugged. "Okay, but beesiness first. The last time I was here, you said, 'come back before Easter.' Did you take Jake's measurements like I taught you?"

"Yeah, I got them." Struss got the measurements from the cubbyhole and gave them to the Jew. The Peddler looked them over and put them in his suit pocket. "How about you, don't you get tired of living all the time in baggy pants? And those under-wear shirts? Do you own any shirts with collars?"

"What do I need new clothes for? I'm not going anywhere and don't want to go anywhere. Case closed."

"I wouldn't want to go anywhere either, dressed like you." The Jew said.

Struss changed the subject. "No packages?"

"No, I had a few that I've already delivered, but I took a lot of orders today, with Easter coming. Easter is good for my wallet."

"You did well on the South Slope. Good. Did you get action from the Outsiders side of the hill?"

"It's okay, but not as good as South Slope." The Jew grinned. "You know those tightwad Republicans, a bunch of cheapskates, they act like Jews."

"Quit with the funny stuff. How about the other Deutschtown neighborhoods?"

"Good on Spatz Hill. Highest Hill and Garden Grove not as well. Pigeon Hill is tops."

"How about Polish Hill, Little Italy? Irish Town? Do they throw rocks at you, or love you like we Germans? I know I must've put at least one of your sons through medical school."

The Jew shook his head. "Not even close. Those other ethnic neighborhoods are okay. What can I say, I make a living."

Struss grinned. "How about Jew Town? Bet you make a million there?"

The Jew laughed. "Where do you think I get the clothes I sell? Jews. I keep my tailor cousins in business."

"Well?" Struss asked. "Are we going to my Rathskeller or are you toting that gift of mine back to Jew Town?"

"You won't be eating limburger cheese down there, will you?" The Peddler pinched his nose. "It's not ventilated, is it?"

"No to both questions. Come on. I've been trying to show off my Rathskeller to you like a Jewish mother shows off her doctor son. I'm proud of it and the hard work it took to build it."

The Jew followed his good customer down into the Rathskeller. Struss turned on the lights and the Jew was impressed by what Struss and his younger brothers had done years earlier in the old house's cellar. The floor had been dug down, increasing the height of the cellar from floor to ceiling. The walls were covered with interlocking planks of knotty pine and were highly varnished. Brass sconces with red, white and blue lighting along the walls gave the room a colorful, festive atmosphere. Six oak tables with four chairs each were well spaced across the tile floor.

The dark, varnished bar top had padded leather edges where drinkers could rest their elbows while sitting on oak stools. Behind the bar was a mirror, surrounded by nooks and crannies to store bottles, glasses and steins.

Underneath the bar, there was a bigger icebox than the one used in Struss' kitchen. This is where he kept the bottled beer and soda pop when partying. A small keg of beer was on tap, but there was enough space for a thirty-gallon keg if need be.

The Peddler was impressed and Struss felt proud showing off his accomplishment. The Jew pulled up a stool at the bar. Struss placed two shot glasses in front of him and poured peppermint schnapps for himself and the Peddler. Struss lifted his shot and made a toast. "Happy Passover and Easter."

"I'll drink to that." The Jew smiled and sipped his drink. Struss gulped his shot down in one swallow.

"Here's your gift." The Jew laid the small wrapped package on the bar.

Struss opened it and read the framed newspaper headlines from a June 10, 1928-edition of the *Pittsburgh Press*. "Pittsburgh Lays Claim to being the Birthplace of Republican Party."

Struss laughed. "This is one of those fake newspapers. Right? The kind people get at fairs. And they can have silly headlines printed about themselves as a joke."

The Jew shook his head and sipped more Schnapps. "No joke. Authentic."

Struss read the rest of the article. "Other cities lay claim to be the birthplace, but from the records of the party itself, the cradle of the Republican Party seems to have been Pittsburgh. The first National Convention met..."

The Jew watched Struss' face. He was stunned that the Outsiders and their political misdeeds were hatched right in his hometown. The Jew drank the rest of his Schnapps.

Struss finished reading, laid the gift on the bar, and poured them both more Schnapps. "You want a beer to wash that peppermint down?"

"No, thanks. Well, what do you say about my gift? Will you hang it on that wall?" the Peddler pointed across the room, "Where all those pictures are hanging?"

"Yeah, in a year or ten." Struss stared at the headlines, not yet convinced that the printed words were true.

"Who are those pictures of?" The Jew became interested in the wall of hanging frames.

"German-Americans." Struss snapped. "After two wars with Germany, many German-Americans downplayed their heritage. Some took on the English version of Deutsche and started calling themselves Dutch, or Pennsylvania Dutch." Struss sighed.

"My brothers and I, influenced by our parents of course, were always told of the great contributions German immigrants made to America. In every field, from sports to science, the Germans made a mark on the character of America. German-Americans are the biggest ethnic group in the United States and from the beginning of the Republic were numerous, especially in Pennsylvania. Benjamin Franklin printed a German language newspaper in 1732 on his Philadelphia presses, which was 44 years before the revolution. Struss drank his shot.

"Don't tell a Jew about casting aspersions on innocent people for the evil actions of others. My people have been blamed for everything, from the death of Jesus, to the poor quality of movies coming from Hollywood." The Jew chuckled. "My family came from Germany before both World Wars like your parents, for opportunity more than hostility against Jews." He chuckled again. "We Jews expect hostility wherever we wander." The Jew drank his Schnapps and slid his shot glass toward Struss. Struss poured him another. The Peddler kept talking.

"Germany isn't the only nation to have brought horror upon the world. The Japanese exterminated the Chinese without guilt as if they were no more than ants. The rape of Nanking is only one horror of many that the Chinese suffered from the Japanese Imperial Army." The Peddler was taking to the Schnapps. He tossed back his head and swallowed the drink and continued to inform his host about the evils in the world.

"Stalin and the Soviets are doing as much with their gulag internment camps in Siberia. One of the biggest differences between the Nazi horrors and other genocides in the past is that there is less or no documentation of non-Nazi crimes available for the world to see. Whereas the Nazi's with their German trait for attention to detail, kept precise logs, photos, and film of their evil. All captured and available for the world to witness."

Struss poured a draft beer and offered one to the Jew. Struss filled a cold glass for his guest.

"Whose pictures are hanging on the wall? I see a big number three, what's that about?"

"The Babe." Struss said. "I'm a crazy baseball fan. I like the Sluggers. I don't have a photo of the Babe, so I just framed a big number three and hung it up. Three was his Yankee number. Most folks don't know he was a German-American. I also have Honus Wagner's photograph, the great Pittsburgh Pirate. Hank Sauer, a slugger born in Pittsburgh, played for the Reds and the Cubs. And, of course, Lou Gehrig, the Iron Horse, played for the Yankee's. All German-Americans. I have other players also, like Ralph Kiner, our Pirate Slugger. You should have brought me a framed photo of Hammering Hank Greenberg. Now that would have been a great gift for my Rathskeller. You know he's a Jew?"

"I'm reminded by my Rabbi often enough." He gulped some cold beer and smacked his lips. "Wunderbar!"

"They're not all German-Americans hanging on the wall, but my family wanted to let our kids know that Germans have made great contributions to America and fought in all of her wars. All of my younger brothers served." Struss said and drank some beer.

"There's photos of Eisenhower as both General and President. World War One Army General Pershing, Admiral Chester Nimitz of World War Two, and a drawing of General Steuben, the German General that improved the effectiveness of

Washington's Continental Army. And last but not least, a painting of Molly Pitcher at the battle of Monmouth, took her husband's place at the cannon after he was killed. Her maiden name was Mary Ludwig Hays." Struss stopped and took a long drink of beer. "Am I boring you?"

"No, not at long as I can drink your Schnapps." He grinned "You're doing well Struss, letting others know that it's really not, like father like son, like Nazi like German, like Herod like Jew. It's good versus evil, and every human tribe has hatched evil people. Thank God. Most never accumulate total power as Hitler and Stalin."

"Another Schnapps?" Struss asked his guest.

"One more, then I got to go."

Struss poured and his guest quickly drank it. "Oh my God," the Jew chuckled. "You eat them too," and pointed to a jar of pickled pig knuckles and feet. "Along with nasty Limburger?"

"Love 'em." Struss laughed. "Want one? It's a new jar, not cracked open yet."

"I'd rather eat my homburg." The Jew was feeling fine, a sort of a permanent smile stayed on his face. "Is that a club standing in the corner?"

Struss laughed. "That's my wife's contribution to the Rathskeller. Her father's shillelagh that he brought from Ireland. It's an Irish walking stick. It's made out of some sort of root. When Jake was small and I was younger, we'd do a lot of partying. Get out of line and she'd threaten you with that ugly stick."

The Peddler saw the big Schnitzelbank poster on the back wall. "That is how my father made me and my brothers learn German." The Jew reminisced. "Everyday we'd practice singing the entire poster. I can still recite the entire poster of pictures by heart. So constantly were those figures and words pressed upon me as a child."

"That's the only German I know well." Struss lamented, "When my brothers and our friends had parties down here, we'd get to drinking and singing the Schnitzelbank. It was great fun."

"Schnapps please," the Jew said, and challenged Struss to prove he knew the German words to the Schnitzelbank as he'd claimed." Struss poured him a Schnapps.

"If I answer them correctly, you must quit calling me Strussberg."

"And if you lose?" the Jew asked.

"I'll buy some pants and shirts from you."

"Deal." The Peddler rejoiced. "In any order I choose?"

"Okay, skip the shaving bench and start anytime." Struss was confident.

"Crooked or straight?" The Jew said.

"Krum und grad."

"Fat sow."

"Oxen blas."

"Cris and cross."

"Kreuz und quer." Struss answered and continued answering in German to each of the sixteen word descriptions the Peddler called out. Struss was victorious.

The Jew was feeling the Schnapps. Struss drank some beer and played big band music by turning some knobs under the bar. They were in a Glen Miller mood.

Struss picked up a deck of cards from off of the bar. "I play Solitaire down here but during the war with Germany, I used to play the War Game with Jake. We never called it War. We called it chasing the old country."

The Jew looked more interested in Glen Miller.

"Get it!" Struss giggled. "We were at war with Germany, the country my parents always referred to 'as the old country.' So we'd call the card game, chasing the old country." Struss laughed hard, thinking that was hilarious.

"Struss." The Jew took on a sad face. "You have younger brothers, I have younger brothers, and they all fought in World War Two. We missed out on the greatest event in our lifetime. Do you ever wish you'd went off to war like your younger brothers? I do. My younger brothers are more in tune with American ways than me. I'm more closely tied to my parents and their traditional ways of living than my brothers. They had a great adventure. I missed it."

"I feel the same as you." Struss murmured. "The war changed everything. My brothers, with the GI bill in hand, have gone off into the hinterland. I feel old fashioned around them, and lost when they talk about their experiences in the war." Struss sighed. "I feel like I took my father's place in the family. I'm the German immigrant adjusting to American life, while my brothers are Americans. When we get together at family events, they talk about the war; where they've been, and what they've seen, and I just sit there listening like an old German just off the boat."

"The Jew nodded in agreement and began tapping his fingers to the music. He finished his draft beer and asked for more beer. Struss opened a bottle of Pilsner. The Jew took a big drink. "I'll tell you another thing, Strussberger," the Peddler uttered. "I'm jealous of them, my brothers. They went to college on the GI bill, got great educations; they're all professionals that work in downtown Pittsburgh, with secretaries. I love 'em, but I'm jealous. I feel like a loser compared to them, do you know what I mean, Strussberger?"

"That's the word I've been looking for," Struss said. "Loser. That's how I feel too. Fate has condemned us to 'losers' as the eldest sons of European immigrants. We didn't have a chance, Jew-buddy." Struss laughed.

"I'm getting tipsy," the Jew smiled. "When your wife comes home from work and finds us drinking with no supper ready, we'll both get our heads banged." The Jew grinned. "You're so German, Struss, I would've never guessed you'd marry Irish."

"I couldn't resist her charm and her sarcastic ways." Struss leaned on the bar close to the Jew as if he were telling an ethnic joke. "Her family takes pride on their abilities to be quick on the draw with sarcastic comments. They even use sarcasms on their own dead at wakes. That's an experience for a modest Jew like you to see, a wake. You wouldn't believe how they enjoy burying their kin. Her folks are either crying or laughing."

"Well, marrying outside of your heritage is common now. You were ahead of your times, Struss." the Peddler uttered. "It's still not an easy step for Jews." He took a long drink from the bottle before blurting, "Oh Strussberger, I forgot to tell you what I heard from reliable sources. There's a big plan brewing for Pigeon Hill. The government is going to demolish most of the South Slope and build projects. Low rent housing, for both Negroes and White people to live in together. What do you think of that?"

Struss chuckled. "That'll never happen."

The Jew roared. "Hoffnung stirbt zuletzt!"

"Huh?" Struss quizzed.

"Hope dies last." The Peddler grinned.

CHAPTER EIGHT
Peek-a-boo

Talk of the creepy snowball attacker lingered on into spring. By Easter season, others claimed to hear "the Whistler" as the snowball thrower had come to be known. The Caretaker was elated with talk about the mysterious graveyard Whistler. He wildly encouraged scary Whistler gossip and stories. Since that snowy ambush, he'd not had to pick up beer bottles, trash, or cigarette butts off of tombs. Petitioning the Almighty for a blustery wind now and then became his nightly prayer.

Mrs. Wernher notified the authorities after listening to Junior and Carl. She reasoned that there might be a connection between the Whistler and her husband's death. Junior convinced himself that the Whistler was in some way responsible for his Dad's fall from the cliff.

The big April raindrops made a rat-tat-tat sound hitting the pigeon coop tin roof. Neither Mr. Vonovich, nor his son Teddy kept pigeons, but the loft, used years before by the previous owner, still had fading white waste splattered on the wooden planks. Rusted garden tools cluttered the inside. Mr. Vonovich sat on a stool waiting for the rain to stop. He'd listened on the radio before coming to the coop and sat patiently knowing the spring shower would pass quickly. After the rainfall, the broadcasting weatherman promised a sunny and pleasant late afternoon.

He was an odd looking man with a skinny frame. Clothes on him hung like a suit on a wire clothing hanger. His thinning hair protruded over his small ears. His head was too large for his stick-like body and his eyes were big and gray. He projected a comic book space alien image. He knew his appearance was shabby, but he believed correcting his grooming habits seldom made people, especially women, react differently when in his company.

He fingered the field glasses, hoping that the rain wouldn't cancel the Bentley's backyard barbecue. Viewing Mrs. Bentley through binoculars became a Sunday ritual. Sometimes he'd feel guilty being a Peeping Tom but dismissed that sneaky-creeper feeling easily, rationalizing to himself that he too had a right to share in the beauty of life. Besides, what harm was he doing? And, if he were inclined to believe in such superstition as scriptures, who could point to a passage that said peeping was sinning? Unlike most Christians, he'd actually read the Bible out of a desire for knowledge. A desire to learn was his constant passion. The state however, did have laws about his peeping habits. He stayed careful with his peekabooing and felt safe from ever being discovered.

He didn't have a German heritage as many of his Pigeon Hill neighbors, but he associated himself with Faust, the German character in Goethe's famous play. Faust who sells his soul to the devil. Like Faust, he too was striving to learn much and have his way with all of his desires. And like Faust, he realized that it's impossible to achieve those goals. If he believed as Faust, that the devil did exist, he'd gladly sell his soul as Faust did. He'd learn everything that can be known and always have his way with whatever. He'd been learning some German from textbooks over the years and by living on Pigeon Hill for many years.

He had no formal education after the tenth grade. He quit high school to help support himself, his parents and his younger siblings. This was expected of elder sons coming from poorer families back before the First World War. He'd been too young to be drafted for that war and too old to be called for the Second World War. Early in his life, he was unable to sustain lasting friendships so he'd found reading to be his only entertainment. Beginning with simple novels, he slowly progressed into the deeper thinking minds of John Locke, Thomas Aquinas, and his most favorite, Johann Wolfgang Von Goethe. Nothing much ever changed for him. Nearing fifty years old he was rejected by his promiscuous wife. She gave him some exciting times for a brief moment in his dull life but now he wanted to move on and start his life over.

He needed friends. He longed to discuss the philosophical questions that tortured his mind. He needed friends to discuss views with, exchange thoughts with, and perhaps be admired. In books he'd found relief to tolerate his empty life, but soon, when he went west to California, he'd have the sort of friendship he desired. He thought about his move. Under floorboards in his house and wrapped with butcher shop paper, lay the vital means to carry out his plan. Seventy thousand dollars. If, by diploma or breeding, he couldn't obtain the comradeship he needed, he'd buy it.

More than a decade ago, he'd planned to escape from his packing house job, his wife and even Teddy. He first began stealing prime cuts of meat after he met his wife. Courting her cost very much, and only because he was able to deliver with the cash to satisfy her desires did they have any relationship at all. He was overwhelmed by her even before she introduced him to sex. She laughed at his seriousness from the moment they met and still continues to do so when she does bother to come home to him and Teddy. After she became pregnant with Teddy, the other men in her life faded away and she found herself alone except for him. She wasn't certain who Teddy's father was, but claimed that the baby could be his. He believed that she would be grateful toward him for not deserting her in her time of need, but the partying with excessive booze and sex never stopped for her. After she'd recuperated from Teddy's birth, she went right back to drinking and having affairs with man after man. And as long as he kept bringing her the money, she'd arrange some relief for him in their bedroom from time to time. Soon he wasn't able to take care of household needs; paying a babysitter for Teddy and paying for sex with his wife. Stealing more meat then he was already stealing would certainly be discovered. He cut his wife off. She cut him off and that is how it stayed. Under the floorboards, he began depositing the ill-gotten money that he used to pay her.

The stealing arrangements with a few truck drivers began out of need for his family. It then became a get-a-way plan for him to break away from the life he inherited by being ugly and poor. The company didn't miss the few cuts he'd mark for special delivery, and the truck drivers would take the meat to prearranged restaurants along their route. As a shift superintendent and an employee of the company for more than thirty years, he merely justified the loss as spoiled meat on the inventory. Spoiled meat was tax deductible and the accountants were always glad to have a big number to record in the loss column at tax time.

He had the persistence to wait a few more years until Teddy was out of high school and could be on his own. He would leave the house to Teddy. It wasn't worth much. It was never maintained properly. The only work he undertook on his property was trimming the pear tree near the coop when its branches grew out and hindered his view of Mrs. Bentley.

Speaking to Teddy now couldn't erase his scars from giggles and frowns he'd already suffered by his mother's actions. He'd read much on alcoholism years ago when he still held out hope of transforming his marriage into some happiness. Teddy was ashamed of his mother's behavior and thought of her as naughty rather than sick. He should've explained that eventually, as her needs for alcohol increased, her promiscuity would also and she'd use men to provide her with booze. He should've prepared Teddy for the anguish he now endures.

The rain stopped. He stood and peeked over the loft opening and into Bentley's yard. Until one summer night, when he sat close to her on the trolley, he'd never spied on anyone. Her beauty so awed him that the compulsion to view her in a quiet setting overwhelmed him. The pigeon loft gave him a perfect view into the Bentley yard and backyard porch. He rushed to an Army and Navy store and bought Army field glasses. Sunday became exciting for him, watching her sit on the porch glider while Mr. Bentley barbecued. He'd never spoken with any of the Bentley's and avoided them when outside just as he did with the rest of his neighbors. He'd nothing in common with any of them so there would be nothing to talk about. He didn't want their pity.

Mr. Bentley came outside carrying cooking utensils.

His heart beat increased, grateful that the weatherman was correct. The sun was shining and would enhance his viewing.

The twins came out. The boy, his hair cut short, wore blue jeans and a tee shirt. He looked athletic carrying a raw roast to his father. The girl, wearing shorts, became visibly upset after her father seemed to object to what she was wearing. She stomped back into the house. Mrs. Bentley came outside carrying the Sunday newspaper and sat on the glider.

Vonovich stood erect against the opposite wall from the loft opening. He took a few deep breaths in the shadow of the loft to calm himself, then raised the binoculars and peered into a face of beauty.

CHAPTER NINE
Fawn

Avoiding the public steps and taking the longer way home up Brookhurst Road, Teddy, lumbering along, his head downcast, was too humiliated by his mother to find anything worthwhile in his life to care about. On his way to school that morning with Jake and the twins at his side, an auto stopped close to his house and let his mother out. All of them watched as she staggered past them without even recognizing her son. No remarks were said by his friends, they just kept walking to the public steps and into school, but he was certain that Carl couldn't wait to blab to Junior and others. After school, he lingered behind, not joining up with the usual group to hike the public steps home. He wanted to be alone.

The back of his head was flat. He camouflaged the flatness by letting his brown hair grow longer, giving his skull a more normal shape. He looked malnourished. His big, dark eyes with long eyelashes dominated his facial features.

"Hi there!" she said, smiling.

He raised his head, while pushing strands of hair away from his eyes. She was standing alongside a pickup truck, dressed in blue shorts and a white top snug enough to show off her gifted breasts. He was startled but uttered softly, "Hi."

"You live around here?" she asked.

"Further up the hill. I'm coming from school."

"What grade you in?"

"Ninth."

"Ninth? You're tall."

Grimacing, he answered. "I flunked last year."

"Oh, what the hell, I just made it myself. Playing hooky today. I'd quit, but my mom keeps talking me into staying. I want a job, earn some money."

"You live here?"

"Are you kidding? My mom hates the city! I'm from the suburbs. We're visiting my grandma. We brought her some stuff."

"Staying long?"

"Weekend."

A man and woman came outside.

"My mother and her boyfriend." she explained the pair. "He lives with us. My real dad took off. I was small. I don't remember him." She moved closer to him on the road and smiled. Her large breasts almost touching him. "What's your name?"

"Teddy."

"Mine's Fawn. What goes on around here?"

"Nothing much. Hang out at the Owl's."

"Owl's? What is that?"

"A corner store, it has a soda bar."

"I like cars, any of your friends have a car?"

"My friend Junior does."

The man and woman began unloading the truck. "Hey Fawn," her mother called. "Move it. We've got work to do!"

"In a minute."

"Get your butt moving." her mother barked. "You can talk all you want later."

"Okay! Okay!" she answered, pulling her white blouse down, tightening the cloth over her breasts. "Are you going to that place tonight? The Owl's?"

"I'm going."

"Are other girls there?"

"Yeah."

"Can I come tonight?"

"Sure."

"Where is it?"

"Go up those steps," he said, pointed to the cliff. "And you'll see it on the corner. Or you can walk up Brookhurst, you can't miss it."

"I'll see you tonight," she smiled and walked away.

He continued his hiking, inspecting his trousers and short sleeve shirt and hoping his Dad didn't forget to buy soap powder again. The few clothes he owned were dirty and he wanted to dress up in clean blue jeans and a pullover like the rest of the gang always wore hanging out at the Owl's.

* * *

It was late when Jake got to the soda bar. He was surprised to see the strange girl standing beside Teddy watching Henry play the pinball machine. Teddy looked polished, well groomed and was not slouching.

"Where have you been?" Susan asked Jake, almost a scolding. "It's almost nine o'clock. I want you to come home with me and Henry, watch television."

"I'm late because I was cleaning wallpaper with my dad." he answered, then lied. "I'm too tired to sit and watch television, I'd fall asleep." He'd decided not to go with Susan and Henry any more as a decoy. It only hurt leaving them alone after her parents went off to bed.

"Come on, Jake." She pleaded her tone and manner suddenly loving toward him. "Milton Berle tonight. You won't need to stay long. After Uncle Miltie's Show, they're off to bed. Please?"

"I'm really tired, Susan." he lied again.

"I'm not going home with you either." Henry said, surprising her with the news.

"Yuk! I feel like screaming!" she yelped.

"Why should I go? Your watchdog parents will stay up all night before they leave me and you alone together."

"See what you did." she blamed Jake for her disappointment.

"Jake." Teddy said. "This is Fawn."

"Hi." She parted her full lips, giving Jake a big smile.

"She's visiting her grandma from the suburbs."

"Wow," Jake said. "Everyone's going that way."

"New people all of time," she commented. "I like it, a lot of teens with cars to hang out with. It's exciting. It's dead here."

"We have the Whistler," Henry said, then chuckled.

"You laugh," Carl said. "But I don't see you going into the cemetery at night."

Fawn was puzzled. "What's that?"

"It's a spook." Henry said and chuckled some more. He lost the pinball game.

"You're putting me on," Fawn chuckled along with Henry.

"Not a ghost," Junior explained. "A man, a rapist and murderer. I think he killed my Dad. Me and Carl saw him. He walks through the cemetery whistling."

Fawn looked at Henry standing behind Junior. He was shaking his head back and forth and grinning. She pulled the same tight top down for Henry to witness her natural blessings as she did for Teddy earlier that day.

"Where's Cathy?" Jake asked Carl.

"She went home."

Teddy didn't miss Cathy as he usually did when she wasn't at the Owl's. Tonight was special to him, so wonderful it was to have a girl stand next to him and talking to him as if he too were a carefree teenager like the rest of the boys.

"Those two have all of the fun." Fawn said to Teddy, nodding her head at Henry and Susan who were cuddling face to face.

Jake saw them too, and turned to Fawn. "Yeah," he muttered. "Henry's a fun guy."

Feathers announced last call.

"Junior," Henry asked. "How about driving Susan home?"

"Okay, but no long bye-bye nonsense. Anyone else?"

Carl nodded that he'd ride along. Jake did also, thinking Teddy would want to be alone with Fawn. He knew three was a crowd better than most. They piled into Junior's four door sedan. Jake and Carl squeezed into the front seat, letting Henry and Susan alone in the rear seat to say their many goodnights with kisses and hugs.

Teddy and Fawn watched them drive away standing under the Owl's entrance light. Teddy moved closer to her.

Everyone was quiet in the car except for Henry and Susan, who were kissing and whispering sweet nothings to one another. Junior was driving fast, in a rush to return to the corner. After they reached Susan's home, Henry hurried his goodnight, and Junior turned the car around talking about Fawn. "She was making eyes at me all night!"

"You're not the only one," Carl shouted. "I had to turn away from her staring."

"She wants it." Henry informed them.

Jake was stunned. This sudden burst of talk about Fawn shocked him. She had smiled at him too, big smiles, but he thought she was just being friendly around strangers, nothing else.

"I'm the only one here experienced," Henry instructed the others like an Eagle Scout would talk to a Cub Scout. "I know what I'm talking about. She's in the mood for some loving."

"But who does she want?" Carl asked.

"Not Teddy," Henry laughed. "Watch and learn fellows."

"Teddy likes her," Jake said. "Maybe we should back off."

"Forget that!" Henry laughed.

"Maybe she's not like you say," Jake said, astonished by how quickly Henry decided she was loose, a ready and willing girl.

"I'll show you." Henry promised. "I know what I'm doing."

When they reached the Owl's, Henry told the three of them to sit in the car and wait.

Henry walked over to Teddy and Fawn just as the Owl and Feathers locked the front door of the Mart and switched off the outside light. "Damn, I was hoping to get back here before the Owl closed. I need a cigarette. You smoke Fawn?"

"Sometimes, but I don't have any. I never buy them," she chuckled. "Just bum 'em."

"Teddy, you live close by," Henry asked. "Your Mom have any smokes at home lying around?"

"Maybe."

Henry smiled. "Mind running home to get some. I could sure use a smoke, what about you, Fawn?"

"Love one."

"Okay." Teddy agreed. "Walk with me Fawn?"

"Naw. I'll wait here."

"I'll be right back." Teddy took off running.

What are those guys doing in the car?" Fawn asked.

"Listening to the radio. I really didn't want a cigarette," Henry grinned. "I have some in the car."

She smiled. "You devil."

"Come along, I'll show them to you. Give you one."

She followed Henry. They both climbed into the back seat. "Show Fawn how your car runs, Junior. Take us for a ride."

"Where's Teddy?" Jake asked.

"He's running an errand." Henry answered, cuddling Fawn. "Drive, Junior, drive."

Junior drove away from the Mart.

It wasn't long before the boys in the front seat heard noises coming from the back seat.

Jake didn't move his head, holding his posture erect and peering straight out the windshield. He didn't want to be accused of peeping. After awhile, the car began rocking.

Carl turned and peeped. "They're doing it!" he muttered to Junior

"I'm parking." He drove into the middle of the Pigeon Hill trolley track loop, turned off the headlights, and parked the car. The boys swiftly vacated the front seat, running away from the bouncy car over the tracks and into an open field.

Carl was excited. "He did it. Really, I saw them!"

"I know!" Junior yelped.

They heard the car door open and close in the night.

Henry called them. "Where are you guys?"

"Over here," Junior answered.

Henry found them. "I told you guys, didn't I?" he bragged. "Who's next? She's easy."

"Are you sure?" Jake asked.

"Yeah man, go get some!" he urged.

The three uninitiated started giggling, more of a nervous laugh.

"Who's first?" Carl asked.

"Go on, you go," Junior urged Carl.

"No, you go. It's your car."

"Damn, one of you go before she changes her mind," Henry said. "Jake, you go."

Jake's heart skipped a beat at being urged onward and into an unexpected adventurous opportunity.

"I'll go! I'll go!" Junior said and walked to his car and Fawn.

Carl went next.

Jake stood silently as Junior danced in ecstasy around Henry. Junior was still skipping about when the sound of the opening car door was heard in the dark. Carl joined Junior in dance while Henry sat in the grass cross-legged, smoking like a victorious Indian warrior chief after a battle.

Jake walked to Fawn like a young brave in Henry's tribe.

CHAPTER TEN
Gotcha

Mrs. Bentley, nestled in the overstuffed chair, fell asleep before the end of the movie. Static noises emitting from the television didn't awaken her and neither did the unlocking of the front door. Her husband looked at the test pattern on the screen briefly before switching the television off. Putting his lunch pail on the coffee table, he walked to the cozy chair cradling his wife under the soft illuminating lamp light. Flowing red hair covered her shoulders, yet couldn't hide the outline of her naked breasts beneath the white pullover. Her bare feet were tucked up in the chair against her fleshy buttocks. Her arms were folded beneath her unrestrained breasts, a sexy posture. Picturing her as becoming and seductive sent him into a rage. He poked her hard with his finger.

"What's this?" he asked, poking again and again.

"What?" She was startled, jumped to her feet, shocked at seeing him at home. "What time is it?" she asked looking at the window, expecting to see daylight.

"Apparently, not late enough!" he raised his voice.

"Shhh, you'll wake the twins."

He lowered his tone.

"What's going on?"

"Nothing." she answered, confused and searching desperately for the right words to ease her dilemma.

"Nothing?" he raised his voice slightly. "Tits hanging out, flashing your butt. That's something to me. You look like a whorish pinup the guys hang in lockers at work."

She walked to the kitchen and switched the ceiling light on. He followed close behind.

"What are you doing home?"

"That doesn't matter. The point is, I am home and gotcha at something."

"Okay, okay, but are you sick?" She feigned concern for his health.

"The crane broke down. I'm glad it did. What's going on? Are you cheating on me?"

She didn't answer and began preparing to brew coffee for something to do other than look at him. He became huffier to her unresponsiveness. His suspicions mounting, he shouted. "Are you cheating? Were you outside like that? You're not dressed like that to clean house!"

He moved toward her. She uttered a soft moan and backed into a corner next to the stove.

"Don't hit me," she cried out, frightened, lifting the coffee can as if to toss it at him.

"You throw that can," he warned, surprised by her spunk. "And I'll whip your ass!"

She burst into tears.

"Quit crying," he said between clenched teeth. "Sobbing isn't going to help you. I want the truth." He pinched her breast hard. "What's this all about?"

"Ouch!" She shoved the coffee can at him, grounds poured over his shirt and onto the floor.

He twisted the tin can from her grip, then pinched her other breast.

"Oh, my God!" she yelled. "Stop it or I'll scream!"

Thoughts of her screams causing community gossip, or the police coming promptly with rumors still flying around about the Whistler, tempered his madness. He put the empty coffee can on the stove. "Sit!" he ordered her. "And start talking!"

She sat defeated.

They heard the twins on the stairs. Mr. Bentley rushed into the hallway.

"Go back to bed," he told them, quickly losing his angry voice. "Everything's okay. We just had an argument. It's over."

The twins retreated back to bed.

He went back to his wife. "Start talking." He sat across from her.

"It's nothing," she said again, closing her eyes and hanging her head. "It's really nothing for you to worry about."

"Jesus!" he whispered. "Don't hand me that crap."

She raised her head and looked into his eyes. "But, it is nothing. I haven't gone outside looking like this, let alone cheat on you. I only dress this way when the kids are sound asleep. And only sometimes. It's comfortable."

"You think I'm stupid? Where did you get the clothes?"

"I bought them."

"When?"

"Years ago."

"I've never seen them. You're lying."

"It's the truth, I swear. I only wear them in the house at night when you work the midnight to eight shifts."

He stared at her, trying to uncover a sign of deception. She stared straight back at him.

"Why?" He was puzzled.

"You'd never understand," she answered. "How old am I?"

"Old enough to know better."

"Thirty-three, but I dress like I'm fifty-three. I could exchange clothes with Mrs. Krombach and who would notice any change in my appearance?"

She looked him over. He appeared calm. "I'm not middle aged, so why should I dress like I am? Because I'm terrified of your temper, that's why. I still remember our honeymoon when you flipped out of your mind about my bathing suit being revealing."

She paused to ponder the effect of her words upon him. She stayed apprehensive, and fear lingered in the pit of her stomach. His calm mood could change faster than a snap of a whip.

"Go on," he said.

"You're too strict. On Sunday, you flew into a rage because Cathy wore shorts. I warned her, but she bought them anyhow with her baby-sitting money. Her friends wear shorts and they're not bad girls. She doesn't want to be different when she goes out shopping or whatever."

"It's the whatever," he interrupted her. "I'm concerned about. I don't understand. You're a wife and mother. I mean hells-bells, how do you think the twins would feel seeing you walk into Miller's Store dressed as you are?"

"I'd wear a bra."

"Bra or no bra, you look flashy. I wouldn't want my mother to look like you do now and neither would the twins."

"Cathy wouldn't care."

"Maybe not Cathy." He was turning irritated. "I'm thinking of Carl. What would his pals say seeing you all dolled up, advertizing your body, showing off your stuff? Those boys are coming of age. It would be humiliating for Carl."

"Then forget about me. I'll throw these clothes away, but you should think of Cathy. And I don't understand. Do Cathy's shorts reveal more of her than when she is in her swimming suit? When she's winning races, you point her out. You tell everyone near you, that's my daughter."

He exhaled, yawning.

"I don't care about myself," she would give up on ever dressing sexy, but not for her daughter. "Perhaps I am being silly for my age. But please, let Cathy wear shorts. She'll be so happy."

"All right! All right!" he said, but followed with a request of his own. "But no more flashy clothes on you. Deal?"

His request sounded more like an order to her. "Deal."

"Good." He stood. I'm going to bed.

Hearing him climbing the stairs, she got up, took a broom from the built-in cupboard, and began sweeping the coffee grounds. "Whew." she muttered. "I'm still alive."

CHAPTER ELEVEN
The Aftermath

Susan quit coming to the Owl's and refused to see Henry when he rang the doorbell to her home. Her mother shooed him away after Susan said she didn't want to see or speak to him. Henry hoped to see her alone and charm her back into his arms. He had total confidence in himself to win her back if he could only get her alone. She wouldn't accept his telephone calls to her home either. After a week, he gave up and quit dialing. He didn't appear greatly upset without Susan by his side. He seemed the same old carefree Henry. To Henry, she had her tactics, and he had his tactics, but for the present, it was a waiting tactic by them both.

How she'd found out about his quickie with 'the Burb Bitch' as Susan referred to Fawn, he had only suspicions, but the number one suspect was Jake. Only one day after their special event at the loop, Susan knew. This was much too fast for the normal pace of grapevine gossip to work its way around. He believed the squealer was one of the benefactors of his gracious gift of Fawn. Jake, with his crush on Susan, had most to gain once Susan found out he had cheated.

Teddy didn't let Henry's trickery to snag Fawn bother him. Ignorant Henry did him a favor, showing Fawn to be as ignorant. There was nothing in his mind to cry over concerning Fawn. Henry did him a favor, showing Fawn for what she was, a person like his mother. In his heart, he believed Jake to be a true friend, his only friend in the neighborhood and at school. He missed

Jake at the Owl's when he went to Susan's house. He hoped for his own miracle. To be with Cathy someday, the girl of his constant dreams. When Jake told him how Susan had asked him to spend time with her at her house, he'd never seen his friend so jubilant. Alone every day with the girl he loved. Who wouldn't be full of joy?

Jake spent most of his leisure time with Susan. They idled their time away watching television or taking short walks. Susan never talked to him about Henry or of his own adventure at the loop. If he'd been going steady with Susan, he'd have never seduced Fawn or gone into the car that night. He was satisfied with Susan just watching Milton Berle on television. He'd rather be holding Susan's hand then making love to Fawn.

Susan and Jake were lying next to each other on the carpeted floor in front of the television. Susan was stretched out on her stomach while wearing blue shorts. She would occasionally lift a bare leg at the knee, and then drop it back to the floor. This was her method of disapproval when she was disappointed with what was happening on the screen. Jake didn't know one character from another watching Susan's favorite soap opera, the Guiding Light. He didn't care for the Soaps, but she followed a few of them faithfully and during those times, she had no interest in cuddling. He waited impatiently in his fast wrinkling khaki pants and tee shirt for the episode to end. Susan's ever suspicious mother looked in on them occasionally as she went about her daily chores. The Soap ended without any of the characters Susan favored in that make believe world being put upon unfairly. Jake was glad about that. He'd see her mood change if the episodes didn't end to her satisfaction.

Jake stretched himself out on the carpet. He could see Susan's mother through the rear window hanging clothes on the clothesline in the backyard. Susan didn't turn off the television and play records like she usually did after the daily soap dramas. It was during those musical interludes of record playing, if her mother wasn't watching, that they'd cuddle and kiss a bit. It was during those scarce, wonderful moments he'd silently scream his thankfulness for being alive. Susan accepted his kisses without resisting or encouraging them, and now and then she'd be kissing him back at the same time. Those were the better kisses and the ones he yearned after.

"No records?" he asked.

"I have a slight headache." She closed her eyes.

Jake couldn't resist her full, moist lips. He leaned over and kissed her. They kissed several more times. He moved his hand across her pullover, exploring.

She opened her eyes. "Stop." she said. "I'm not the Burb Bitch."

He stopped his exploration and rolled onto his back. He was secretly pleased that she had resisted his advances, believing she'd also deterred Henry when he tried moves to go beneath her clothing.

Mrs. Mallhauser was coming back inside. Susan stood up. "Want a pop?"

"Sure." He was thirsty. He watched her walk away with her big brown hair curls bouncing and her body and strong legs concealing her pudginess with the taut skin of youth. He sat up, but stayed on the floor. She handed him a cold glass of orange pop before sitting in the rocking chair.

Her mother walked by and gave him a smile. He smiled back and swallowed some pop.

"My headache is getting worse."

"Take two aspirins." he advised.

"I think I will and lie down awhile."

"Should I go?" He placed his glass of soda on the coffee table.

"Maybe you better."

He stood up and walked to where she sat, looked around for her mother, and not finding Mrs. Mallhauser lurking about, quickly kissed Susan on the lips. "See you tomorrow. Love you." He had welcomed the beginning of summer vacation as never before. So much time to be with Susan.

"I'll call you tomorrow." she said, touching his hand.

Jake left the house.

Susan telephoned the Owl's and spoke with Cathy.

The announcer on the television screen was talking about troubles in a place called Korea.

* * *

"It's a sin now if you lied." Feathers warned. She handed the Bible back to the Owl after having Carl and Junior swear on its cover that they saw the Whistler that past winter. She still didn't believe them. She wiped her hands on her pink apron, as if to rub off their swearing lies. "You're both going to hell."

"We're not the only people that heard him!" Carl said.

"The two of you," the Owl said in cross examination, waving his family Bible in front of them. "Are the only people that claim to have actually seen him?"

"That's because people are afraid to go into the graveyard at night." Junior answered in rebuttal.

"Who's afraid?" Henry laughed.

"Y-o-u." Junior smiled. "That's who!"

"Me?" Henry answered, pointing to himself.

"If you're not, go now, it's getting dark." Junior challenged. "See for yourself."

"I'll go if you will." Henry accepted the challenge, and then raised the dare. "I'll walk!"

"I'll go if Carl goes!" Junior answered, hoping Carl would decline.

"I got an idea," Feathers chuckled. "Why don't you all go? It's almost closing time."

"Who's going to chicken out?" Henry searched their faces.

"I am." Cathy said. She was happy wearing her white shorts.

"Come along." Henry teased, displaying his fingers catlike toward her. "I'll protect you from the big bad whistling wolf."

Cathy smiled. "You better."

The boys, with Cathy close to Henry, left the store. After taking a shortcut, a dirt path through thick tall grass, they came to the cemetery stone wall. Henry helped Cathy over the wall. They followed a grassy track to the dirt road and continued walking until they came close to where the Caretaker had ambushed Carl and Junior. The group halted at a bend in the road, huddling close together and silent. The sun was setting below the Western Pennsylvania hills.

"Which way?" Teddy asked. "Where was he?"

Carl pointed in the twilight. "That area near by the flagpole."

They all peered up the hillside, but stayed where they stood. All sunlight had vanished, but they could still see each other in the clear moonlit night. A faint sound traveled through the summer breeze.

"Hear that?" Cathy squealed. "Far enough for me."

The boys remained silent. Teddy found himself unexpectedly happy at finding the others afraid. He was weary too, but knowing the others weren't as bold and brave when the chips

are down, when courage really counts, sent a wave of content-
ment through his mind that he'd never experienced before. They
heard the noise again, somewhat louder, but were unable to fix
what section of the steep slope it was coming from.

"I'm not going any further." Junior informed them.

"We agreed to find him." Teddy burst out.

"I only agreed to walk here." Henry said. "Not confront him."

"Yeah," Carl chimed in. "If you want to find him Teddy-boy,
go ahead. We'll wait here."

Teddy glanced at Cathy, her pale face in the moonlight, the
outline of her ponytail bobbing with each movement of her head,
and accepted the mission. "I'll go." he said calmly and started
walking up the steep grade without another word. Cathy watched
him march into danger, witnessing his valor. This might change
her view of him. He was hoping they'd all change their view of
him now. Dying for a chance to get Cathy's love was a risk he
was willing to take.

The closer to the flagpole he got, the more the shrill increased.
He walked directly to the flagpole, stood still and listened. The
noise was coming from above. He looked up and heard the faulty
ball whistling. He knew he had solved the mystery of the Pigeon
Hill Whistler. He looked back down toward the others, still
grouped together on the road in the pale moonlight. He turned
and walked the remaining steps to the very top of the hill,
silhouetting himself like a dark shadow against the moonlit
horizon, praying that the others would see his fearless posture
and be awed by him. After a few seconds, he walked over the
horizon, out of the sight of the less brave.

He sat next to a gravestone plotting strategy. He didn't
want to risk losing the respect they have for him now by revealing there wasn't a Whistler. He went forth alone, bold as brass,

challenging a Phantom as a David against Goliath. Knowing the truth, they'd all climb the hill to hear the flagpole ball and soon it would be forgotten that he ventured first.

He stood and charged up and over the crest of the hill. He passed the whistling flagpole and yelled as loud as he could, "He's here! Run, run, run, he's coming!" Running down the hill, over graves, sometimes into grave markers, he didn't see the others dashing for the cemetery wall. Neither did he see Henry pulling Cathy down into the tall grass.

The boys gathered at the closed Mart, breathing heavy.

"Where's Cathy?" Carl gasped. "And Henry?"

"Holy hell!" Junior yelped. "Owl! Owl!" He called up to Owl's place above the Mart.

The Owl opened his third floor window.

"Call the police! The Whistler got Henry and Cathy!"

"Hurry, hurry!" They were all screaming up at him.

The Owl was flabbergasted. At first hesitant, but hearing their frightened voices, he had come to believe that the boys had witnessed something. He shut the window and called the police.

Before the Police arrived, Henry and Cathy appeared out of the darkness. Carl saw them first. "There they are!" he yelled.

"The Owl called the Police." Teddy said looking at Cathy. She had grass stains on her white shorts and pullover and a blade of grass in her hair. "Did you fall?" He was suspicious, smelling funny business.

"A lot!" She lowered her eyes.

"I thought he got you." Junior chuckled at Henry.

"Almost." Henry began lying. "Cathy couldn't keep up with me. I had to slow down. He got close to us, but fell over a gravestone and we got away. Cathy was exhausted, so we hid in the grass for a while."

"What's he look like?" Teddy asked.

"Tall, wore a white shirt. Right, Cathy?"

"Yeah, Henry saved me."

"Better get home, Cathy," her brother warned. "It's way past nine."

"Dad's at work, he's on the four to midnight shift. I'll go soon. Mom won't tell on me. Don't you."

The police arrived and Henry retold his story. The police patrolled Pigeon Hill regularly and reports of the Whistler were becoming tiresome. They didn't hurry getting the facts or driving to the cemetery.

After the police left, Carl and Junior huddled around Henry, asking one dumb question after another. Cathy was wide-eyed and glued to every lie Henry uttered. None of them cared that Teddy went to the flagpole first. That he was the White Knight, while they were piles of chickenshit.

He walked away and headed home; wishing Jake had seen his gallantry. He didn't bother saying goodnight to any of them.

CHAPTER TWELVE
Mints

Henry abruptly became a full time workingman, making a good hourly wage and laboring on a coal barge. He had no intentions of ever returning to high school. Transporting coal on Pittsburgh Rivers, feeding the mills and manufacturing plants with the black lumpy source of energy offered steady employment. Sometimes he would be gone for two weeks before showing at the Owl's. When he did come to the soda bar, he had plenty of folding money to show the others. He talked to Junior about getting a car soon; asking if he could get a good price from his mother's used car lot. Junior assured him of a good price.

Susan maintained her stubbornness, steadfastly remaining away from the Owl's, even when told Henry seldom showed there since he became a full time workingman. Staying away from the hangout, she boasted, was her guarantee of avoiding someone so detestable. Jake visited her every day. They walked and talked, watched television and listened to the radio, played records and kissed. They celebrated Jake's seventeenth birthday together by going to a movie, *The Asphalt Jungle* staring Marilyn Monroe. He got many unrestrained kisses on that special day for his gift from Susan. In the back of his mind however, he had a slight worry about her and Henry. Was she avoiding him because she disliked what he did with Fawn? Or didn't she trust herself or her resolve in his presence not to crumble and forgive him and begin their romance anew? He tried not to think crazy thoughts, like she still loved Henry, and he had never been more than her second choice. He dismissed such craziness. They were growing older; she was outgrowing childish flirting with the likes of a showoff as Henry. Besides, Susan was honest and pure, a wholesome gal through and through.

Carl and Junior drove away from the Owl's earlier in the evening, enjoying the cool summer dusk cruising the slopes of Deutschtown, persistently honking the horn at girls, and blasting the radio. As new initiated teenagers constantly hoping to run into another Fawn. They never invited Teddy to join them on their lusty hunting trips, but as long as Cathy kept coming to the Owl's, he would never want to be any other place on earth.

Lately, circumstances had been favoring Teddy. With Jake at Susan's, Henry working on the rivers, Junior and Carl stopping only long enough for Junior to feed himself full of ice cream and other sweets, he had been alone with Cathy a lot. When Cathy told the Owl and Feathers that he faced the Whistler first while all the others were frightened, he felt like he had won the Congressional Medal of Honor. Her praising words showered him with happiness and giddiness stayed with him for days. Her sudden change toward him, her open friendliness every night at the soda bar, left no doubt in his mind that his courage must've impressed her, since he'd done nothing else out of the ordinary. With each passing night alone with her, he became more relaxed and slowly he began losing his backwardness. He was less hesitant or afraid of saying something stupid, and there were befuddling questions on his mind that he wanted to ask her soon.

It was getting close to quitting time. They left the soda bar and stood close to each other on the street corner. Again, she wore shorts, her shapely legs suntanned from going with her dad to the community swimming pool on a regular schedule. He loved looking at her graceful moves, her bright eyes, her perfect lips, and her face of beauty, her ponytail, and the way it swayed when she moved her head. There was nothing about her that he didn't adore.

He needed to get more money. His Dad had been giving him an allowance for housecleaning chores, but it wasn't enough. He needed more clothes. He had been washing the blue jeans he was wearing every other night. His entire wardrobe of summer wear couldn't fill a bushel basket.

Cathy looked at her watch.

It was still thirty minutes until the Mart closed. He had been walking her home after the Owl locked up at nine for over a week. It was a short distance. He didn't make any romantic moves on their slow strolls to her front door, just friendly chat passed between them. Tonight would be different. Tonight he would kiss her and hope upon Saint Valentine's spirit that she would kiss him back. He was anxious for the store to close for once. He had jitters in his stomach, but he was determined to feel her pink moist lips on his.

"Are your parents going to Owl's wedding next Saturday?" he asked.

"Mom is. She is taking Mrs. Krombach. My dad's working overtime. His job is considered vital, and since this Korean thing started, he'll be working long hours. Are we at war?"

He pondered her question. "I guess so. Someone said it was a police action, I think the President did. What's a police action?"

"Don't know." she shrugged. "Me and Carl are going to the wedding. Are you?" She avoided inquiring about his parents.

"Yeah."

She was playing with her watch again.

He wished he could learn to dance overnight. She would be asked to dance plenty of times at the wedding while he would just sit and watch her being caressed and twirled by who knows who. It would be a big wedding, driven by German customs galore. There would be a huge crowd. She could even meet a stranger, a fellow who would sweep her off her feet. Loving Cathy would always mean having a worry to be worrisome about.

"We'll all sit together. Junior's coming too." she said. "His mother and older sister are not attending, still in mourning I guess." She opened some of her secret inner feeling to him. "He makes my flesh creep."

"Who?" Teddy perked up. "Junior?"

"Yeah. He's always staring at me." She chuckled. "I don't think his eyes blink."

"I guess they'll never find out about his Dad." Teddy said. "What really happened?"

"He still believes it's the Whistler." she said and again looked at her watch.

"Yeah, I know he does." Teddy uttered, contemplating whether he should reveal the secret of the flagpole. He was still confused about her support for Henry's lies about being chased by the nonexistent spook. He poked for the truth. "Were you frightened that night?"

"At the cemetery?" she asked.

"Yeah." he said.

"At first." she answered.

"Weren't you scared when the Whistler chased you?"

"I saw nothing," she smiled. "I was ahead of Henry. I can outrun any old Whistler." Then said more then she intended.

"Henry too." She caught her error and turned away from Teddy, fingering her watch.

He jumped at her revelation. "Why didn't you?"

"Ahh, cause Henry, ahh, we had a secret plan from the rest of you." she lied. "Ahh, hide ourselves. Scare everyone, pretend the spook got us." She gave a nervous laugh.

"Oh," he said. "I was wondering how your clothes got grass stained that night."

She blushed.

He didn't go further with his questioning. He had plenty of time to find out the truth. He had to keep the secret of the whistling flagpole to himself. Being thought of as gutsy had gotten him this far with her; he would never give that secret away. She was looking at her watch again. "Something wrong with your watch?"

"I think it's running fast. I hope so."

He thought what she said was odd. "Why?" he chuckled.

"Ahh, so I don't have to rush home." She turned away from him. "It's a few minutes from nine."

It was time to prepare himself. He needed mints. He didn't think he had bad breath, but why take a chance. "Want some chewing gum or anything else before the Owl closes?" he asked her.

"No, thanks." She seemed disappointed.

Was she feeling bad because she had to go home? Maybe, hopefully it was because she didn't want to leave him. He hoped that was why she suddenly got down in the dumps. He went into the store just as a shiny, sporty-looking car parked outside.

He served himself, picking up a pack of chewable peppermints. He dropped them on the checkout counter and handed Owl a quarter. "Don't close yet, Owl. A customer just pulled up outside."

The Owl gave him his change. "Better hurry, with the wedding next week, my nights after closing are full of things to do. Too much planning."

Teddy put a mint in his mouth and went to Cathy.

"Hi, Teddy-boy." Henry was standing very close to Cathy. She didn't seem to mind and she no longer looked sad. "See my car? Nice, huh?"

Teddy was too stunned to answer him.

"Come, Cathy, take a good look at my car."

She wasn't looking at Teddy and with bowed head; she followed Henry to his car.

He could hear Henry talking to her. Cathy turned and started moving away from him. Henry took her hand and whispered closer to her ear. She remained beside him.

The Owl locked the door and turned out the lights.

Teddy heard the car door open. "Goodnight, Teddy-Boy," Henry called to him. "I'm driving Cathy home." Cathy didn't say "goodnight Fool," or even give a tiny wave goodbye to Teddy before climbing into the car. Henry drove away.

Teddy stumbled down Brookhurst Road, torn, with tears gushing, and barely able to see his unsteady way. He continued walking until he was off of Pigeon Hill. In Deutschtown Community Park, he laid on a public bench. He cried the night away. At dawn, the pigeons gathered around him cooing. He tossed the mints at them.

CHAPTER THIRTEEN
Revelations

The Owl and Feathers wedding was a typical Deutschtown celebration with all of the German traditions, plenty of food, drink, music and dancing. However, with both the Owl and Feathers coming from large German families, their festivities were being magnified tenfold. Each had relatives scattered over the hills and through the valleys that comprised Deutschtown, with Pigeon Hill having most from both families. Some of their kin arrived as refugees only five years earlier, since the end of the World War. Owls' distant cousins came from Stuttgart, one of the most heavily bombed cities by the allied forces during the war. Feathers, of Bavarian blood, said the only acceptable location to celebrate their bliss was at the Ancient Society of Teutons. Their Great Hall had an attaching Biergarten, to be used if the July temperature rose too high. Then the guests could retreat outside and continue enjoying themselves, sitting on benches at long wide tables. Tables that could hold an abundance of food and pitchers of beer.

The wedding day weather was grand. Sunny, but not too hot, and every now and then a cool breeze blew across all of Deutschtown. The late afternoon Wedding Mass went as smooth as a precise German-made machine. Handfuls of rice were thrown at the newlyweds when leaving church and every piece lodged in Feathers' hair was counted by her Maid of Honor, as was customary with the Germans. Eight grains were found and announced to the cheering crowd. "Eight children!" The

Owl laughed, and said he planned to get started fulfilling that omen that very night, to everyone's loud cheers.

At the Great Hall, guests and the working staff gave prolonged applause when the Bride and her entourage entered. The Owl, dressed in a tuxedo, was aglow with joy. But he still had on his black framed peepers, showing him more as a nearsighted penguin than a Hoot Owl.

Feathers white gown had a short train. She looked beautiful, like Cinderella. She was transformed from a skinny Soda Jerk with bunched up hair, wearing a house dress and pink apron, to a blooming white lily. She had a flowery headpiece pinned to her dark, curly hair. Her bridesmaids wore blue and white, the colors of the Bavarian flag. She followed her mother and grandmothers' tradition, choosing a gold wedding band over a diamond ring. After the obligatory first waltz by the bride and groom ended, the party started in earnest with musicians striking up the band, playing *The Beer Barrel Polka* to much hoot-and-hollering.

Women from both families prepared the food. It was a help yourself feast. Bratwurst, knockwurst, spatzle, sauerkraut, braise red cabbage, hot German potato salad, and more filled warming trays positioned one after another on table after table. Trays of American favorites; hotdogs, cold potato salad, baked beans, fried chicken, and macaroni-and-cheese covered another tabletop. Sweet baked cookies of many sorts as well as thin sliced pieces of apple strudel were laboriously placed on blue and white paper plates, on all of the guest tables. Big urns of coffee were strategically placed about the hall for easy access to the merrymakers. And big bowls of salty hard pretzels were on the tables in easy reach from every chair.

Bavarian blue and white was the decorum. Blue and white crepe paper was strung. It stretched inside the hall and outside around the Biergarten. Blue and white paper plates and drinking cups for soda pop and coffee were in abundance for both children and adults. Many men brought their own personal stein with them into the Great Hall, but for those that didn't, plenty of thick glass mugs were available at the bar. Busy as bee bartenders, wearing stiff straw skimmer hats and tightly wrapped aprons over portly bellies filled and refilled tall pitchers with lager and dark ale. Youngsters, in Hansel and Gretel costumes, circled around the Great Hall and Biergarten. Each was carrying a shoulder bag full of small boxed matches, handing them out to guests as keepsakes as a memento to remember the marriage. Each white box showed the newlyweds name in a gold print, as well as the date of their blessed union as man and wife. The women pocketed the matches while most men used the matches to light cigarettes, cigars, and pipes. Huge ceiling fans kept the smoky air circulating. Gretel, in a red poplin and alpine trimmed apron with blond braided pigtails and a white head scarf smiled a lot and was enjoying her role. Hansel, in brown short pants with suspenders over a white shirt, didn't seem as enthusiastic with his role but the women fussed over him and his green alpine hat with a red feather.

Everyone seemed to be happy with the celebration and they were enjoying themselves except Jake. He sat at the bench feeling grumpy, uncertain about his future with Susan. Cathy, Carl, Junior and Henry were talking and laughing, but his mind wasn't following along with their conversations. He just daydreamed while watching stout women going back and forth from the unseen kitchen, replenishing the trays of food.

In his mind, he was going steady with Susan, yet she asked him not to sit with her and her parents at the reception without very convincing reasons. She told him that her parents didn't want any boys sitting at their table, which also had many of her relatives. Anyhow, she explained, her family gathering would be boring to him. He had suspicions about that reason. Mrs. Mallhauser, a parental watchdog, nevertheless, always treated him fine and was friendly when he was lounging about her home. Her follow-up excuse was more thought out. She claimed that this would be the first time since breaking up with Henry that they would both be at the same place. She believed that Henry would come to where she was sitting under the pretense of seeing his buddy Jake whom he had not seen for quite awhile. He believed the second excuse revealed some truth and she was unsure about her true feelings toward Henry.

Events with Susan weren't developing the way he thought they should. He would often tell her that he loved her, but seldom got the same message returned. When she would say those three magical words to him, they sounded forced and flat. He had little money to take her anywhere, but she would never ask to go anyplace. When they weren't together, she stayed at home helping her mother and talking on the phone, most often with Cathy.

Cathy was the only girl at the table and she was more dressed up for the occasion then the boys, who were wearing trousers and short sleeved shirts. She wore a white blouse and yellow skirt that fell just below her knees. She sat across from Henry. Her face lightly made up, enhancing her sparkling eyes. She also used a pink shade of lipstick. Her French braid hung below her shoulders. Because Teddy hadn't been seen since the night she rode home with Henry, her tightening relationship with Henry was still a secret to the others.

"Hey Jake!" Henry called out. "Snap outta it. You're in a fog."

"I'm okay. Just daydreaming."

"About Susan?" Henry smiled. "I'll bet."

Jake grinned without answering.

"This is really a dull wedding." Junior uttered.

"For us." Henry answered. "The adults are having a grand time. We need some booze." Henry stood up. "Watch this." he boasted with confidence and walked to the bar with a lit cigarette hanging from his lips, thinking that would make him look older.

The boys watched with wide-eyed envy over Henry's brashness. After a few minutes, he returned to the table with a dry pitcher. "That's a smart ass bartender," he chuckled. "But I like him."

"What happened?" Jake asked.

"He asked me how old I was. I said twenty-one. Then he leaned over the bar and said, and I'm the Burgermeister of Deutschtown." Henry chuckled again. "But he offered me a Pigeon Hill Special."

"What's that?" Cathy asked.

"An orange and cherry soda mix." Henry was laughing hard, thinking the bartender was funny, but also hiding with cheer his disappointment at failing his stated mission. "I should have gotten a Pigeon Hill Special for you, Cathy."

She gave him a big smile. "Thinking of me, Henry?"

He didn't answer her. "I'm thinking, there's gotta be a way to get some brew." He eyeballed the Great Hall. The Band was on a break and guests were gathering by the stage. They were being entertained, watching one man and two women twisting and turning doing the dreisteirer. The threesome never let go of each other's hands, while constantly looping and weaving themselves through intricate patterns. The audience clapped and cheered for them after each hard move. Many tables were abandoned by the drinkers as they gathered by the stage, a perfect time for the boys to strike. Henry gave the order to act.

"Grab some cups, guys and follow me into the Biergarten. Snatch a pitcher of beer from a table along the way."

They were excited and played Henry's game of following the leader. Carl told Cathy to stay put as he hustled to his leader's side. She went and sat with her mother and Mrs. Krombach.

While many watched the man wearing leather lederhosen short pants with suspenders and two women in wide skirts, embroidered bodices, and low-cut shirts showing cleavage, their pitchers of beer were hijacked into the Biergarten by the Katzenjammer Kids.

The giggling group, each with their own pitcher of lager, found an empty table in the corner of the Biergarten with shrubbery between them and the doorway into the Great Hall. Behind them was an engraved marble Egyptian obelisk with the names of the Deutschtown war veterans that fought in America's wars. The servicemen killed in action had a star next to their name. Each of the four Deutschtown communities had a side of the obelisk. Every year on Decoration Day, the names of the heroes were spoken aloud to all assembled in the Great Hall for a special remembrance dinner. All of the boys knew neighbors with family members on the obelisk. Inside the Hall, the Band returned and began by playing *The Just Because Polka*.

They sat and filled paper cups with beer from the big pitchers, gulping the first mouthfuls.

Henry, wiping foam from his lips, expressed his successful plan with gusto. "Am I good? You bet I am. Pigeon Hill Special, my ass." He grinned and swallowed more beer.

"Where's Teddy been? He doesn't have a girlfriend, does he?" Carl asked. "Cathy said he hasn't been seen."

"Naw," Henry answered. "Teddy loves your sister."

Carl choked on some beer. "He hasn't a chance!"

"I know he doesn't." Henry said. "She likes me."

"Want me to put in a good word for you?" Carl asked.

"I'll think about it." Henry said turning to Jake. "Why ain't you sitting inside with what's-her-name?" the beer already beginning to loosen his lips about Susan.

"I don't want to sit with her parents." Jake lied.

"I saw her dancing inside with her Dad. She never even glanced in our direction during the whole dance. That tells me something." Henry smiled at Jake. "You'd think she'd have given you a smile, after all the time you two spend together."

"What does that tell you, genius?" Jake asked.

Henry smiled and drank more beer. "Maybe I should ask her for a dance. Do you think she'd dance with me, Junior?"

"Hell no, she's too peeved about Fawn. Gosh, I wish I knew where she lived. I'd drive to her house right now." Junior said. "I'm needing a little Fawn right now."

Dusk came. Strings of electrical wire with dangling light bulbs crisscrossed the Biergarten overhead. More people were coming outside into the cooler air, with beer and pretzels, and settling around wooden tables.

Jake took a big drink of dark beer. Junior worked himself up with more remembrances of Fawn, while interested in turning the table talk more sexual. "Did you get far with Susan?" he asked, grinning at Henry.

"That's top secret." Henry stared into his paper cup.

"Come on!" Carl said. "We won't blab."

"Jake would."

"Knock it off, Henry." You got nowhere." Jake said.

"And you'd know?"

"I'd know."

"How? Think she'd tell you?" Henry chuckled.

Jake raised his voice to Henry. "Think every girl gets silly over you? Well, Susan's showing you. You're not Casanova."

"Hey, hey, hey," Junior intervened. "This is a party. Let's not fight amongst ourselves. Drink more beer. We never fought while we were growing up, now that's all we do. What happened?" They didn't answer. "I know." Junior answered his own question. "Girls. I've changed. Since Fawn, all I think about is getting laid."

There were some chuckles.

Junior continued with his beer loosening thoughts. "Jake, you take everything too serious. Hell, it's not like you really go steady with Susan. I mean, you both just sit around her house talking and watching television."

"How would you know?" Jake quizzed.

"Susan tells Cathy everything. Cathy tells us. It's not like we're sworn to secrecy. To tell you the truth, she still loves Henry. At least that is what I think."

"I think she does too." Henry said. "I still like her."

Carl perked up. "Go in and ask her to dance, Henry. Or are you a chicken?"

"She won't." Jake said.

"Maybe later." Henry said, uncertain in his heart if Susan would come into his arms. The thought of her rejecting his dance request would be hard on his ego and especially in front of the others. "Right now I'm only concentrating on drinking beer and planning on how to get more."

Junior started another conversation. "Did you hear the new release by Teresa Brewer? *Music. Music. Music.* I like it."

They agreed, all liking the new song. For a good while, they talked music. Especially newer songs such as *Candy Kisses*, a favorite of Junior's, Nat King Cole's, *Mona Lisa*, and funny tunes like *Goodnight Irene* and *Pistol Packin' Mama*.

Jake turned the talk to sports. "My Dad heard a sandlot football league might be forming from Pittsburgh neighborhoods. He said in the twenties and thirties, there was a league and Pigeon Hill had a team called the Arrows. Players must be between eighteen and twenty-one."

"I'm not interested in football," Henry said. "Only making money."

"Me too." Junior said. "Miss Brewer's song is *Music, Music, Music*, well mine is Money, Money, Money."

They all laughed and drank the last of the beer. "We need more." Henry said. "What's going on in the Hall now? I don't hear the band."

"It's another one of those traditional things." Carl said.

"It's Schuhplattler." Jake said, more aware of German customs than the others because of his father.

"Good." Henry said. "Time for another raid." They all walked quickly into the Great Hall. As the guests and wedding party watched men dressed in leather short pants with suspenders over white shirts wearing alpine hats, the beer raid occurred. The performers, rhythmically slapping their thighs, knees and feet, while stomping, had the copycat crowd slapping themselves in 'a monkey see, monkeys do' fashion.

The successful raid gave them each a pitcher of beer and after more drinks, the talk again came around to Susan. Getting himself full of alcohol and courage, Henry's desire to go to Susan was increasing. He let out his plan. "When the band starts up again, at the first slow tune, I'm going to ask Susan to dance."

"Watch yourself, Henry." Jake warned. "You're half smashed and she's with her parents."

"They're half smashed too." he answered and started walking toward the entrance into the Great Hall to wait for the right tune. The others followed him to watch.

The band was taking their place on the stage.

Jake was elated with Henry's intentions. Certainly, his approaching Susan in front of her parents, tipsy from booze, would end forevermore any lingering feelings she may still have for him. They huddled at the entrance of the Hall, waiting for the band to start, all hoping for slow dance music. Henry hit the jackpot with a slow beat. Carl and Junior slapped Henry on the back for support. "Go get her," Carl said. "She's all yours."

Henry walked to his love. She was wearing a dark blue dress, her head full of curls. She saw Henry coming her way, getting closer and closer to her table. The other lads stood staring, alternating their stares between the sitting Susan and the slow walking Henry. They didn't let out a sound and they became tenser with each step Henry took. When he got a table length away from Susan, the unexpected happened. Without Henry saying a word, Susan rushed to him and into his arms. Cuddling each other, they walked to the dance floor.

Instead of screaming, Jake followed Carl and Junior back to the table and the beer.

Henry kept Susan on the dance floor for a few more dances before bringing her to their table. "Well, we're going steady again." Henry put his arm on Jake's shoulder. "Sorry, Jake, but we never stopped loving each other."

Jake didn't look at Susan and no words passed between them. He drank some beer and swallowed hard. Never in his life did he feel so bitter.

Cathy joined them at the table, visibly shaken. Her face white.

"What do you want?" Susan was nasty. "My friend! You're a sneaky bitch! Henry told me you've been playing up to him."

Cathy remained stunned, saying nothing in her defense.

Susan continued her violent denunciation of Cathy. "Ohh," she mocked. "You were so sorry to tell me about that whore, Fawn."

"Yeah!" Henry looked at Carl. "Big mouth!"

"Watch it Henry, before you say something I won't ignore."

"Well, why did you tell Cathy about Fawn? It was none of her business. She caused all of the trouble between me and Susan."

Cathy burst into tears and ran away.

"Don't call me names, Henry! Understand?" Carl ordered.

"Sorry, buddy." Henry said and gave Susan a squeeze. "But Cathy did start my troubles."

"Forget it!" Carl raised his voice. "Let it go."

"Okay, okay." Henry mellowed

"I'm getting something to eat." Junior guided his big body toward the food trays. Henry, Susan, and Carl followed him into the Great Hall.

Jake sat alone with a stone face, angry and thinking. He had been used. He was just someone to keep her company until makeup time with Henry. Someone good looking enough to put a scare into Henry that perhaps she didn't want him back. And she says Cathy's a bitch. What did Cathy do that was so awful? Tell her friend that her boyfriend cheated on her? Both of them blaming Cathy because Henry cheated with Fawn. He closed his eyes and couldn't figure out their reasoning.

Carl and Junior returned to the table with overflowing plates of food.

"Where's Henry?" Jake asked.

"He's sitting at Susan's family table." Carl said.

Jake's head was swimming with bitter thoughts shouting for vengeance.

"Hey, Jake." Junior said between bites of food. "Your old man's on the dance floor, staggering more than dancing. He fell, almost pulling your mother down with him."

Jake didn't know whom he was more sickened of, his lifelong friends or himself. He wanted to leave the Biergarten and the Great hall, but not go home to his lonely bed. Anywhere but home. He heard Junior talking about Susan.

"I'm thinking Feathers isn't the only woman getting feathered tonight."

"He never had her!" Jake raised his voice at them, and then wondered why he had spoken in defense of the witchy Susan.

"I think tonight." Junior explained. "At the food table, he got a rubber from me. They're leaving soon in his car." He chuckled. "I always have one in my wallet. You never know."

They sat listening to the music. Big band music was being requested by most of the guests. Arrangements by Benny Goodman, Kay Kyser, Harry James and Glen Miller filled the Great Hall. Junior interrupted their trance. "I wish I could dance. You can really make out if you can dance. Maybe I'll take lessons."

"Have Jake's old man teach you." Carl snickered.

"Yeah," Junior chuckled. "How to fall on my fat ass."

Jake had enough. "Your Dad wasn't so great, Junior!"

"My Dad was a hero!" Junior snapped. "Your Dad couldn't pin the tail on a donkey."

Carl giggled.

"What are you happy about? Your family isn't perfect either."

"You got something to say about my Dad?" Carl challenged. "Say it."

"It's not your Dad I'm speaking about!"

"What?"

"I said, it's not your Dad I'm talking about. It's your mother."

"What about my Mom?" Carl snapped, posed like a tiger, ready to pounce.

Jake stared at them. "It's not what I said. It's what I saw." He pointed at Junior. "I saw your Dad," he paused. "Making out with Carl's Mom before he fell over the cliff."

Carl ran around the table to get to Jake. He swung a round house punch that missed Jake by inches. They locked in an angry embrace before falling onto the floor. Carl was screaming "I'll kill you!"

Junior stood over the wrestling teenagers. Now and then he'd kick Jake while yelling. "Liar! Liar!"

Men rushed into the Biergarten and separated them. They were ordered to leave the Great Hall or sit with their families. Carl and Billy left. Jake sat with his parents. He stayed quietly sitting and hating, wishing he had never been born. He sat there for hours while his parents and their friends continued celebrating. He had seen Cathy and Mrs. Bentley leaving in a rush. He was already sorry for telling on Mrs. Bentley and prayed Mr. Bentley wouldn't kill her. He didn't even notice that the band quit playing and his father and others had a schnitzelbank poster on stage. He decided to go home to his lonely bed. A bed he could no longer lay covered in warmth and dream of a future with Susan. Walking out of the Great Hall, he could hear Struss' strong voice amongst the singing group.

"Ist das nicht ein schnitzelbank?
Ja das ist ein schnitzelbank!
Oh, die schoen heit an der wand
Ja das ist ein Schnitzelbank!"

CHAPTER FOURTEEN
Polka Dots

The old windows in the kitchen rattled from the pounding on the door. Mrs. Strussberger sat up in bed concerned, wondering who would be hitting their front door so hard. Struss, still a bit intoxicated from celebrating was sleeping soundly and he wasn't awakened by the determined beating on the door. She tried to arouse him. "Struss, wake up!"

He didn't move.

"Struss," she said, shoving him hard. "Get up." She continued rocking his limp boney body back and forth until he awoke.

"What?" he moaned.

"Hear it? Somebody's beating on our door, like a bill collector after a poor debtor."

He groaned. His throat was sore from the excessive talking and singing at Owl's wedding reception. He rolled into a sitting position and slipped his bare feet into slippers. He was in his pajamas, grumbling under his breath while looking at the bedroom alarm clock. Eight o'clock. "Christ, The Almighty," he mumbled. "Who visits at this hour in the morning?" He slowly walked downstairs and opened the door. It was Mr. Bentley, dressed in work clothes, his angry looking son behind him on the stoop. They barged into the kitchen.

"Struss!" Bentley was mad. "Where's Jake?"

"What?" Struss looked dumbfounded. "Come back later, at a decent time."

"No! I intend to stop his hideous lies!"

Struss yawned. "What lies?" Struss slammed the door shut.

"Lies about my wife! Where is he?"

"Wait one goddamn minute now," Struss' mind was clearing. "You'd better back off and start from the top! I don't like your attitude right now!"

"Well, I don't like what Carl told me either!" Bentley shouted.

"And that is?" Struss asked, placing his hands on his hips just as Bentley had his hands.

"Carl told me that Jake said that my wife and Otto Wernher were making love on the city steps before Otto fell to his death."

Struss looked at Carl. "Why would Jake say something like that?"

"He's mad because Susan jilted him for Henry, that's why!" Carl sneered, his shirt pocket ripped from fighting with Jake at the Great Hall.

"That doesn't make any sense." Struss said, waving his arm as if shooing a fly.

"Yes it does!" Bentley raised his voice. "Jake lost out to Henry, and when Carl and Junior teased him a bit, he flipped out and started making up hurtful tales to get back at them." Bentley threw his arm in the air. "I mean, calling my wife a slut, that's horrible!"

"I'll wake Jake."

"Jake!" Struss shouted up the stairway. Mrs. Strussberger, in nightgown came out of their bedroom. "What's wrong?"

"Go back to bed. I'll handle it."

"Jake in trouble?"

"The Bentley's are claiming he's spreading lies about their family."

"Our Jake? He'd been broadcasting? Never! Tell 'em to be coming back at a more convenient hour."

"Go back to bed." Struss told her. "I'll get to the bottom of it."

She went back into the bedroom.

Struss called louder. "Jake!"

"What?" Jake heard the pounding on the door and supposed it was Mr. Bentley.

"Come down, the Bentley's are here with some disturbing issues."

Jake walked into the bright kitchen in bare feet, wearing pajamas, and blinking his eyes.

"Why are you telling dirty lies about my wife?" Mr. Bentley demanded.

Jake looked at his Dad.

"We need answers, Jake. Carl said you're lying about Mrs. Bentley and Otto Wernher having sex on the public steps the night Mr. Wernher died? Why would you say such a thing?"

"I didn't say they were doing it." Jake said, hanging his head and speaking in a low voice. "I meant they were kissing and hugging."

"Still lying!" Bentley howled.

"Shut up!" Struss snapped back. "I know my boy. We'll get to the truth." He put his hand on Jake's shoulder. "Son, if you saw Mr. Wernher fall, why didn't you say so before last night?"

"Mrs. Bentley asked me not to tell. She said she was afraid of him." Jake nodded his head at Mr. Bentley.

"More lies." Carl yelled, shaking his fist at Jake.

"It's not a lie!" Jake responded.

"Have you talked to your wife?" Struss asked.

"Not yet." Bentley made a disgruntled face. "She's in bed. And why would I speak to her about such filth?"

Struss continued his interrogation. "Jake, tell us everything you can recall about that night. Everything."

Mr. Bentley threw his arms into the air. "You're starting to believe him!"

"I am." Struss answered.

Bentley reached for the door knob and nodded at Carl. "We're out of here. I'm suing."

"Stay until Jake finishes, then I'm calling the police." Suddenly Struss began feeling pleasurable, acting out his hidden desire to be a lawyer. The Bentley's stayed.

Under Struss' prodding, Jake told details on the night of Otto Wernher's death, but skipped Mrs. Bentley's comeliness behavior toward him in her living room.

"Proves nothing." Bentley said. "My poor wife is going to be tormented by his lies!"

"I remember something else." Jake looked at Mr. Bentley. "On your honeymoon, you wouldn't let Mrs. Bentley wear her new bathing suit. A suit with green and yellow polka dots."

Mr. Bentley looked stunned, as if he'd been hit in the face with cow manure. The flabbergasted father and son tramped out the door.

"The defense rests." Struss murmured and called the police.

Jake sat with his father at the kitchen table waiting for the police. Struss opened a beer bottle and took a long drink. Jake was nauseated and heavyhearted. He was in such a blue mood he wished he could disappear, run away. Go somewhere. Be anywhere else but Pigeon Hill.

CHAPTER FIFTEEN
Consequences

The embarrassment Mrs. Wernher suffered after the details of her husband's death were revealed to the public hastened a desire she had long nourished. She sold her home and bought a new ranch style home in the suburbs. Her home on the better developed side of Pigeon Hill was well maintained by her late husband and she received a swell price for the old structure.

She pushed down hard on the folded clothes, trying to make more space inside the cardboard box to pack additional garments. She wore shorts and a matching short sleeve pullover with the logo of her company on the back. She heard her daughter's voice calling her.

"Mom, what about the toys and board games? Are we taking them?"

She didn't answer immediately. The toys from Jean and Junior's childhood were stored in the attic. She was frugal and always planned to give the toys to her grandchildren someday. Now, being a single independent woman with a growing business, she didn't dwell on thoughts of becoming a grandma.

"Mom!" Jean called again. "Can you hear me?"

"Yes, have Junior give them to the neighborhood kids."

"When is he coming home to help?" Jean asked, coming down from the attic wearing summer shorts and a soiled tee-shirt. She was developing into some woman of voluptuous design. Her big blue eyes, with dark long lashes caught onlookers' attention. She resembled her mother in stature who also had a regal overbearing way about her. She kept her auburn hair short like her mother.

"Soon, I hope. It shouldn't take long to say goodbye to Carl."

"Where is Mrs. 'Drop-Her-Drawers Bentley' going?" Jean smiled contemptuously.

"Junior said she's staying put."

"What nerve, she's without shame. Where is Mr. Bentley going?"

Mrs. Wernher taped the flaps on the box closed. "Take a break."

They both sat on Junior's double bed. "He's already moved into an apartment. The twins are moving in with him today."

"Do they own their house?" Jean asked.

"I don't think so."

"Who's going to pay her rent? I hope she gets evicted."

"I guess she'll get a job." Mrs. Wernher answered.

"I hope they work her ass off!"

"Jean!" Mrs. Wernher disapproved. "That's no way for a college girl to speak."

"I haven't taken my entrance exam yet."

"You'll pass dear, no need to worry."

Jean began talking about her plans in college. Her Mom had her own thoughts.

Mrs. Wernher had thoughts about Mrs. Bentley herself, and they weren't all bad. Although she didn't mention it to her children, she was grateful to Mrs. Bentley for not lying. It would've been more comfortable to claim she had never seen Otto before that night, to say he tried to rape her. She admired her in court, giving her straightforward answers to the Judge. They didn't speak to each other in court. There wouldn't be further inquiries since Otto died instantly, incurring a broken neck with massive head injuries. And he hadn't been abandoned to suffer an ago-nizing death alone. Mrs. Bentley sobbed while the magistrate scolded her for not reporting the accident to the authorities and for inducing a youngster to do likewise. She heard Junior's car outside.

"Hey Mom! Jean!" Junior yelled running into the house. "You'll never guess what happened!"

"We're in your bedroom."

"Cathy!" He stopped in the bedroom doorway to catch his breath "Cathy Bentley's knocked up!" He flung his fat body onto the bed, exhausted.

"Junior!" Mrs. Wernher frowned. "The way children talk these days. And get your sweaty body off the clean bedding."

"She's not going with her Dad." he gasped. "She's staying with her mother."

Jean was delighted. "Who's the Daddy?"

"Henry!"

"Ha ha ha." Jean mocked.

"Carl and Mr. Bentley are screaming madly at her."

"Well, let's finish packing, Mrs. Wernher said. "We have troubles of our own. Go finish packing in the attic."

After the teens went up into the attic, Mrs. Wernher sat on the bed awhile longer thinking about her late husband. He had surprised her, going on the hunt for sex outside of their marriage. As hard as she tried, she couldn't picture him kissing the beauti-ful Mrs. Bentley.

* * *

Two months after the Owl's wedding, Henry eloped with Susan after she too announced her pregnancy. Cathy was further along with her pregnancy than Susan. The two-soon-to-be mothers both quit high school. Cathy stayed at home and did house chores while Mrs. Bentley worked at her new job. Teddy visited Cathy every day after school. He kept talking about quitting school too, like everyone else did, and going to work at one of Pittsburgh's Mills. With money in his pocket, he could start planning on leaving his parents home and go out on his own. Cathy and Mrs. Bentley kept pleading with him to stay and graduate. With a high school diploma, he would be able to get a better job. A cleaner job to look forward to, rather than working on some scrap metal pile at a dirty mill. Cathy helped him with his studies and he was doing well in school, getting above average grades. Teddy looked upon Cathy's pregnancy as a gift from God. With her friends abandoning her, he was able to step right up and fill her need for an understanding friend. In time, after the baby is born, and after graduating and finding a good job, he would marry her and be a great father to her child. He was glad others would look on her as soiled. He would be her hero.

Cathy, after being rejected by Henry, was depressed and downhearted, but slowly recovered with constant motherly advice and reassurances that all would turn out okay. She looked forward to Teddy's visits, having someone young to listen to music with and share teenage talk. She had not seen Henry since the Owl's wedding reception. When she telephoned him, giving the news of her pregnancy, he said it wasn't his child and hung up. At times, when alone in the empty house, she would remember that not long ago she had been a happy teen. Without Teddy's visits, she would be alone and lonely most of each day.

Mrs. Bentley hoped the hot September heat wouldn't cause her to sweat and stain her new blouse as she waited at the trolley stop. She looked herself over. The new low heeled shoes fit well as did the nude nylons, showing her shapely feminine legs. The snug skirt that ended at her knees pleased her too, as well as the men waiting at the trolley stop behind her. A low hubba-hubba sound was murmured several times. She didn't acknowledge their approval of her derriere, but was glad it was noticed. She saw Mrs. Krombach coming toward her, and although she usually didn't mind speaking with her, today she would have rather not have her thoughts interrupted.

She was glad that Henry eloped with Susan and not her daughter. Cathy's teenage crush on Henry was fantasy, just like the fantasy she had on her husband as a teenager. Cathy was slowly getting over Henry, and with each passing day, seemed to be recovering from her broken heart. She explained to Cathy that her mistake with Henry wasn't enough to ruin her life. She only needed the resolve to wait out the storm. She told her that Henry was only an infatuation and someone she really didn't know. She conveyed the importance of not thinking of herself as defiled when she started dating again in the future. And not to let any date be disrespectful to her because she had a child out of wedlock.

In her heart she had a hidden wish that Jake would visit her and Cathy when he came home on furlough. He didn't visit them before he ran off and joined the Marines. At the inquiry he looked so sad. She wanted to hug him, comfort his heart and mind. She felt ashamed in the courthouse while being scolded by the Judge, especially when rebuked for leading Jake astray. Her Christian teaching, sin cast long shadows on others as well as yourself, had come to pass in her life.

Even through Carl was like his father, she missed him and his vicious remarks screamed at her had been painful. In some ways, she missed her husband too, and knew how crushed his heart was by her behavior with Otto. He had always been a good father to the children. He was old fashioned with his controlling thoughts about women, but he had been a great provider and his family always came first. He had plenty of imperfections, but doesn't everyone?

Her sudden freedom, obtained by death and sorrow to many, was never something to be giddy over. But it was nice to dress like an appealing woman of her young age. Several men at her job, a receptionist in training at the Pittsburgh Century Hotel, were quick to ask for a date. She refused them with a smile. At this difficult period in Cathy's life and for a good portion of the next several years, her daughter must not be allowed to believe life is easy, without responsibilities, without sane planning for the future. The most terrible thing that could happen to Cathy now would be for her mother to date many men, give off impressions that fun is the most important thing in life. Should Cathy, as a single mother, become pregnant again by another phony like Henry, her life would indeed be ruined. She would continue to refuse dating offers, but looked forward to buying clothes. Mrs. Krombach was approaching.

"Guten morgan." The old lady, dressed all in black waved to her. "Ya lok'ink vunderbar!"

"Thank you, Mrs. Krombach. How are you?"

"Gout, fur mein age, gout." The elder stood next to Mrs. Bentley. "Go'ink vork?"

"Yes."

"I pick'in der garten today. I giffs sun Catsee."

"Thank you. You've been so kind to me and Cathy, giving us vegetables from your own garden. Fresh vegetables are just what the doctor ordered for a pregnant girl."

"Tank Gott I can." She gave a toothless smile. "Chust eaten 'em raw. Dem gout fur baby."

"Dot's all ve can ask fur, gouten health. Catsee strong Frauline. Like ven I jung Frauline, I strong." She bent her arm making a muscle for Mrs. Bentley. "Oh my Gott, nein can food 'en! Start cook'in supper morgan, backen bread, waschen, mend'tink sock, mak'in jelees, ve vos strong."

Mrs. Bentley smiled. "I don't think I could do all of that."

"Ya vold, ya coud, it dot or not'ting."

Mrs. Bentley patted her hand. "They don't make them like you anymore."

"Dot bussard help Catsee?"

"Who?"

"Dot Henry."

"No, he doesn't. Says he's not the father."

"Dot bussard, Catsee better mitout der bum."

Mrs. Bentley wasn't sure if she was calling Henry a buzzard or a bastard.

"I think so too, Mrs. Krombach."

"I 'member Catsee go'ink schwimmer v'en jung mit her daddy. So cuttee in baden suit."

"Yes, she still loves to swim."

"Vell, she von't now. Der bussard Henry!"

"Here comes the trolley. It was nice talking with you Mrs. Krombach. Have a nice day."

"I ve'll. I go'ink pick sum tomato now, giff to Catsee."

"Thanks for being so kind. Bye." Mrs. Bentley boarded the trolley and sat in front, near the conductor. She was aware of passengers looking her over. What wasn't known to her was if she was being mentally strip teased because of her sexy posture, or mentally rebuked because of her bad behavior with Otto. Perhaps both causes.

CHAPTER SIXTEEN
Chance Meeting

Standing on the back porch with Cathy, in front of the grill, Teddy held a plate of hotdogs for her as she placed each wiener, one by one, on the smoking gridiron. He had no memories in his past that were more pleasant than his present life. He enjoyed helping Cathy with her household chores as much as if he were a little boy getting to play with a shiny new toy. It was like playing house, pretending she was his wife, school was his job, and after a hard day at work, he would come home to his beautiful mate. He couldn't recall ever eating so well as he did at the Bentley house and when he looked into a mirror, his complexion showed wholesomeness that he had never seen before. Each Sunday's cookout with Mrs. Bentley and Cathy was a holiday to him, a fourth of July with Cathy's sparkling eyes his fireworks.

If he had remained at the public park never returning to Pigeon Hill as he had planned after Cathy entered Henry's car and drove away at the Owl's, paradise would've passed him by. Those weeks hanging around the park, begging money, looking cruddy, staying unwashed the entire time, were becoming a fading memory. All of this new life would've been lost had his father not filled out a missing person report. When arrested after fighting over a half of bag of shelled peanuts, he was found to be Teddy Vonovich, the missing seventeen-year-old boy. He was given a choice; return home and stay out of trouble or be put into a juvenile correction system. He chose to go home and Cathy's troubles became his salvation. Peanuts left on a park bench for bums to fight over saved him from carrying out darker thoughts of taking his own life. Taking a leap from a Pittsburgh bridge and into one of its three rivers crossed his mind nightly laying on the park bench. He told Cathy about those suicidal wishes and about the half-filled bag of peanuts that caused his arrest. She said the peanuts were left there by his Guardian Angel.

"How are those dogs coming along?" Mrs. Bentley asked from the glider where she sat reading the Sunday newspaper.

"Soon." Cathy answered.

"After we eat," Mrs. Bentley asked. "Could you both cut down those high weeds along the fence? I'm afraid of snakes and I saw one the other day. I know garter snakes aren't poisonous, but they give me the creeps."

"We'll need something to cut them down with." Cathy said.

"We have a sickle." Teddy said. "I'll run home and get it."

"Hurry," Cathy said. "The dogs are almost ready."

Teddy ran at full speed to the old weather worn pigeon coop, through the unkempt yard of tall grass, and passed underneath the pear tree. Reaching for the door knob, he heard his father's voice. "Beautiful."

He opened the plank door and saw his father shudder, drop the binoculars, and give off a whimpering cry. In the loft opening, Teddy saw a fine view of the Bentley home, as well as Cathy and Mrs. Bentley, both in shorts and sleeveless pullovers.

"Teddy! It's not what you think!"

Teddy charged his father. They both fell to the floor, rolling around on the stained planks, grunting and groaning. Mr. Vonovich lost his glasses, but managed to grab and hold onto Teddy's arms. "Stop fighting! Please Teddy, let me explain."

When exhausted, they laid side by side on the floor. Teddy was the first to speak.

"You and Mom ruin everything for me. What if Cathy found out you're looking at her? It's creepy."

"I wasn't looking at Cathy. I was looking at Mrs. Bentley. I think she's beautiful."

Teddy didn't answer him. They both got up and dusted themselves off. Each of their white tee shirts was badly soiled. Teddy hoped he had a clean shirt in his bedroom.

"I won't look at her anymore." his father said, raising his right hand as if to seal his promise to his son. "I promise."

Teddy picked up the binoculars and smashed them again and again until the lens shattered. "No more!"

His Dad didn't try to stop him.

Teddy picked up the rusty sickle and ran outside toward the Bentley house forgetting that his shirt was awfully stained.

Mr. Vonovich picked up his glasses and took one last look at Mrs. Bentley, then left the loft. Entering his home, he instantly smelled the strong odor of urine coming from his wife who was sleeping on their queen size bed. She was snoring. His eyes wandered over her body. She still had a trim, curvy figure, but her face was puffy. He undressed her, drew a bucket of warm water, and wiped her entire body with a soft wash cloth. After he finished cleaning her, he wrapped her nude body up into a clean sheet. He lay on the bed beside her and thought of his plan and the ill-gotten money under the floorboards. Thinking about his runaway plans was his cheap therapy. He intended to carry out his plan in a few years. Enough years to accumulate more money and then Teddy will be on his own. Yet, years away from becoming an old rooster and being too old to flap his wings.

CHAPTER SEVENTEEN
Semper Fi

Struss sat with his stein of coffee in front of his bay window, watching a flock of pigeons swooping close to the old roofs of the row houses. Fallen autumn leaves, gathering on cobblestone streets, looked quaint under the old cedar trees. Struss loved what he saw, recollecting the old Germans and their big families living in the same row houses that still stood outside his bay window. He could recall with ease running on those streets with his childhood pals, remembering their nicknames and the row houses they lived in. It didn't seem that long ago.

It did seem long ago that Jake left for the Marines, but it was only three months earlier. He missed him. His mother prayed her rosary every day for his safe return. He prayed for him also, but in a lesser display of piety. She was against Jake joining the Marines at only seventeen and foregoing his high school education. He had agreed with his son to join after what had occurred with Mrs. Bentley. With the Korean War escalating, he was having second thoughts about his support for Jake's enlistment.

In Jake's last letter home from Paris Island, South Carolina, he'd wrote that he would be ordered to Camp Lejune, North Carolina for Advanced Infantry Training after basic training. Struss never served in the Armed Forces like his younger brothers, but the heavy training his son was undergoing probably meant he would be shipped out to Korea soon after his training ended. If Jake's fate was to go into combat, there would be nothing else to do but pray, just as his parents prayed for his brothers during World War Two.

He sipped his coffee, watching more big leaves falling to the ground. If Jake would be killed in action, he wasn't certain if he could go on living like the old-timers he knew did during the Great War after losing their kin. Mrs. Krombach and her generation were from a different world, a world incomprehensible to Struss. Perhaps that is why he loved and missed them. He drank the rest of his coffee. It was time to cook.

PART TWO
Easter Week 1954

"Nothing Endures But Change"
Heraclitus, Greek Philosopher

CHAPTER EIGHTEEN
Darkening Days

In the more than three and some half years since Jake joined the Marines, Struss and his Pigeon Hill neighbors were tormented with a rumor that the City of Pittsburgh intended to build low income housing in their community. This was the politician's answer to the many complaints from Struss and other residents about the lack of sidewalks, decaying wooden public steps, and street repairs. Complaints for years by the Negro community leaders about the poor housing prospects for their people were brushed off in the same manner, with promises of soon-to-be big changes.

Sitting in the Rathskeller, Struss read the reality of those promises being kept in the newspaper. Pigeon Hill's South Slope would be the site of a low income housing project. The massive project would be funded by the Federal Government. He tossed the newspaper aside and read the church bulletin his wife brought home after Palm Sunday Mass.

A meeting of concerned citizens will be held April 8, 1954
at Saint John's lyceum to review the Pigeon Hill Project.
An Official from the city will be present to answer inquiries.
Father Levalle will moderate the event. Pastor Mall of
Iona Street Lutheran and Reverend Moser of Diana
Street Congregational will attend.

Struss grabbed the telephone and dialed his ward boss. No answer. He kept dialing over and over until his call was answered. "This is Struss... Oh, you know why I'm calling? ... Not answering questions?... Go to the meeting?...That's all you got to tell me? Go to the meeting." Struss hung up on the party ward boss. "You're damned right. I'm going to that meeting!" he yelled at his baggy pants and undershirt image in the mirror behind the bar.

After sulking for a period of time at the bar, Struss left the Rathskeller and returned to his duties in the kitchen. He would dye eggs. Not as many as past years, but enough for an appearance of Easter being celebrated while living with pending doom. He wondered what sort of das osterfest could be enjoyed with such a dreadful future to look forward to. He checked his mail and opened an Osterkarden from Mrs. Krombach wishing the Strussberger's a Happy Easter with a message inside that she was praying for Jake's safe return. It wasn't in her handwriting. She would always enlist someone to write her English messages. Few people gave Easter cards anymore. He took a beer from the ice box. It was time to play Easter Bunny and dye eggs.

* * *

Unlike Saint John's Roman Catholic Church with only street curbs parking for its automobile owning parishioners, its Lyceum was only ten years old and had a substantial parking lot. The building was used for wedding receptions, wakes, and community meetings. Many cars were driving into the parking lot for the meeting that would determine Pigeon Hill's fate. The church grounds were at the bottom of Brookhurst Road, far enough away from Struss' home that he rode the Deutschtown trolley to the gathering, and took Mrs. Krombach along with him. Mrs. Strussberger stayed home, spouting that she had wee use for politicians and their malarkey. They came early, wanting to get a seat up front so that Mrs. Krombach could hear the speakers. Their promptness was rewarded with seats in the first row. Mrs. Krombach leaned to Struss. "Struss vas ist mit Saint John's?"

"Saint John's won't be torn down." He patted her hand. "Don't worry."

To everyone's surprise, Struss wore a suit to the meeting. Discussing the destruction of Pigeon Hill was as solemn as an occasion could get and equal to a death in the neighborhood. People were moving into the room and the long rows of folding wooden chairs facing the stage were quickly being filled. On stage, Struss saw three clergymen and a man in a slim lapel suit sitting behind a table with microphones, water pitchers, and glasses on its top. To Struss, he had the appearance of an undertaker. When everyone was seated, Father Levalle spoke into the microphone and attempted to silence everyone several times before the room became quiet.

"Thank you." he said. "Before I introduce our guest, I have a request. No smoking tonight in the Lyceum. This building needs to be clean in the morning for an assembly of the Deutschtown Gold Star Mothers Association. That's why the Lyceum is ablaze with red, white, and blue. Certainly, if any group deserves a clean place to assemble, these mothers do, who lost a son in battle for our freedom." He smiled. "If I can go a few hours without a smoke, so can you. And besides," he flashed a devilish grin. "I had the altar boys take away and hide the ash trays." The smoking ban was met with groans and grimaces.

Father Levalle introduced the Mayor's representative. Struss watched him stand and sit back down. He was fat.   "The gentleman," the priest continued somewhat sarcastically. "Said to tell you that he can answer questions regarding the planning and construction deadlines of the housing project, but he cannot answer why Pigeon Hill was chosen. That decision was made by his superiors. Please stand when asking your questions. Thank you."

The fat man spoke. "The Mayor is aware of the inconveniences this will cause and he and his administration intend to make your relocation as stress free as possible. You will be compensated for your moving expenses and your home if you own it. On the North Slope of Pigeon Hill, no projects will be built. On the South Slope, most of the buildings and houses will be demolished. I know many of you are concerned about the fate of your beautiful churches. The churches are not to be taken down."

Sighs of relief could be heard in the audience.

The Mayor's fat man continued. "If you are required to move, you'll be given notice explaining the deadline for the property to be vacated. If you own your home, an appraiser will visit, and set compensation. Now I'll take questions."

There were questions. Questions after questions and Struss sat listening to the end of his world by words from a fat stranger. Struss never planned to leave Pigeon Hill, he expected to die there. But now it was going to die first and leave him. Seldom did he leave Pigeon Hill in his lifetime. Only once or twice had he gone beyond Pittsburgh's city limits and never beyond the State border. Everything he needed or wanted was on the South Slope or nearby. Telling him it would all be gone in a year was the same as saying he had twelve months to live.

"Did the Mayor pick our neighborhood?" an angry man shouted.

"I'm not privy to those decisions."

"The Whistler picked it!" a voice cried out. A few chuckles followed.

The Owl was nervous. He had rushed from the Mart and got to the meeting late. He fingered his bow tie to ensure it was on properly before he stood. "I have a small business. A Mart."

"Excuse me?" the man interrupted. "A what?"

"A Mart." the Owl answered. There were chuckles. "A general store."

"Oh, I apologize." the Mayor's man smiled. "I never heard of a Mart before."

"My Mart is on the South Slope, near the top of the hill. Will it be taken?"

"If it's on the South Slope, it'll be demolished. Businessmen will be given assistance to reestablish themselves back into business."

The Owl was glum and sat down. Opening a Mart off of Pigeon Hill with the Mart sale money wouldn't lead to riches with the supermarket competition growing stronger each year. He must come up with a way of staying in business on Pigeon Hill. In addition to all of his established white customers, he would have access to an entirely new community of hungry Negroes.

"When can we expect these notices?" someone asked from the back of the room without getting up.

"Construction will begin in the large open baseball field adjacent to the Deutschtown High School. Some of you have already received notice. Those living higher on the hillside, near the cemetery wall, will be notified this summer. The people whose homes are taken and haven't found a place on their own have preference for housing in the projects as they are completed."

"What's the rent in these projects?" a woman shouted.

"Your rent is based on your income, and that'll include all utilities."

An elderly lady stood along with her daughter. She spoke in German. Her daughter translated. "My mother wants to know what these projects will look like."

"They'll be two stories high and made of brick, landscaped, and well insulated, warm in the winter. Roads will be much wider and have sidewalks." he smiled. "Missing sidewalks have been a constant complaint to City Hall from South Slope. You'll have sidewalks! Beautiful, wide sidewalks!"

A young man stood. "I'm a recent home buyer from the North Slope. Can I be assured that these projects won't be built beyond the cemetery wall of the South Slope?"

"Yes."

Mrs. Wernher stood dressed in her new brown suit with a hem a bit above her knees. "You mentioned businessmen." she felt slighted. "You should have said businesspeople." Chuckles rippled through the Lyceum. "My business isn't located on Pigeon Hill, but most of my customers live here. I have a quality used car lot. I depend on people from Pigeon Hill for my business. If most of the South Slope population moves away, my business will suffer. Will I be compensated?"

"You won't be compensated. Many residents of Pigeon Hill will remain, especially after they see how beautiful the new housing looks. Also, many more people will be living on Pigeon Hill as the Negroes are relocated here from across town. Your business will grow."

"I don't believe that will be the case." She sat back down.

Mr. Vonovich felt like a Judas sitting amongst the people in despair over losing their homes, while he personally found the news of the Projects heartening. With the news that his home would be bought by the government, he decided to advance his plan. With his hidden floorboard money and government compensation for his house he could move west and be financially independent living his new life. He started improving his appearance in anticipation of moving west. He brought new slacks and shirts, some of which he wore to the Lyceum. He bought new glasses with a gray plastic frame. He also went to a barber which is something he had not done in years. Usually, to save money, he would trim his hair himself.

The good news for him however, couldn't contain the resentment he felt stirring up inside of himself while watching the crowd. They sat worried about their future because some know-it-all authority, probably with some sort of highfaluting degree, thought he knew what was good for people he didn't even know. Academic intellectuals with no common sense would destroy America. Social engineers planning how humans should live in brick hives, as if they were ants or bees, would certainly crumble. Classroom theorists with no world-wise wisdom are nudging ethnic groups together before they're ready to merge instead of letting them ooze together over time. This wouldn't work either. He felt with his lifetime of studying, mixed with enduring hardships, he grew wise. And he knew better than the educated socialist nincompoops swarming into the government since Roosevelt's New Deal.

Vonovich wished he could warn them by predicting the consequences of destroying the Pigeon Hill community. He guessed the colored across town and the working class citizens in the Lyceum would vote the straight Democratic ticket as faithfully as the priest on the stage crossed himself before prayer. Now they were being rewarded with better housing if they wanted it or not. His older German neighbors had the perfect words for what was happening now between the Democratic Party voters and the Democratic Party leaders. "Vorsicht vor falschen freunden." he thought, and muttered the saying in English under his breath. "Caution of false friends."

Vonovich was awakened from his thoughts by an angrier voice. It was Struss.

"What about old people, people in their seventies and eighties?"

The mayor's spokesman smile widened, beaming with confidence that his answer to Struss' question would be received as a blessing for the elderly. "The building for the old people will be wonderful. It'll be a high-rise. It'll have elevators so they won't have steps to climb."

Struss huffed. "What's an old lady like Mrs. Krombach going to do on the tenth floor of a high-rise, caged like a canary?"

"Everything she does now, but she'll be warmer and safer."

"Safer from what? She comes and goes now around Pigeon Hill without worrying about her safety. I check in on her if she isn't seen around the streets. She doesn't want to be warmer or safer. What she wants is to be left alone, go to her church, and live in the house she shared with her family. All of your step saving elevators don't mean anything to her. Hell, in nice weather, she'll walk to the cemetery and care for family graves. She doesn't need your elevators. She needs her home!"

"Well sir!" the man lost his smile. "We have citizens living across town that need warmth in the winter and escape from rats. Let us take care of the living and quit worrying about the dead!"

Struss leaped to his feet. His Prussian face tense by his anger, his blue eyes glaring. "Okay, Mister Big Shot, now listen to me." Struss started to recall reading one of the city's newspaper editorials about rare pockets of Republicans living inside of the city limits. "You won't say why Pigeon Hill is the site for these dreamland homes of yours, but our nightmare. Well, I know and I'll spill the beans right here, right now." Struss turned and faced the seated crowd. "South Slope has always been democratic, but the fancy homeowners and businessmen on the North Slope are Republicans. By relocating the Democratic Darkies to Pigeon Hill, the Republicans are overwhelmingly outnumbered and our district seat on City Council will no longer be a race, but a shoo-in for the Democrats." Struss turned back to the Mayor's Messenger Boy and pointed his finger at him. "That's why, so don't go getting nasty with us about our neighborhood and cemetery. And don't talk down to us. We know what's going on! Tearing down South Slope is a fool's idea!" Struss, short of breath from hollering, sat down.

"You're absolutely wrong." the man said.

"No, he's not!" a voice boomed from the rear. Heads turned to see who was speaking. It was Vonovich. "What Mr. Strussberger said may or may not be true about why Pigeon Hill was chosen, but his statement about demolishing Pigeon Hill is a foolish act is correct. You disciples of dishing out goodies for votes without personal financial penalties on yourself, who plan and think for the poor, do most harm by thinking. You think that ruining this community will do more good than harm. You think you can eliminate slums by doing away with half of a community as this one and all will be warm, content, and live without rats. You'll destroy our homes. Offer us space inside a building which has no resemblances of what we believe is a home. You'll move in the colored and they'll be better off for a while. When people here tonight move into your buildings, they won't stay long. They'll do whatever it takes to move back into communities that they're accustomed to. Your projects will become predominately colored.

After that happens, the homes around the projects will begin being placed up for sale. Landlords will gobble them up as their value diminishes, and then rent them out to Negroes. Soon, the entire community will be colored just like the community you're relocating them from. Eventually, because the colored are too poor to repair the homes they live in, and the landlords won't, the area surrounding your new utopia of brick will be another slum with broken windows, inoperable furnaces, shabby yards, littered streets, cold children and rats. What have you accomplished? Can nothing grow old in America? Communities in Europe as Pigeon Hill stand for centuries. Your projects will become modern day catacombs, where surely the meek and innocent will fear to venture outside of their allotted space, or unlock their doors." Vonovich sat down.

The crowd applauded.

The fat man tried to get a word into the microphone, but the people began booing. He walked off the stage. Father Levalle, Pastor Mall, and Reverend Moser ended the meeting with a prayer for the community and the audience filed out of the Lyceum. Mrs. Wernher stayed sitting in her chair watching Vonovich speak with a few people that cornered him. His speech moved her to introduce herself after the crowd thinned.

CHAPTER NINETEEN
Love Is In the Air

Mrs. Wernher was infatuated with Vonovich. She probed into his personal life through her son Junior and knew about his troubled marriage. After they talked at the Lyceum, she offered him a ride home, which he gladly accepted. On the drive to his home, he told her about his plans to relocate to California. He said that he would soon need a car, a station wagon and asked to be contacted when one in good condition was available. They talked for over an hour inside of her Cadillac while parked in front of his house. She became fascinated with his ability to converse about every subject she brought forth, including the pros and cons of being a small businessperson. She became excited by his presence, his voice, and his vast knowledge. She had been pierced by Cupid's arrow. After they parted on that first night, she resolved to lasso him, pull him into her life.

She allowed other intelligent men to fade away in her life without them knowing how intensely she desired them. If she hadn't been reserved in those situations, too slow to show her emotions, perhaps an intellectual beau would've asked for her hand in marriage. Never again would she end up married to a boring Otto. Lying on her bed while in her bathrobe, she took the telephone from the night stand and dialed his number.

"Hello," his commanding voice came to her.

"Hi," she said softly.

"Well hello."

"I have a very nice station wagon on the lot if you're still in the market."

"I certainly am, thank you."

"You're still going west? That's a bold move." she paused. "But you're a bold man."

"I won't change my plans. Already quit my job."

"Is your wife going with you?"

"No, she doesn't want to go." he lied. He had no intentions of telling his wife where he was headed or when he was leaving. "Our marriage isn't the best."

"Oh, sorry. I didn't mean to..."

He cut her off. "Don't concern yourself, it's okay."

"Your son?"

"No. He's practically on his own. Between his job and girlfriend I seldom see him."

"It must be beautiful in the west, the wide-open spaces," she said, and then added in a playful voice, "Can I come along?"

Vonovich ignored her request and began describing America's west to her. She asked to go west with him in a kidding manner, but she wasn't pretending in reality. She applied to Detroit and the banks to open a new car dealership in the suburbs, but her application was rejected. She believed she had been refused because of her sex. The pending destruction of Pigeon Hill would ruin her business and she wanted to sell as soon as possible. Colored don't get bank loans. He finished explaining the Spanish missions of California and their original purpose and history.

"It sounds wonderful." she said. "I called you for another reason also. To invite you to my party. It's a combination birthday and spring welcoming party. Please come."

"I haven't been to a party since dating my wife."

"It'll be good for you. Get out of the city for a night. Come to the new world of suburbia."

"I'll come."

She wanted to scream like a Bobbysocker, but started rambling on and on about who would be at her party for him to meet. She also talked about what finger foods, cocktails and wine would be served.

Vonovich knew she was running after him. No woman had before. She didn't fit into his plans, but he wouldn't discourage her persistence to become close to him. He was enjoying the sought after status and believed he would eventually obtain a bargain price purchasing a car from her lot. His years of saving for his getaway plan continued and carrying on a friendship with some silly woman was just another way of saving money. She finished her party-planning spiel in a schoolgirl manner. "I'll make sure jumping into spring with me isn't boring."

He ignored her coy hint of offering him sex.

She gave the date, time, and her suburban address.

"See you then." Vonovich hung up.

She pulled her bathrobe tightly around herself. "I love him." she laughed at herself.

* * *

Vonovich pressed the button and heard the chime. He could hear the chattering and laughter inside the house. He saw his reflection in the narrow glass pane alongside of the entrance doorway. He was a bit uncomfortable wearing his new suit he bought at a Goodwill store. He had no idea of current fashions and wasn't certain if his suit was in style. He hoped the cost of the cab he rode to her suburban home would save him money when the time came for buying one of her automobiles. The door swung open.

"You should've let me come for you." she smiled.

"You're the hostess. You were needed here." He stepped into the vestibule.

"Well, I'm your taxi home."

Vonovich became transfixed and didn't hear his hostess. A vivacious young lady in the center of the next room took hold of his mind. She was wearing a cherry red mini cocktail dress with a black petticoat slip beneath, enabling him to see the hemline when she moved briskly about the room. It had a haltered neckline.

"Do you like my dress?"

"Huh, yes, it's beautiful." He feigned looking at his hostess' black and emerald cocktail dress with a sweetheart neckline.

She spun around so he could get a total view.

"Very nice." he uttered, still mesmerized with the lass in the next room, laughing and smiling while moving around the room, serving drinks. It was dreamlike. Years ago, his wife was gay and breezy as that girl. She even looked like his wife did back then, with her short reddish-brown hair and trim curvy figure.

"Me or the dress?"

"What?"

She took him by the arm. "You said 'very nice.' Did you mean me or the dress?"

"Oh, you of course." he smiled.

She winked. "Did you notice my dress has a rear zipper?"

He ignored her remark. "Do you think we should join the guests?"

She guided him into the spacious living room taking him from group to group around the room, shaking hands, and exchanging a few insignificant words at each encounter. After they circled the room, she stopped the young beauty carrying a full tray of drinks. "And this is Jean. My daughter. It's her birthday we're celebrating."

"Hello," she sang smiling broadly. "My mother's always speaking of you."

Vonovich was perplexed. He remembered her mentioning something at the Lyceum about children, but not a grown daughter. However, he usually stayed inattentive when she spoke.

"I'm delighted." he smiled. "Happy birthday."

"Thank you. Allow me to deliver these," she said, nodding to the tray of drinks. "And then I'll return and we can chat."

"Wonderful." he answered and watched her walk away and go about the room putting glasses into waiting hands. He looked at Jean's mother. "I'm really glad I came. Can I have a simple highball?"

"You can!" she answered joyously and let go of his arm and walked to the bar.

Jean finished her chore and returned to his side. "When I offered to help my mother entertain," she cheerfully said. "I had no idea I would end up her innkeeper."

"House parties haven't changed much since I last attended one." he smiled at her.

"When was that?"

"More years ago than your age," he grinned. "How old are you?"

"Twenty three."

"A lovely age for a lovely Miss." Out of the corner of his eye, he could see her mother at the bar holding his highball, but trapped by a talkative guest into conversation. Be thankful for small gifts, he thought. "Do you work or go to college?"

"Pitt."

"Your major?"

"Liberal arts, general subjects, math, history, etcetera. I suffer through those classes but they don't excite me. Classical art excites me."

"I have some art appreciation." he smiled, holding up his forefinger and thumb. "A tiny bit. Religious works."

"Great!" she exclaimed. "I'm only a novice, but I love the Italian renaissance and the late Gothic periods. I think Duccio and Capin are breathtaking."

He could see she was excited being able to speak with someone about her passion for art. Vonovich didn't lose the moment to impress her further. "To say nothing of Hubert and Jan Van Eyck. Especially the Ghent Altarpiece."

Jean covered her half-opened mouth, astonished by what he said. "Oh my God," she gasped. "I love them, too. I hope I can travel to Europe someday. There is so much I want to see."

"Are you two discovering anything in common?" Jean's mother handed Vonovich his highball. He sipped the drink while looking at Jean.

"Many things." her daughter answered. "He's wonderful, Mother."

"I told you." She took a hold of his arm.

"I'd better circulate." Jean smiled. "I hope you don't leave early Mr. Vonovich. We have much to talk about."

"I'll be around." he answered, eyeballing her as she walked away.

"Shall we get involved in some of the many conversations? I am the hostess."

"Lead on, brave hostess." he was bubbling over with gladness.

They moved toward the nearest group of partygoers. "Before we mix with others, I want to tell you something." he said. "Please do."

"Don't telephone me anymore. I'll call you." he gave her a wink.

She cuddled him. "You won't run off early?"

"I'll stay as long as you wish."

Giving him a squeeze, they strolled arm in arm to the closest group of partygoers.

* * *

Getting off the Deutschtown trolley, Mrs. Bentley hoped Cathy had supper ready. She was hungry. She still had not dated since her husband and son walked out of her life. But with Cathy proving to be a good mother, meeting her responsibilities, taking care of their home, doing the washing, cooking and cleaning, it was time to begin thinking of her own future. Her concern for Cathy was her relationship with Teddy. He was responsible also, graduating from high school and finding work learning a trade as a typesetter for the Sun-Telegraph morning newspaper. He liked the work and the shift, midnight to eight, because he could spend a good part of the day with Cathy and the baby at her house.

She wasn't certain if the romance between Teddy and Cathy was authentic. Certainly with Teddy it was unquestionable, but she wasn't as sure about Cathy's love for Teddy. Cathy loved him in many ways that was clear. She was full of gratitude to him for being there for her when others weren't. He was there during her pregnancy and the hectic days that followed when she and her daughter felt pilloried by many with gossip and head-turning stares. She worried that Cathy felt emotionally blackmailed. She believed that she owed Teddy and fearing with his deep crush on her, what he would do if she didn't marry him.

Her own life was fine. She loved her job as a receptionist because she got to come in contact with many interesting people. Offers came daily for dates by men on business trips to Pittsburgh who were staying at the Century, but with a smile, she'd turn them away. At work, she began wearing her wedding ring to put a halt to the requests and it worked for some men, but not all.

One man that sent her heart fluttering was a sports writer for the last German language newspaper in Deutschtown called *The DeutschAmerikaner.* He hung around the hotel seeking out professional ballplayers in town hoping to get interviews. Every now and then, he'd take her to lunch. With her divorce final, she'd been considering his invitations to go on a date. She told him everything about her life, including the Otto Wernher incident. He remembered reading about it in the newspaper, and of the reporters speaking of it at his work. None of her past seemed to concern him. He was single, never married, a few years younger than her, smart, bilingual, funny, and good-looking. He always complimented her and her clothes, especially the clothing that revealed her sexy figure. She often wondered what he would have thought of her loose fitting wardrobe that her ex enforced upon her figure. He seemed a little giddy today over what she had on, a skirt and blouse. The blouse neckline showed more cleavage than what she normally allows people to see. She disorientated his usually bright and humorous comments at lunch, and they both knew her breasts caused his giddiness.   She was smitten and she knew it.

She was taking the upcoming demolition of her rented house calmly. Her new project home would be easier to keep clean. Maintenance would be handled promptly, not as at present with the landlord fixing nothing since the house is going to be torn down. And the last winter heating bills were a hardship on her budget. She made extra noise entering the house, wanting to send Teddy and Cathy a warning that she was home. She didn't want to catch them kissing and cuddling on the sofa as she did once before.

"I'm home." she called out while still in the doorway.

"Hi." Teddy and Cathy answered from the kitchen.

"How was your day?" Cathy asked.

"Fine. Where's my granddaughter, Colleen?"

"Upstairs, sleeping."

"Is supper ready?"

"Oh yeah, spaghetti."

"My God, Cathy!" Mrs. Bentley said. "Spaghetti again?"

"It's cheap, Mom."

"Yeah, I know."

Cathy put the bowl of pasta on the table. She removed her apron and looked radiant in the printed house dress she wore. She maintained her trim firm figure and stayed partial to putting her hair into a ponytail. She never indulged in wearing much makeup and only used it lightly.

They sat down to eat like a family as they did every evening over the past few years. Teddy dressed in new blue jeans and a Pittsburgh Pirate pullover. He had grown taller than Cathy, into a lanky good-looking man. He would stay with Cathy until nine o'clock and then go home and get dressed for work. He had little to do with his parents, seldom seeing his father and his mother rarely came home.

"It's hard for me to believe this house will be gone soon." Cathy said while turning pasta with her fork.

"I'm looking forward to moving." Mrs. Bentley said. "This place was freezing last winter." She looked at Teddy. "Did your parents get their notice to move yet?"

"I think so, but I'm not sure."

"I expect our notice any day." Cathy said. "Time really does fly."

"Yeah," Teddy said. "I heard Jake Strussberger is coming home from Korea."

"When?" Mrs. Bentley asked, putting her fork down onto her plate of noodles.

"June. I think."

"Is he getting out of the Marines?" Cathy asked.

"On furlough."

"I wish he would've visited us when he came home a few years ago." Mrs. Bentley said. "I still have bad feeling dragging that boy into trouble like I did."

"When I see him," Teddy said. "I'll ask him to stop by."

"Thanks, Teddy." Mrs. Bentley answered. She lost her appetite to bad memories. "Is Jake's parents moving into the projects?"

"Yes." Cathy answered. "That's what Mrs. Krombach told me."

"Then I guess they are." Teddy chuckled.

"She's upset about moving." Cathy said. "It's sad."

"The price of progress." Teddy said. "She's so nice. Plenty of people will miss her gifts of fresh vegetables and cookies."

"She was here today." Cathy said. "Brought us some cookies she made. That's our dessert. She's always asking if I'm going swimming when the public pool opens."

"You should." Mrs. Bentley said.

"Maybe."

They finished eating and together they cleaned off the table. Teddy and Cathy did the dishes while Mrs. Bentley went and showered.

"You should do as your mother said." Teddy said. "And go swimming."

"What about you?" she asked.

"I can't swim very well. Go early, when I'm home sleeping. Then you'll be back home when I wake up and come here."

"We'll see." she said and gave him a quick kiss on the lips.

Colleen awoke and was crying. They both went to get her.

CHAPTER TWENTY
On Leave

People from the lowest section of the South Slope and some colored from across the river moved into the first completed projects. The Owl lost his encounter with City Hall. The Mart would be torn down. He didn't know what he was going to do. He asked around about opening a store on the North Slope, but was firmly advised against it by the residents. They didn't want Negroes wandering into their neighborhoods even if only to shop.

The North Slope homeowners felt somewhat secure. The projects wouldn't go beyond the South Slope cemetery wall. Resurrection Cemetery became a barrier against intrusive government madness. The dead were looked upon as unmoving centurions guarding a way of life cherished by the sons and daughters of the German immigrants who settled the hilly slopes.

Houses were being torn apart and hauled away in huge trucks. When they began demolishing the house where Struss lived as a child, he watched at a distance. He could see the bedrooms which sheltered him and his brothers when the wrecking crews ripped into the wood and plaster walls. To his surprise, the bedrooms were painted. Somehow he pictured them eternally wallpapered like when he was a child. He could see the stairs, remembering the many times his mother had climbed those steps to get him up for school. He turned away, walking past workmen building a new public school. Destruction and construction would continue till winter.

It all seemed unreal to Struss. Street after street was gone and also the lower part of Brookhurst. The streets were as much a part of him as his family. He had walked their winding ways thousands of times in rain, snow, and sweltering heat. It was a nice cool day so Struss walked some of the remaining South Slope roads. He wandered under the cemetery steel arch entry and strolled its winding dirt road, passing grave markers with names of people he had known. He stopped at some graves and spoke.

"Struss here, Mr. and Mrs. Henline. Thanks for being so understanding when I threw a rock and broke your window." He walked over the grassy hillside and stopped and spoke again.

"Struss here, Mr. and Mrs. Stritzinger. Thanks for always finding room at your table for a good meal. They were some of the best potato pancakes I ever ate." He walked awhile and stopped again.

"Struss here, Mr. and Mrs. Hoffmann. Thanks for letting my family be free from worrying when we came up short for our monthly rent." He walked on for a short distance.

"Struss here, Mr. and Mrs. Freiss. Thanks for always giving me a nickel when I went to the store for your family. That was a lot of money. With those nickels, I was able to see talkie movies."

He walked on hiking most of the cemetery while passing headstones in the oldest burial grounds with inscriptions in German. He stopped at some and said a few words to their spirits. He stopped at Mrs. Krombach's family tombs. He knew she'd been there recently by the fresh flowers planted on the graves. When he came to his parent's grave, he crossed himself and talked to them for a while. He told them that Jake was home on leave from the Marines and the awful news about the South Slope. He crossed himself again and headed home, taking a shortcut by walking a well-worn pathway through tall grass on the unused portion of the cemetery grounds. When he got to the Mart, he saw Jake in uniform speaking with the Owl.

"Hi, Dad. Where you going?"

"Home, to get a beer." Struss answered without slowing his pace.

"I'll see you later." Jake told the Owl and yelled after his Dad. "Hey Dad, wait!"

Struss stopped and waited for his son.

"Where are you coming from?" Jake asked.

"Just walking around taking in the sights, before it's all gone and forgotten."

"Did you see the new homes going up?" Jake asked.

"Projects, not homes." Struss sort of growled.

Mrs. Krombach was sitting on her porch. They waved to her.

"Corporal Strussberger. That's great." He put his arm around his son's shoulder. "I'm proud of you."

When they got home, Struss took an official appearing envelope out of the mailbox. He tossed it onto the kitchen table and got himself a beer from the icebox. He would read the notice later.

From the kitchen window, Jake saw Cathy Bentley walking on the street with a small child. He opened the door and yelled from the stoop. "Cathy!"

She turned. "Jake! My God, how are you?"

"Fine. Where are you headed?"

"Swimming."

"Wait. I'll get my trunks and come along."

Within minutes he was at her side. "Is this your little girl?"

"Yes. Colleen."

"Hi, Colleen." he said, picking her up and carrying her as they walked.

"How long are you home?"

"I'm on a ten day leave."

"Why didn't you write?" she asked, smiling up at him.

"Why didn't you?" they both laughed. Before reaching the Deutschtown community swimming pool, Cathy invited him to supper. He accepted.

* * *

Teddy, gripping the cyclone fence, peered through its diamond shaped openings searching for Cathy and Colleen. The pool was crowded with many mothers and their small children in the shallow end of the pool. Cathy told him she was taking Colleen swimming, but that she'd be home early afternoon. When he went to her house and she wasn't there, he decided to meet her at the pool.

He spotted the three of them. Jake was holding Colleen's hand and walking her slowly through the low water. Cathy was splashing them. He watched them laughing and splashing each other for a long time through the fence holes before Jake stole a short kiss to Cathy's cheek. It was a sudden kiss, a kiss on an impulse. Cathy appeared startled at first, but then said something to Jake and smiled. Her face couldn't hide the joy she got from his kiss. Teddy turned and walked away.

* * *

Cathy carried sleeping Colleen upstairs to her bed. The child was tired from her wet day at the swimming pool. Jake sat on the same sofa remembering the night Mrs. Bentley controlled his mind and titillated his hormones. He was apprehensive waiting for Cathy's mother to come home from work. He hadn't seen her since the inquiry of Mr. Wernher.

Cathy entered the room. "I wonder where Teddy is? I know he'll be glad to see you."

"I'd like to see him, too."

"I've got to start supper." Cathy said. "Come into the kitchen."

Jake made a funny face and teased her. "If I watch you, maybe it'll ruin my appetite."

"Suit yourself, Marine!" she snapped and walked briskly to the kitchen.

Jake followed close behind. Her appearance hadn't changed much to Jake. Her figure was a bit heavier, which he thought gave her a more wholesome and healthy look. And there was something about her personality that moved him. She seemed void of false pretenses. She wasn't the girl he had known when he was a silly boy running after Susan. She was a beautiful woman.

"Do you see Junior or the others?" he asked without knowing what sort of relationship she had with Henry concerning Colleen.

"I only see Teddy. I saw Susan at the Mart a few times and tried to speak with her, but didn't get very far. She and Henry live with her parents. I guess they'll be moving into the projects also when their house is demolished. I never see Junior since his mother moved to the suburbs. He called me a few times right after I delivered Colleen because he wanted to go out with me. He quit calling after awhile."

"What about Carl?"

She stopped what she was doing at the stove. "Hadn't seen him or my father since the day they took their belongings out of this house. Mom tried to telephone Carl several times but he hung up on her. He's a brat and won't talk to me either, nor will my father."

Jake could see she was furious with her father and twin brother. She had fire in her belly and he liked what he saw. He asked a lighter question. "Shouldn't you be wearing an apron over those pretty shorts and sleeveless blouse?"

She stopped stirring and looked at him. "You're right." Her apron was hanging over a chair and she grabbed it and put in on. "It's your fault, got me gabbing so much. I don't know what I'm doing."

"For the sake of my stomach, I hope you know what you're doing." he chuckled. "I can see that it looks like spaghetti, but the question is, does it taste like spaghetti?"

She grinned. "I make a lot of spaghetti." She turned off the stove top burner and her smile turned to a serious look. "I really had a good time today, Jake. I haven't been swimming in years." She started setting the table.

Her obvious joy at being in his company pleased Jake, but it also confused him. Several times at the pool she expressed her delight at being out and away from the house. He didn't ask her, but from the way she spoke, he got the impression that she hadn't been out having fun for years. He couldn't grasp what she and Teddy did for leisure and fun. Their relationship seemed strange. After he kissed her at the pool, she told him that Teddy was her steady, but he could feel from her reaction that she liked his kiss. "Don't you and Teddy go swimming?"

"Teddy can't swim very well. I don't think he likes swimming, and I, well, I just didn't have the nerve for a long time to face people. I know it's crazy."

"I'll say." Jake shook his head. "Just hanging around here?"

"Yeah," she murmured. "Except to go shopping."

"Are you and Teddy planning to marry?"

"Yes. Someday."

Her answer didn't sound convincing to Jake. "Teddy's a lucky guy. Smarter than me. He had his eye on you since high school."

"What do you mean, smarter than you?" she asked, finishing the setting of the table and sitting down across from him.

"It should be clear what I mean. You were always cute, but looking back now with my horse blinders off, the truth is you were beautiful."

She stared at him in his uniform. He could've been a recruiting poster, she thought. "I had blinders on myself back then." she smiled. "Thanks for your compliment, Jake." Then she broke into a laugh. "That's if you meant it!"

"I did."

She came around the table and gave him a peck on the cheek. "I forgot what it feels like to get compliments. I haven't had one for a long time."

There it was again. The strange responses she uttered in their conversations. If she's planning to marry Teddy, and they saw each other every day, it was difficult for him to understand why she wasn't getting compliments. "Come on." he said, watching her go back to the stove and move pots around trying to look busy. "Teddy tells you sweet things every hour." She flushed. "You never gave me compliments in high school or when we hung out at the Owl's."

"I told you. Teddy's smarter than me. My romantic thoughts were for Susan," he chuckled, and watched for her reaction. "And your mother."

"Who?"

Jake laughed, rubbing his cheek. He needed a shave. "I was in love with Susan and your mother."

"I don't believe you!" Cathy said, a frozen smile on her face.

"I was," he said, laughing at her stunned stance over the steaming pasta.

"Jake, if you're lying, I'm going to dump these noodles on you."

"I'm not."

"Jake Strussberger," she dropped the ladle into the pot. "I thought you were bashful."

"You can be bashful and still be in love." he said.

"Mom will be home any minute now. Maybe I'll tell her."

"Don't." Jake cautioned. "I'm nervous already about meeting her after all these years." He didn't want Mrs. Bentley to think he told Cathy about their intimate moments after Mr. Wernher's accident.

"Don't be silly." she said. "I got the best mother in the world."

"The prettiest too."

"Enough is enough, Marine!" Cathy warned with a smile. "Are you here to see me or my mother?"

"Well, you're spoken for, but your mother's free."

Cathy's eyes were gleaming. "You better hurry, then. She has a newspaper sports reporter interested in her and she is interested in him."

"A sports reporter?" Jake reached out and took her hand. "Then I better make my moves on her tonight."

They heard the front door opening and heard Mrs. Bentley calling out. "I'm home." Jake let go of Cathy's hand.

* * *

Mrs. Bentley was feeling good about the previous night in Jake's company. He changed into a mature and amusing man.

The three of them had talked late into the evening before Jake went home. Jake's presence as a man, and no longer a teen, was a shock to her senses when she saw him in uniform standing in her kitchen. But after awhile, he put her at ease with a friendly hug.

She looked around the lobby from the receptionist desk. The DeutschAmerikaner reporter hadn't arrived and her lunch hour was about to begin. She had hoped to go to lunch with him.

She was worried about Teddy. He didn't show for supper. Cathy telephoned his home, but got no answer. She feared something triggered Teddy's despondency. He had a habit of going into dark moods, especially when Cathy spoke about Henry's unwillingness to acknowledge being the father of Colleen. He still harbored a jealousy about Henry's affair with Cathy and it was a deep enough bitterness that he couldn't hide it even when he tried. He had nothing to worry about. Cathy had no love for Henry, she detested him. Teddy knew how Cathy felt about Colleen's father, yet she believed it troubled him that Henry had been intimate with Cathy. That was a worrisome fear to her. She thought again of her strict German father and his warning. Sins and misconduct cast long shadows into a person's future. Mistakes leave wounds. Wounds leave scars. Scars leave reminders.

She could see her lunch date entering the lobby. Her heartbeat told her she cared for him. She would date him soon.

CHAPTER TWENTY ONE
Pickle Juice

After he left the swimming pool fence, Teddy went home and packed a suitcase with plans to take a train somewhere, anywhere. Yet when he got to the train station, he only sat on a bench. Perhaps he was overreacting to Jake and Cathy's fun in the water? When he saw Cathy talking to Jake after he kissed her, maybe she told Jake, warned him, not to kiss her again because she was in love and faithful to him. Thoughts zoomed through his mind, alternating between innocent and devious behavior by Cathy at the pool. He recalled her skilled underhanded tactics as a teen when she crossed Susan and allowed Henry to make love to her. He thought she learned her lesson, but he wasn't certain.

A sailor walked by carrying his duffle bag with a cute girl holding his arm. He watched them strolling to the gates for the departing trains. The girl had been crying, her eyes red with sadness. He was obviously returning to his ship after being home on leave. Teddy felt sad for both of them. The romantic pair gave him adventurous thoughts of his own. Maybe he should enlist in the Armed Forces. Perhaps the Navy. See the world. Soon he would be drafted anyhow. Would Cathy wait for him? Cry and sob like the girl on the sailor's arm? He hoped she would, but he doubted her love for him.

The tiny incident at the pool, seeing her face aglow from a peck on the cheek spoke wonders to him. Did Cathy love him out of sympathy rather than deep desirous feeling, like the girl clutching and sobbing inconsolably onto the sailor's uniform? He sat still, staring at the couple, wishing he was the sailor and the girl was Cathy. The "all-aboard" announcement came over the intercom. The couple embraced and kissed one last time. Then he was gone and she stood lonely and brokenhearted.

How fortunate they were. He could only wish for such beautiful moments to enter into his life. He went to the restroom and changed into his work clothes. After changing, he walked to a homeless shelter run by the Sisters of Saint Joseph. He gave the nuns a few dollars and bunked with society losers until Jake went back to the Marine camp. Then he'd visit Cathy and have it out with her once and for all about their relationship. He giggled nervously to himself. He felt right at home with Saint Joseph's misfits.

* * *

Opening the door into his house, Teddy immediately smelled the repugnant odor. In the kitchen, he found the same old dirty dishes in the sink and the same half of a loaf of stale bread on the table as when he was last home over a week ago. He went to his parent's bedroom and the smell overwhelmed him. He rushed past his sprawling mother on the bed and opened a window. Pinching his nose, he looked down upon his mother's body. She was dead. There were dark spots on her skin. Her mouth was partly open and full of something. It looked like vomit to Teddy. He touched her arm. She was hard, like a stone.

The fresh air had lessened the smell. He released his nostrils. He looked at his mother's face again. It was grotesque, her sunken cheeks covered with powder and rouge, lips twisted with bits of dark red lipstick. He wasn't Catholic or of any religion, but crossed himself anyway for wanting to do something respectful. Yet, he wasn't certain he did the crossing in the correct way. He left the room.

In the kitchen, he opened the refrigerator. A pickle jar with only juice in it sat on the shelf, just as he left it the last time he was home. He shut the fridge door, looked about, and checked for clues that his father had been home. There were none. He went to his bedroom and found a note tacked to the door from his father, listing a telephone number to call.

He dialed the number. Junior answered.

"Junior?" Teddy asked befuddled.

"Yeah?"

"This is Teddy. Is my Dad there?"

"Yeah, he's here." Junior sounded sassy. "He lives here."

Teddy waited for his father's voice. "Hello, Teddy."

"Hello." Teddy muttered.

"I'm glad you called. I've been trying to get in touch with you, but you never answer the phone. The house has been sold to the government. We've got to vacate within sixty days."

"Okay." Teddy said unconcerned. He planned to move in with the Bentley's and go with them into the projects. "Mrs. Bentley said I can live with them."

"The good news is, only if you want to. I'm divorcing your mother and marrying Mrs. Wernher. We're moving to California and Mrs. Wernher wants you to come along. Her children, Junior and Jean, are coming with us. We could be one big happy family."

"I don't want to go out there." Teddy answered. ""I'm not leaving Cathy. We're going to get married someday."

"Well, if you change your mind, we'll always have room for you. Are you sure about you and Cathy?"

"Why are you asking that?"

"Oh, it's just something that Junior said about your relationship with her."

"What?"

"He said that she played you for a fool before, and will again. I don't want you to get hurt son. That's all I meant."

"Junior should keep his mouth shut! He's jealous of me because he likes Cathy too, and she'd never go out with him." Now more than before, Teddy wanted to have it out with Cathy about the depth of their relationship.

His father changed the subject. "Is your Mother home?"

Teddy said nothing.

"Teddy, are you still there?"

Teddy wanted to leave the house and go to Cathy and have his say about their romance. Was it real on her part or pretend? Telling his dad about his dead mother now, calling the undertaker, the coroner. All the commotion would just delay his needed confrontation with Cathy.

"She's in her room."

"Sleeping?" Mr. Vonovich asked. "Don't awaken her. Leave her sleep."

"I will." Teddy murmured.

"Well, goodbye. Please call me again and let me know how you're doing. And good luck learning the printing trade. I'm proud of you, son."

"Bye." Teddy answered.

"Teddy!" his father blurted his name.

"Yeah?"

"I'm sorry I failed you."

Teddy could hear his dad's voice breaking.

"You're a victim of your mother's partying ways and my self pity. I'm sorry."

Teddy wasn't in the mood for explanations about his befuddling life. "Bye, dad."

"Bye, son. I love you."

"You too, dad." Teddy hung up the receiver.

He planned to get out of his working coveralls and shower before seeing Cathy, but he was too impatient to see her. He rushed outside and dashed to her house.

"Cathy!" he shouted upon entering the house.

"Where have you been?" she shouted back at him from the kitchen. "I've been worried sick."

He entered the kitchen. "Sick enough not to kiss Jake Strussberger goodbye before he marched back to camp?"

"You're jealous of Jake?" Cathy asked confused. "Why?" She went into the living room where Colleen sat on the rug watching television. She sat on the overstuffed chair and folded her arms. Teddy followed her into the room, pacing behind Colleen. Cathy scolded him. "Sit down Teddy. Cool off, and then we'll talk."

He didn't stop or sit down. "Did you spend his entire furlough with him?"

"No, he came for supper a few times."

"Yeah, I'll bet. How many times did the two of you go to the pool? Huh?"

She didn't answer him.

"Plenty. Right?"

She looked away from him.

Teddy started rambling, overreaching with sassy remarks to find out the extent of their time together. "Your silence tells it all. Did he see you in anything other than a bathing suit and shorts while he was home? Bet not! Did you wear those sexy shorts and blouse you're wearing now while feeding him supper?

How about lunch? Was he here for lunch? I'm fed up to here with people!" He sobbed while tapping his forehead.

"Teddy. Calm down. Please."

"Calm down!" he mocked. "It's easy for you to say. You! You! Ohh, forget it!"

"Go on and say it!" Cathy shouted. "Whore! Slut! Bitch! Say what you feel. What you wanted to say since Henry." Colleen started crying.

Teddy started crying too. He brushed his tears away, stooped and picked up the child, caressed her and began pacing again.

"Well?" she asked.

"Well what?" he whispered. "I have a right to be mad. I saw the two of you in the pool. He kissed you and you loved it."

"Oh, my God." she chuckled. "He kissed me once on the cheek."

Colleen stopped crying. "Once that day. How many times while he was home?"

"Why didn't you come around and find out. Spy."

He put the child back onto the floor. "Because I got sick seeing him with you."

Cathy came to him, put her arms around his waist and laid her head on his chest. "When he kissed me in the pool, I was surprised. I told him I was going steady with you. After that, he never tried to kiss me again. Honest. He came and visited me and Mom while you were off sulking, but he also wanted to see you. He's your friend, Teddy."

"Did you tell him we're going to get married?"

"Yes."

"When are we?" he whispered, putting his arms around her.

"When are we what?" she teased.

"Both." he squeezed her. "I know you want to wait till our wedding night, but it's hard for me, especially since you aren't a virgin. I can't understand why I have to wait."

"Because I changed, Teddy. I'm not a slut. I only did it one time with Henry and I was scared out of my mind in the back of his car. I got nothing from it but life-changing troubles for five minutes of nonsense. And I gave stupid Henry bragging points. There is no person sorrier than me for being Henry's stooge. I'll marry you when I'm sure about how you feel about me."

"That's crazy talk." he said.

"Come sit on the sofa. I want to tell you what's bothering me." They sat. She held his hand. "Sometimes I think you're only infatuated with me, but believe it's love. I get a feeling that if another pretty woman came into your life, you'd fall for her too, like you did for Fawn after just a few moments with her. I remember how thrilled you were over her, I understand, I acted the same way with Henry. I know better now. I'm not sure you do."

Teddy tried to interrupt her thoughts. "Ahh, that's..."

She put her finger to his lips. "Shhh." she continued. "When I am sure your love for me is true love and I'm not a short-lived passion after a few times in the sack together, I'll marry you."

Teddy smiled. "I don't know how else I can show my love is true, other than how I have over the past few years."

"Get rid of the green monster inside of yourself. That creature changes you in an instant from a sweet guy into someone I don't know. You befriended me during terrible times, when facing people was a chore for me, and some facing me had little compassion in their hearts. I'll never forget how you kept me company and helped me with Colleen." she laughed. "Heck, how many times did you change her dirty diapers? As much as me? I do love you Teddy."

Teddy didn't like the message she delivered, but promised to change. "I'll try never to be jealous again."

"Please. We'll get along much better."

"Are you going to write Jake?" he asked.

"I told him I would."

"Has he changed much?"

"Haven't we all?" she chuckled.

"Did he say much about Korea?"

"Nothing."

Teddy turned remorseful. "I shouldn't have stayed away. Jake has always been my best friend. I think there's something not right with me."

"Listen to me and my mother and we'll heal you. I love you, Teddy."

Teddy looked at Colleen. She'd fallen asleep holding her favorite blanket.

He took Cathy in his arms and they began kissing. He forgot to tell her about his mother.

CHAPTER TWENTY TWO
Targets

Sitting behind the firing line, his M1 rifle sling looped high on his arm, Jake had time before leading his squad onto the firing line for their annual qualification. His squad was lounging about on a grassy knoll off to the side of the rifle range, awaiting their order to move into firing positions. He thought about Cathy and her letter in his rear pocket.

He couldn't get Cathy out of his mind. Those days on leave in Pittsburgh were treasured now. Even though he only kissed her briefly on the cheek on impulse, the touch of her skin on his lips became an overpowering moment he brought back to Camp with him. His letters to her were short. Writing to her about his day to day activities as a Marine would be written in terminology she wouldn't understand, so his letters were mostly composed of a lot of questions about what was happening on Pigeon Hill.

Her letters to him were lengthy. She answered his questions, told him about her Mother's blossoming romance with the Sports Reporter, but she didn't say much about Teddy. She only told him that he moved in with them and made a make-do bedroom for himself in their attic until they all moved into the projects.

Her words made him homesick. She would write about how she relished autumn when the leaves on the trees of Pigeon Hill and Pittsburgh turned bright colors. She thought that was the most beautiful season and it was her favorite. She wrote how she loved walking the winding dirt paths that zigzagged through their community when the leaves were radiant. There was one sentence that caught his attention; it was when she wrote about how she regretted that he would miss walking with her under the fall leaves because his discharge would only occur later in the fall, when the trees would be bare.

Why wouldn't she mention walking the dirt paths with Teddy? Was she daydreaming about him holding hands and strolling the paths, taking in the glory of nature? That daydream became his fantasy away from home. Even with her constant acknowledgment that Teddy was her beau, Jake couldn't shed the feeling that something passed between them when he was home. She enjoyed his company, her face and mood displayed that she more than liked him. And although she showed concern that Teddy didn't visit her while he was home on leave, she didn't fall to pieces or do anything like try to contact Mr. Vonovich as to Teddy's whereabouts. And they weren't engaged yet either? Their strange courtship was confusing.

Her letter had sad news also. Teddy's mother died and Mr. Vonovich had his wife cremated without funeral home visits beforehand or religious services. She enclosed a newspaper clipping of Mrs. Vonovich's death notice along with other clippings about the community. One clipping he found most enjoyable was an article written by Mrs. Bentley's DeutschAmerikaner sport reporter. Cathy wrote how her mother bribed him with a promise of a homemade supper of sauerbraten and kartoffelknodel if the reporter would cover the opening game of the Pigeon Hill Arrows sandlot football team. He agreed and they all went to the game to watch the Arrows lose.

Jake took her letter out of his pocket. The thought of the German dishes of sour roast and potato dumplings that Cathy wrote about got his mouth watering and stomach growling. He'd be glad to be discharged. It was time to go home after seeing some of the world and being at war. He took the article written by Mrs. Bentley's Reporter and read it again. Jake liked the FritzDerLip handle used by the reporter.

FritzDerLip

To my faithful followers, I confess. I was bribed away from my normal beat at the Century Hotel, cornering big league players for interesting insider information by a promise of homemade sauerbraten, karoffelknodel, and a sprinkling of spazle. Add to that, the redheaded lady cook, who was more irresistible to me than the food. This all sent me, notebook and pencil in hand, rushing to Garden Field to cover a sandlot football game between the home team, Pigeon Hill Arrows, and the Crosstown Crushers.

The final score of the game, a Crosstown victory 42-7, in a comical way, revealed that the teams were properly named. Crushers sounds foot-ballistic. The Arrows, on the other hand, brings to mind an anarchy team of clean young gentlemen dressed in white pants, vee neck sweaters, with perfectly groomed hair. The sandlot league isn't a recent organization; it was being reestablished as it existed before the war. During the war, the need for service to our country superseded many of the local sport activities.

I couldn't stop wondering why such an odd name for a football team. Being curious, I nosed around, and the best I could get from the locals was that at one time there was a German immigrant archery club of some quality from Pigeon Hill. The Arrows name probably came from that defunct club.

At that time, archery club rules, as well as references to the club were in German. Archery club translates in Deutsche to bogenshutzen klub and sounds somewhat threatening in German, but not as menacing as Arrows Football Team in German. Pfeile Fuballnationalmannschaft. There's a name that would make any Crusher run to his coach crying.

Before the game, I investigated the whereabouts of the Arrows training facilities and their coaches in a sort of under-cover way, a day before the opening game. What I discovered by the training, scrimmages, and coaching was that I could predict defeat for this rebirth of the Arrows team as assuredly as death itself. I surmised at the end of a day watching them practice that the only way the Crosstown Crushers could lose to the Arrows is if they were already dead and positioned onto the field as cadavers.

I took the trolley to Pigeon Hill, all the way to the end of its line at a loop where the tracks circle around and head back through Deutschtown to Pittsburgh. Close by, I spotted a tavern with a dangling sign above its entrance, Herman the German's Saloon. There I went, like an investigating reporter, hoping to strike up some conversation with the locals. I wanted to get their feelings about the Arrows, small tidbits of information that'll make a newspaper column more interesting to the reader. And to get a lager, of course.

Bingo! I hit the mother lode. The entire Arrows coaching staff was inside the saloon, circling the bar, drinking, smoking, laughing, and bickering about planned plays to be used against the Crushers. And what player should play what position. I must've heard "do what you want, you're the coach," as much as I heard calls to the stout bartender to refill their glasses of draft beer.

It was a horse-shaped bar and from where I sat enjoying my beer, I could see and hear everything said. Had I been a

Crusher spy, not only would I have known the Arrows short list of uncomplicated plays, the player's strengths and weaknesses, but I would have also known the sizes of their body parts, so freely did the information flow about the team.

On one occasion, I marveled at one coach who showed another coach his idea of a good play, tracing out the formation and its benefits with beer foam on the bar surface. Taking foam from a heady head of draft beer (I think it was his beer), he spread the bubbles on the bar and worked his fingers fast, showing the other coach the action. No Crusher spy could be quick enough to glimpse that bursting bubbling play.

Inside the saloon I discovered that the practice field for the Arrows was none other than the somewhat grassy area of the trolley loop, a few steps away from the saloon. The equipment storage and team dressing facilities were Herman the German's shed behind the bar. No investigative reporter ever had it so easy. With no loss of shoe leather, I was in the center of Arrow action, capable of observing both the makings and obstacles of sandlot football.

The practice began with simple calisthenics, the normal stuff; sit-ups, pushups, running in place, and a lot of hollering by the partly inebriated coaches. The plays, tee formation, hand-offs to the fullback, or a halfback, with short passes over the middle, could've been conducted on a cement school yard. The hitting and blocking were mostly against imaginary opponents and few players expected to be hit hard at practice or knocked to the ground. It all seemed like a lackadaisical effort by the entire team.

The only parts of their uniforms that were uniform were the jerseys. They were all the same colors. Black and gold. The pants and helmets were a variety of different looks from the forties.

Padding for the pants or anywhere else chosen for protection, came from huge boxes of extra large Kotex, provided by the head coach. I thought a Kotex might present some difficulties for an Arrow if one fell from his pants in front of a Crusher.

Game day: The Crushers took the kickoff and ran past midfield before being brought down by the Arrows. On their first play, the Crushers ripped through the Arrows line like stampeding cattle. The Crusher halfbacks, cutting off a tackle or running the ends got good gains before being dragged down by multiple Arrow players. The Crosstown fullback pounded the Arrows center for never fewer than two yards. One Arrow defensive line player, being lectured by his coach, was heard to say, "But coach, they gotta run somewhere." At the end of the first half, the Crushers had ran up 28 points, came back in the second and scored two more touchdowns.

When the Arrows got their hands on the ball for the first time and for many plays thereafter, they were often confused, sometimes running into each other. Only once, in the first half were they able to achieve a first down.

When the final whistle blew, it seemed like an embarrassing blowout and a humbling experience for the Arrows and Pigeon Hill, but that is not the case. What I saw while watching this sandlot game in such a "no glory league" for any player or team, was heart. The Arrows were in a league with age limits, 18 to 21. What I observed, and found to be true, was that many Arrow players were not yet 18 and some were only 16.

On the other side, the Crushers looked bigger, and older. Some had heavy beards, and they revealed themselves as an experienced team. Were ringers in play? Possibly, the league should look into it. The Arrows held the Crosstown lads to only two touchdowns in the second half and scored themselves. That's a fair beginning for a bunch of green neighborhood youngsters and their beer drinking coaches.

Pigeon Hill is no longer an entirely German community. Many nationalities now call it home. Names on the back of Arrow's jerseys reveal a mix of ethnic heritages. A quote from Goethe, which I'm going to write for this 1954 Arrow team, is a tribute to them. It may have never been heard by people other than us German-Americans, yet it nonetheless could've been written by Goethe himself for this Arrow's team. "The deed is everything, the glory naught."

Jake watched the range non-commission-officer take his stance on the firing line and knew it was time to put silly romantic matters aside and focus on being a Marine. He put Cathy's letter and clippings in his pocket and stood waiting for the command. He alerted his men to stand ready.

The range Gunnery Sergeant barked the command. "Sixth relay, move to the firing line!"

Jake lay on the hard ground, the rifle sling loop high on his arm, above his biceps. He kept tightening the loop until it hurt and wouldn't tighten any further.

The Gunnery Sergeant barked again. "This will be ten rounds, rapid fire, 300 yard line, 50 second time limit. Make your adjustments!"

Jake swung the butt of the rifle into his shoulder. It was tight, his elbow directly under the rifle. The sling cut into his arm and hurt. He ignored the pain, knowing the tight sling was necessary to keep his body and weapon as one, allowing him to drop back onto target after each recoil. He removed the rifle butt from his shoulder, checked his rounds, and waited for the command. It came.

"Ready on the right?" There was a pause.

"Ready on the left?" Another pause.

"All ready on the firing line?" A pause.

"Watch your targets!"

"Targets!"

Jake saw his target appear in the distance. He pushed a clip into the receiver, let the bolt slide forward, and swung the rifle butt into his shoulder. He took a deep breath, exhaled half of it, and sighted the target. The black bulls-eye looked like the head of a pin. Jake squeezed the trigger. The explosion lifted his rifle and strapped arm as if they were welded together, then lowered smoothly back onto target as he squeezed again, and again, and again, until all rounds were fired. He waited for the cease fire command before moving off of the firing line to await his score.

CHAPTER TWENTY THREE
Nut Gatherer

Mrs. Bentley's ex-mother-in-law answered the phone. "Hello."

"Hello, is Carl home?"

"Just a minute."

Mrs. Bentley waited for the sound of her son's voice.

"He won't talk to you," the old woman said.

Carl shouted in the background. "Tell her to quit calling!"

She hung up the receiver. As before when she telephoned, Carl refused to talk with her. She had learned to live with his rejection, but occasionally she would weaken and attempt to make contact. She went outside and joined Cathy and Teddy who were grilling hamburgers on the back porch.

"Come to Grandma," she said to Colleen, picking up the four-year-old and rocking her in her arms.

"Did he talk?" Cathy asked.

"No."

"He's like Dad. Hardheaded."

Mrs. Bentley sat on the glider, pulled her short dress up and bounced Colleen on her bare knee.

"They finished the high-rise." Teddy said. "Mrs. Krombach's moving tomorrow."

"Poor woman." Cathy said. "What memories that house must hold for her."

"I hope she adjusts well." Mrs. Bentley commented.

"She must've picked the last of the vegetables from her garden. She brought us some this morning. It's so sad." Cathy said.

Mrs. Bentley changed the conversation. "You should wear shorts more often, Teddy. You look good in them." she teased. "I can't make up my mind on which one of you has the best looking legs."

Teddy laughed.

"I told him that too." Cathy said. "He has nice legs. I read in a magazine that guys out west wear shorts and so do the mailmen. We're too old fashioned around here."

"I still feel funny in them." he said. "But I'd wear anything your daughter bought for me."

"Speaking of out West." Mrs. Bentley asked. "When is your father moving to California?"

"I don't know the exact day. A month or so."

"The Strussbergers? When are they moving into the projects?" Mrs. Bentley asked.

"About the same time as we're moving." Cathy answered.

Teddy was surprised. "How do you know?"

"Jake wrote me." Cathy chuckled. "Isn't it crazy? My neighbor is moving and I find out about it by way of North Carolina."

"What else did he write?" Teddy mumbled under his breath, trying to hide his concern from Mrs. Bentley.

"Nothing much."

"I'll bet." he mumbled louder than before.

"Stop it, Teddy." Cathy warned him.

"I can't." he said and went into the house.

"Mom, watch these hamburgers while I talk with him."

"Sure." Grandma sat Colleen on the glider.

Cathy went directly to the kitchen where Teddy stood by the sink. "Teddy, you're driving me crazy." She touched his shoulder. "You were doing so good controlling that green monster."

"You think so?" his eyes watered. "I've been faking it."

"My God, Teddy. You scare me. I think you need professional help."

"No. What I need is you. Marry me, please. Then I'll know for sure that you love me. I won't have to worry about another man coming and taking you away from me."

Cathy put her arms around him and her head against his chest. "I can't, Teddy. I just can't."

"And why not?" he asked sharply.

"It's you that stops me. You scare me."

"Then you don't love me." He was getting nasty again. "At least not like you loved Henry."

"God, please help him to understand. I love him more than I ever loved Henry."

"Then you did love Henry." He was becoming sassier.

"No! I didn't love him. I was infatuated with him." she said, pulling away from him. "I never loved him."

"But you love me?" he asked facing her.

"Yes."

"Then marry me." he begged while putting his hand underneath her sleeveless blouse.

"We've been over all of this before. I won't marry you until I feel it'll work out between us. And I love you, I've never loved Henry. I wish I'd have never known him. Get that through your head, please."

He felt her bare breast. "Then you wouldn't have Colleen. Are you sorry you have Colleen?"

She pulled his hand out from under her blouse. "That's not fair, Teddy." She moved away from him.

"Fair." he chuckled. "You're going to lecture me about fair. Well, tell me, Wizard, how can you wish you'd never seen Henry, yet glad you have Colleen?"

She didn't look at him or answer his burning question.

"You love me like you'd love a retarded brother. You believe you owe me for being here for you after Henry rejected you for Susan."

Cathy started to cry. "Please, Teddy." she pleaded. "Its complex, I know. I hate Henry but I love Colleen. I don't know how a mind works, mine or yours, we feel what we feel, but ..."

He cut her off. "It doesn't matter. We're getting further and further apart."

"I know." she sobbed. "And I don't want it to happen."

"You can't stop it. You think I like the way I am? Full of bitterness and discontent. I try not to be. I want to be nice like Jake and other guys I meet. There's something wrong with me, a word, a thought, a remembrance will set craziness circling in my mind. I think I'm crazy."

"You can try." she sobbed and moved against him again. "We can try together to overcome whatever's troubling you."

"It's not only your past that bothers me. It's also my life. I know I'm goofy, but I can't seem to do anything about it."

"You can." she whispered. "After we're settled into the projects, we'll seek help from a psychologist. Mom will help us to find out what we can do."

He put his arms around her and chuckled. "A shrink! I couldn't." he laughed louder. "Want people to think I'm a nut or you're a squirrelly nut gatherer?"

She laughed with him.

"I'm just a miserable fellow on a trip to a disaster if I can't get myself under control. I haven't taken the plunge off Point Bridge yet, but I thought about it."

"Teddy!" Cathy hugged him tight. "Please don't talk like that. I love you."

"Maybe." he whispered. "But it's not like it'll be with Jake."

"Me and Jake?" she asked looking into his eyes.

"Yeah, I saw it. I don't know why I could see it, but I did. When you were in the pool together."

She put her face back into his chest. "What did you see, Teddy?"

"I don't know. Something. A feeling. I saw a feeling."

She muttered into his tee shirt. "Silly, you can't see a feeling."

"I did."

"I'll always love you, Teddy."

"We'll see. Jake comes home soon."

Cathy hung onto Teddy's arm while walking back outside to the grill. It reminded Teddy of the sailor and his girl at the train station. It made him feel swell.

CHAPTER TWENTY FOUR
Westward Ho

After Jean's birthday party ended and the guests departed, Vonovich, Jean, and her mother sat in the living room drinking coffee and talking for several hours before Jean tired and went to bed. After Jean left and Vonovich and Mrs.Wernher were alone on the sofa, he developed a strategy to bring Jean into his life. He couldn't let her get away from him after suddenly finding such a treasure as Jean. She brought him back vicariously to better days, in his otherwise dreary life, when his wife was as energetic and beautiful. Being near Jean was like beginning life anew from the happiest time of his life. He made love to Jean's mother that night and moved into her suburban home the next day.

He decided at Jean's birthday party he would marry Mrs. Wernher. With Jean's mother as his wife, he could be assured that Jean would be in his life forever. Teddy's mother's death worked to his advantage and two weeks after he cremated her, he married Jean's mother. His new wife was as excited about him as he was about Jean and she agreed to go along with everything he proposed, including moving to California.

He was certain he'd be able to interest Jean in Indian Art and together they could make excursions into the California desert searching for artifacts. He already had the new Mrs. Vonovich interested in establishing some sort of beach business, keeping her busy and away from him and Jean.

Jean was excited about the move. Junior, not as thrilled, hated his mother's decision to marry Teddy's father. It embarrassed him and going west gave him some comfort knowing he'd never have to face friends like Henry anymore. Henry would tease him by asking him if he called Teddy's father "Daddy." Vonovich looked forward to the long drive. He'd have Jean as his captive audience for twenty-five hundred miles.

There was a morning chill in the autumn air, but they all wore clothes befitting their destination. Jean and her mother wore shorts and a sleeveless blouse. Vonovich and Junior wore loose-fitting beach clothes.

The sun was rising and Junior finished putting some pillows into the new station wagon.

Jean locked the door and hid the house key under the porch mat for the real estate person.

"Ready?" Vonovich asked. "Let's hit the road before morning traffic."

Junior climbed into the back of the station wagon facing the rear window. He made himself a cozy spot to lounge, along with a stash of candy bars to munch along the way.

"Want to drive?" Vonovich asked Jean. "Take the first leg on the trip?"

"Sure." Jean said.

Vonovich would sit in the front with Jean. He insisted that his wife take the roomy back seat for herself where she could stretch out and nap. He brought along sleeping pills.

Jean climbed in behind the steering wheel and Vonovich sat beside her. He turned to his wife in the back seat. "Would you like a sleeping pill?"

She smiled at him. "You think of everything. After a bit, honey."

Junior made a face of disgust.

Jean started the station wagon, pulled out of the driveway and onto the main road.

Vonovich unfolded the map and laid it across his lap. He faked glancing at the map and studied Jean's legs. Jean and her mother began singing *"California Here I Come."* Junior covered his ears.

* * *

As soon as Struss' wife left for work, he poured himself a stein of black coffee and sat on his stool at the bay window. She was in a good mood because Jake was coming home, but he wasn't. He would hate the projects and would miss his rathskeller. All the government money couldn't take the place of his cellar jewel. He would miss his bay window too, and as soon as Jake came home they'd have to move. Houses all around his own were disappearing, and very soon after the people vacated them.

He heard the rumbling before he saw the bulldozer and trucks coming near his home. They stopped in front of Vonovich's empty house. Many men got out of the trucks. The supervisor checked the house address against some papers in his hand. After a moment, he gave the wrecking crew the signal to go to work. Vonovich's house was coming down and Struss had a front row seat. Struss emptied his stein of black coffee and filled it with beer. He sat most of the morning, watching the servants of evil-doings at work.

* * *

Vonovich stopped at the red light. The small northern Arizona town was bright with lighted store fronts and business' catering to travelers going east or west on Route 66. They already passed through countless small towns on their trip and it was time consuming. They used up so much time adjusting to various speed limits, being held back by local traffic, and watching for route signs. The traffic light changed to green. He drove by the signal and spotted another red light ahead. He slowed, hoping the light would change to green before he reached it. He glanced at Jean sitting, but sleeping, in the seat beside him. She looked beautiful to him as town lights and passing headlights reflected off of her fair face. The light ahead of him changed to green. He sped through the intersection, and in the distance sighted the last light before leaving the small town. It was a yellow blinking caution light, warning traffic to slow down. His wife was sleeping soundly, but he could hear Junior moving his bulk around in the rear.

Vonovich knew that Junior disliked him, and he had big plans for Jean's fat brother. He could afford to keep Junior busy with parties and girls and out of his way. He packed the ninety thousand in cash from under the floorboards into a locked leather suitcase and tied it on the roof rack with the rest of their luggage. He secured the suitcase so thoroughly; the roof of the station wagon would fly away before his suitcase broke loose. The others didn't know about his secret money.

When his wife changed her bank account to a joint account, he deposited the money he received from the government for his house into their account. He would've never dreamed of being so rich. Money seemed to come from everywhere, his first wife's insurance, the government money, the used car lot sale money, the sale of the suburban home, and his new wife's considerable savings. The sum was almost two hundred thousand dollars and that wasn't counting his suitcase money.

Junior woke. "Let's stop and eat."

Hungry again, Vonovich thought, but spoke politely to him. "I'm almost through this town. Can you wait until the next town?"

"How far is it?"

Vonovich smiled, thinking of Junior's agony. "Fifty miles."

"That's too far. My stomach's growling. Why are we rushing? We should stop at a motel instead of driving late at night."

"Because we want to get there sooner than later. Living out of suitcases is hard on your mother. It gets her down in the dumps."

"Starving and being squashed back here, gets me down too."

"We'll cross into California before sunrise, and then we'll get a motel."

They passed under the blinking caution light and Vonovich accelerated. The station wagon headlights beamed into the night and empty highway. A jackrabbit crossed the road. "A jackrabbit just now crossed the road." Vonovich said to Junior. Seeing a jackrabbit was another new experience for him and he relished it as much as he enjoyed viewing the new types of scenery on the trip.

"Big deal." Junior said. "I'd rather see a hot dog."

Jean stirred in her seat. Vonovich watched her shifting her legs for a few moments, before putting his eyes back on the road.

Junior moaned. "I'm starving."

"Take your mind off of food. Turn on the light and look at those brochures I gave to you and dream of the pretty girls you're going to meet on the beaches."

"I'm tired of looking at photos. I want the real thing."

"The less we stop, the sooner you'll get the real thing."

"You're a lucky fellow," Vonovich said, encouraging Junior to plan long stays away from home while leaving him alone with

Jean. "Able to hang out at the beaches all day, help your Mom with her beach business, meet the girls, bathe in the Pacific. That is unless you're afraid of sharks, and who isn't?"

"Right now, I'd eat the shark."

Vonovich quit talking and increased the pressure on the gas pedal. Talking to Junior was a waste of his time. He thought about Teddy and intended to keep in touch with his son. Inside of a rented post office box, he put a package with ten thousand dollars bundled up with Christmas wrapping. Also in the package was a family photograph, taken soon after he was born. He wished to show his son that for a brief moment in his life when they had been a happy family.

The key to the locker was in the suitcase with the secret money. The key was going to be an early Christmas gift for Teddy. He thought about giving his son the gift before leaving Pittsburgh, but had second thoughts. He thought that fatty Junior might find out about it and say he was giving away his mother's money. He would mail the key to Teddy as soon as he was settled in his new California home.

Headlights suddenly appeared ahead. Oncoming bright lights would give him a quick view of Jean when the beams passed over her. If he glances at her figure at a precise moment, as he'd been doing at night on the road trip, he'd be treated with a titillating image when the light reflected off of her face and bare legs. The car was approaching fast and luck was with him. The eastward bound automobile didn't click high beams to low. The time came. He turned and saw the light pass over his love. He sighed with pleasure.

He missed seeing a big warning sign. Slow down. Bad curve ahead.

CHAPTER TWENTY FIVE
Big Spender

Teddy sat inside the undertaker's office waiting for Junior and the bodies to arrive from the airport. The office was dreary. The furniture was dark and heavy and the drapes were pea green and thick. He wore a dark brown suit. Cathy went with him to the department store and helped him select the suit. She sat next to him, wanting to be by his side throughout his sudden shocking ordeal. She wore a black mid-length dress. The contrast between her blond hair and glistening blue eyes against the black cloth sharpened her beauty. Mrs. Bentley arranged to be excused from work to watch her grandchild throughout the funeral. She asked Fritz to keep her company while babysitting Colleen. Fritz brought along his portable typewriter, toothbrush and high hopes.

Teddy tried to feel grief, but was having difficulty finding the sadness a son should display. He knew his father cared for him as a child, yet he still felt as if he were awaiting the remains of a distant relative. Perhaps when he saw his father's body, the mourning feelings he sought would come into his heart.

"Did you notify Carl?" Teddy asked Cathy.

"No, he won't talk to me. You know that."

"I know. But I thought, well, I don't know what I thought."

"You thought maybe this tragedy would be an excuse for me to see my brother?"

"Yeah, with him and Junior being close friends, I thought he'd want to come for his buddy's loss."

Through the window, they saw the three hearses. Cathy tightened her hold on his hand.

Junior, wearing a well fitting gray suit, stepped out of the first hearse and was met by the undertaker. They shook hands and came toward the office.

"Junior looks good." Cathy said. "I mean, he looks like he hasn't a scratch on him."

"He was thrown free somehow, out the back door of the station wagon." Teddy said.

Junior came into the office, followed by the undertaker. They all greeted one another. Junior fixed his eyes on Cathy.

"Sorry about your loss, Junior." Cathy said.

"Thanks for your thoughts." he answered, taking his eyes from Cathy's legs and bringing out a cigar from inside a suit pocket. He lit it to everyone's surprise. The undertaker hurriedly placed a standalone ashtray near him.

"How's Carl doing?" he asked, blowing smoke toward the ceiling.

Cathy looked away from him. "I never see him."

Junior chuckled. "Still mad at you and your Mom?"

Cathy perked up. "I don't know what his problem is and I don't care."

"It's childish to stay mad." Junior lectured.

The undertaker sat behind his desk. "You're so right, Mr. Wernher." he said. "Life is too short."

"Ask them." Junior nodded, blowing smoke toward the window and the parked hearses.

The undertaker was a thin, middle aged man in a cheap suit. "If everyone is comfortable, we'll get on with the arrangements. He looked at Teddy. "We can forgo selecting a coffin for your father, that is, unless you're not satisfied with the casket his remains were transported in and selected by Mr. Wernher."

"Fine." Teddy said.

The undertaker continued looking at Teddy. "I've already received most of the necessary information from Mr. Wernher, but there's still a few questions I need answered. "Your father's religion?"

"He never went to church." Teddy said.

The undertaker smiled. "Was he baptized?"

"I don't know." Teddy answered. "When I was packing to move, I found a picture of him in white knickerbockers holding a rosary. I guess he was Catholic."

The undertaker looked at Junior. "Ahh, this may cause a problem."

"Why should it?" Junior snapped. Clouds of smoke were filling the room.

"Excuse me." The undertaker stood and opened the window behind him to the cool outside air. He sat back down and smiled at Teddy. "Mr. Wernher wishes only a simple service at the grave site. If you want a requiem mass for your father, I'll have to make additional arrangements."

Before Teddy could answer, Junior spoke. "He don't need a mass, a bunch of mumble-jumble. Right, Teddy?"

Cathy was becoming annoyed by Junior's smart attitude. "Teddy will decide what's best for his father's funeral!"

"Why?" Junior grinned at her. "In a way, he was my father too."

Cathy didn't answer, only shook her head in disbelief over how Junior was behaving at such an awful time.

"I guess Junior's right." Teddy said.

"Good." Junior said, taking another puff on his cigar. It had gone out. He didn't relight it.

"I can have a priest come here and pray a rosary," the undertaker said. "If you'd want something like that."

"I think you should." Cathy told him. "It'll be giving your Dad some sort of respect."

"Okay." Teddy agreed.

The undertaker turned to a disappointed Junior. "The praying of the rosary won't interfere with your mother's or sister's visitations."

Junior nodded his consent.

The undertaker again turned to Teddy. "Mr. Wernher has arranged with me for his mother and sister to be viewed together in one viewing room, and your father in another. It would be a bit crowded with three remains in one room."

"Much too crowded," Junior remarked.

"Fine." Teddy agreed.

"Fine, just fine," the undertaker commented. "There is just one last question. Did your father have life insurance? Mr. Wernher hasn't been able to locate any policy amongst your father's belongings."

"I don't know." Teddy shifted in his seat, concerned about the cost of the funeral.

"Well, not to worry," the undertaker said while standing. "Mr. Wernher has agreed to pay all expenses."

"Thanks, Junior." Teddy said, relieved, taking his hand from Cathy's grip while standing up. He extended his hand. "I really appreciate what you're doing. Maybe someday I'll be able to make it up to you."

"Forget it." Junior replied. They shook hands.

"I won't forget it."

"One other item," the undertaker said to Teddy. "Mr. Wernher asked, and I concur, that the caskets will be closed to visitors. You can understand, the time since the accident, the injuries?"

"Okay." Teddy murmured. He wouldn't get to see his father, or perhaps shed some tears.

"Is that it?" Junior asked the undertaker, "I got business at the post office."

"Yes sir, it is." Junior and the undertaker shook hands.

"I'm calling a taxi," Junior smiled at Cathy. "Can I give you a lift?"

"No." Cathy blurted before Teddy could accept Junior's offer.

"You two living together?" Junior grinned.

Cathy asked. "Is it any of your business?"

Junior took the telephone from the desk and dialed for a cab while chuckling.

Teddy, Cathy, and the undertaker walked outside. The undertaker motioned for the coffins to be taken inside to the hearse drivers smoking cigarettes nearby. Teddy and Cathy watched the two polished bronze caskets and the one drab gray casket being wheeled by transport gurney into the funeral home.

* * *

When Teddy and Cathy arrived at the funeral home, Mrs. Krombach was sitting near Mr. Vonovich's casket praying her rosary. There weren't any other visitors in the room. Teddy and Cathy went to the closed casket and made an attempt at silently praying for the dead before sitting. Many voices were heard coming from the adjacent room. Teddy expected few people. He knew his father was a loner.

Two baskets of flowers were placed by the casket. One from Teddy and Cathy, the other from Mrs. Bentley and Fritz. Two Mass cards lay by the register. Teddy went to see who had sent them. One was from the Strussberger's and the other from Mrs. Krombach. The undertaker placed more ferns than usual around the coffin because of the lack of floral arrangements. He had taken the extra potted ferns from the Wernher room, which was bursting with flowers given by old North Slope neighbors and relatives.

"My regrets." A female voice came from behind Teddy. He turned. It was Susan holding a framed picture. "Junior asked me to give this to you. He said he found it among your Dad's stuff."

"Thanks, Susan." Teddy was surprised. It was a long ago picture of him as a toddler with his smiling parents. He felt a sadness overtaking him, tears swelling up in his eyes. It made him happy to be crying for his father.

"Are you holding up?" Susan asked. "Not so good, I see."

"I'll be okay." He brushed the tears away.

"It must be awful. So sudden, a shock."

"Yeah." Teddy agreed. "Is Henry with you?"

"He's with Junior outside in the parking lot, smoking. They're talking like long lost souls."

"How's everything with you, Susan?"

She tapped her stomach. "Pregnant." She saw Cathy sitting by Mrs. Krombach and went to her. "Hi, Cathy."

"I'm so glad to see you, Susan." Cathy smiled. "It's been too long."

"You look great, Cathy. Striking."

"You look good too, Susan."

Susan chuckled. "In maternity clothes, fat, pregnant, and I look good to you? You're sweet."

"How's your little boy?" Cathy quickly changed the subject.

"A devil. Your daughter?"

"Fine."

"Where are you living, Cathy?"

"At home, with my Mom."

Susan was surprised. "Your house is still standing?"

"In two weeks, we're moving into the projects."

"I live there. My parents bought a small house in the suburbs. It would be too crowded for us, especially with a new baby coming. Me and Henry decided to live in the projects. At least for awhile."

Cathy was curious and full of questions. "Do you like living there? Are they nice? I hear they are."

"They'll do until we can buy a house of our own." Susan didn't appear enthused with the projects.

"Teddy boards with us." Cathy said.

Susan ignored what Cathy said and exclaimed. "Ohh, guess who I saw today?"

Cathy shrugged. "Who?"

"Jake. His parents live in the same building, down the corridor from me. He's out of the Marines."

Cathy nodded. "I knew he was coming home any day now. We've been writing to one another."

"Oh," Susan was surprised. "I didn't know you stayed in touch. He's looking for a job."

"I expect to see him soon."

"Ohh. I see. Well, I gotta get Henry away from Junior and get home. I need my rest."

"Thanks for visiting." Cathy said. They hugged.

Susan went to Teddy's side. "My regrets again, Teddy." They hugged too.

Susan departed the room without acknowledging the late Mr. Vonovich's casket.

Teddy asked Mrs. Krombach. "How are you?"

"Hassen dot platz dem put me. Vot a luff."

"I'll be living there in two weeks." Cathy told her. "I'll come and get you, show you where my apartment is, then you can visit anytime. Okay?"

"Dot's vunderbar."

Cathy looked up after patting Mrs. Krombach's hand and saw the Strussberger's coming into the room. Jake was wearing a dark blue suit. Cathy kept a solemn pose, yet her heartbeats began leaping after seeing Jake. Father Levalle came in behind them.

Seeing the priest, a few elderly people came from the Wernher room. After Father Levalle and the Strussberger's offered Teddy their condolences, the priest knelt and began reciting the rosary. "The first sorrowful mystery," Father Levalle prayed. "The agony in the garden."

With Jake behind them, Teddy and Cathy knelt side by side holding hands.

CHAPTER TWENTY SIX
Godspeed

The old furniture looked outdated and out of place in the white painted rooms with low ceilings. Struss' aversion to his new home was taking a toll on his health. He was drinking more, eating less and filled the bottom shelf of his new refrigerator with Pilsner. The old icebox, stood next to the refrigerator like a worn down aging father alongside a robust son and was now used by Struss for storage of non-perishables. The kitchen was tiny, lit by florescent bulbs, and had a small sliding glass window. He missed the sunlight shining through large double-hung windows.

The decision to have a refrigerator was made for him. It came with the apartment and the iceman lost all customers on the South Slope and expected to go out of business. He wanted some variety, wallpaper or colored painted walls, but through and through, the living spaces in the projects reminded him of a white sanitized mental institution.

At night, his wife was troubled as strangers walked the long corridors and staircases. He didn't know who lived on either side of him. Many people lived in the building and it was difficult to match faces with door numbers. All the corridors, all the doors, and all of the buildings looked alike to Struss.

More and more, colored were moving into the projects and that upset him. His only contact with colored in the past was a weekly pickup of trash by the city garbage men; otherwise he had never interacted with them. Living amongst colored for Struss was as if he'd been dropped into a foreign land with people that spoke differently, dressed differently, ate different type foods, listened to different music, and even worshiped the same God differently.

There was a knock on the door. "Who's there?" Struss hollered from the built-in kitchen range where he was making a pot of coffee. Many changes came into Struss' life, but not his way of dressing for housework. He still preferred baggy pants and an undershirt.

"Susan," she said, loud and clear, like a soldier giving a password traveling through dangerous territory.

Struss unlocked the deadbolt.

"Is Jake home?"

"In his room. Come in, I'll get him."

She stepped inside. Struss went for Jake

"Good morning, Jake." Susan smiled. "I came to tell you the mill where my Dad works is hiring. Thought perhaps you'd be interested."

"Thanks. I'll look into it." He was wearing his Marine fatigue trousers and a green sweatshirt.

"Well," she hesitated turning toward the door. "I guess I'll go."

"Wait." Jake said. "I'll walk with you to your apartment." Jake opened the metal door, and side by side they strolled slowly along the corridor.

"I like your maternity outfit, Susan, with all those cuddly teddy bears imprints. You look very motherly, for lack of a better word."

She turned her face from him and started to cry.

Jake stopped walking, took her chin, and turned her face to himself. "My God, Susan. What's wrong?"

She sobbed. "Henry left me."

"I saw you both last week at the funeral home. What happened?"

"He quit his good job with the river barge company. We fought. Quitting when I'm pregnant. He's crazy. She turned her face from Jake. "Please Jake, I don't wish to bother you with my troubles."

"We're friends. Bother me if you think it'll help."

They started walking again. "You can't, but thanks."

"When did he leave?"

"After we came home from the funeral home last week. It's that lamebrain, Junior. He has Henry all excited about working for him."

"Working for Junior?" Jake asked. "Doing what? Does Junior have a business?"

"He wouldn't tell me anything, except that he's leaving and he'll send money."

"What are you going to do in the meantime? Do you think he'll come back?"

"No, he's not coming back." She started crying again.

Jake took her in his arms.

"I won't miss him. I haven't loved him for a long time now. He cheated on me right from the start. He's disgusting. I'm crying for myself and my children, for making a mess out of my life. My life is over. Who'll want me with two children?"

"Are you divorcing him?"

"As soon as I can. With his good job, I could stomach him for my child's sake. Without a job, we'll be on welfare, mother's assistance, I don't need him. I'm moving in with my parents in a few days. To the suburbs. So I guess I won't be seeing you often, if ever."

Jake was lost for words, but tried to encourage her. "Susan, there are plenty of good men in the world. I know, I've been serving with many for the past four years. Don't give up. Kids for some men are a joy, not a burden." He cuddled her harder. "The important thing for you is to be smart," Jake tried to make a bad situation lighter with a bit of humor. "Smarter than the average bear, as Yogi would say. You still have your good name, protect it. A good name cannot be taken away; it can only be given away. Please don't rush into a quick relationship until you're absolutely certain."

"Like Cathy. Right?"

He hesitated. "Yeah."

"Have you been with her yet?" she asked close to his ear. "Since you've been home?"

"Only at the funeral home. She's busy packing. I'm invited to supper after they're moved in. I'm hoping they get an apartment in this building."

They parted but stayed holding hands.

"My parents just make it themselves. I hate going home, dumping my problems on them."

"My God," Jake said. "I wish I could help."

She sobbed again and into his sweatshirt, now with wet spots from her tears. "You never had much yourself; it makes me cry, because I know you'd help me if you could."

Jake kissed her on the forehead. She mumbled what she'd wanted to confess since first seeing him after his discharge from the Marines. "Oh, Jake, I was so stupid choosing Henry over you. You were too sincere, you always have been. I think that's why I went for Henry. You were too real. I was longing for the unreal. I got that with Henry."

Jake didn't remark to her confession. They just held each other, both remembering when their feelings for each other were reversed, when he loved her and she liked him. Life can be a soap opera after all, Jake thought.

Struss burst into the corridor. "Jake, watch the stove. I have a meatloaf in the oven."

"Where are you going?"

"Father Levalle called. Mrs. Krombach had a stroke. She's dying."

"I better go," Jake said, releasing Susan.

"Thanks for holding me, Jake." She smiled. "I needed more than a quick hug. I needed strong arms." She kissed him on the lips. He embraced her again. "Jake," she whispered into his ear. "When you think of me in years to come, if you do, remember me kindly, will you?"

"Always. Susan. And promise me something. That you won't give up, or allow yourself to be used by little men with big egos."

Tears were streaming down her cheeks. "I promise." she sobbed.

He kissed her on the forehead again and released her. "I'll check on you."

She smiled at him, tears gushing from her dark eyes. "Bye." she murmured, bravely turning, and walked away from Jake without looking back.

* * *

Struss rushed along the sidewalk to the high-rise. He was breathing heavily and his heart was beating fast. The Priest said her death was imminent. He entered the building and took the elevator to the sixth floor. After a few seconds of confusion, he located Mrs. Krombach's small apartment.

She was lying on her bed, head propped up with pillows. He stood with the doctor at the foot of the bed watching Father Levalle administering the sacrament of Extreme Unction, anointing her body with the oil and balm mixture.

When the priest finished the last rite, Struss approached the dying lady. She couldn't speak and he didn't know if she could see. Struss took her hand into his, but said nothing. The woman, withered by time, lay peacefully awaiting the change to eternal life promised by Jesus. He patted her hand. "Godspeed." he whispered.

Her chest quit moving. The doctor pronounced her dead, and Father Levalle recited a passage from John, "I am the resurrection and the life, he who believes in me, through he may die, he shall live." Struss kissed her hand and crossed himself. His friend was gone as was his Pigeon Hill neighborhood. He'd never hear her say, "vot a luff again."

CHAPTER TWENTY SEVEN
Wedding Bells

Fritz and Mrs. Bentley sat on one side of the table while Teddy and Cathy sat on the opposite side. Jake felt awkward as a guest sitting at the head of the table. Cathy made pork and sauerkraut with tasty dumplings for dinner. It was prepared especially for him as a small thanks for his service in Korea. She had telephoned Struss and asked about his son's favorite meal. Pork and sauerkraut with dumplings was on top of the list that Struss rattled off. Struss told her that Jake was an all-around meat and potato guy like his father.

During the meal, there were a lot of silent moments and the chit-chat stayed to a minimum. Jake hadn't met Fritz before and he was dressed more formal than Jake. He was wearing a burgundy colored sport jacket and light brown slacks. Mrs. Bentley looked like a mature cover-girl, with thick curly hair gathered on top of her head, revealing a slender bare neck. She wore yellow slacks and a white long sleeved sweater that buttoned up in front. Cathy wore a brown wool skirt and a burnt orange sweater. Her hair was pulled back into a long ponytail and it was hard for Jake to keep his eyes off of her. He was glad to see Teddy casually dressed like he was, wearing slacks and a short sleeved shirt.

When Cathy invited him to dinner after connecting at the funeral home, he didn't think much of it. He never expected to meet Fritz at dinner or have accolades given to him for his service in Korea. He didn't want to seem dismissive of the sportswriter's questions and it wasn't that he wouldn't talk about his service as a Marine. He just found it clumsy saying what he did while serving. He found it impossible to speak with people about being a Marine, in combat or otherwise, unless they had also been a Marine. It was just one of those things in life that couldn't be shared with outsiders. Not that it's a mystery, but because it's a feeling that only another Marine could feel when speaking of service in the Corps.

Teddy wasn't very talkative, but he told Jake how glad he was to have a buddy in his life once again. Out of loyalty to his childhood pal, Jake made a double effort to avoid looking at Cathy as much as possible under the circumstances. He put down his fork and sighed, while looking at Mrs. Bentley.

"That was great. Better than my Dad's pork and kraut." Jake chuckled. "He's been slipping with his cooking talents since moving into the projects. Drinking more, too. My mother's worried he may not be up to cooking our Thanksgiving dinner next week. He hates these projects."

"Don't praise me." Mrs. Bentley said. "Cathy did it all."

Cathy chimed in. "Teddy helped."

Teddy laughed. "Yeah, I washed the pots and played with Colleen."

"Where is Colleen?" Jake asked.

"Fritz's mother's watching her." Cathy said. "She hasn't any grandchildren and spoils her terribly."

Everyone finished eating and Cathy began serving coffee.

"Are you a sports fan Jake?" Fritz asked.

"Sure, but not as much as you, I'm sure." Jake answered. "But I really enjoyed your columns in the GermanAmerikaner that Cathy would send me. I especially liked the one about the Pigeon Hill Arrows."

"I have to be a fanatic. Without sports and a pencil, I'm a poor fella." he smiled and took Mrs. Bentley's hand into his. "Have you got a job lined up yet?"

"No. I haven't tried finding anything. Taking a little vacation."

"I might need a job soon myself. The GermanAmerikaner might be going under. It's expensive running the paper in both English and German. The German written issue at one time was the money maker with plenty of readers. Fewer and fewer people read German anymore. The old-timers are gone. Heck, few people speak Deutsche anymore. Advertisements are getting harder to find. Ads keep a newspaper operating."

Teddy joined the conversation. "Typesetting German is a nightmare."

Cathy finished serving coffee and sat back down. Teddy took her hand. Jake felt somewhat left out without a soft hand to hold.

"You'll get hired by another paper." Jake said. "You're too good."

"Oh, I'm not worried about being unemployed. I have offers from three other Pittsburgh newspapers. Two of them have given me a sort of open invitation to come and work for them, whenever I wish."

"Wow," Jake said. "You'd probably make a lot more money with a bigger paper."

"Sure, and I'll need the bigger dough soon." He looked at Mrs. Bentley. To Jake's surprise, he lifted Mrs. Bentley's hand to his lips. He joked. "Fritz der lip I am, I am. I love this woman, Jake. In case you haven't noticed."

Mrs. Bentley laughed. "Jake doesn't want to hear about your longings."

"I've noticed." Jake laughed.

"My favorite sport is baseball." Fritz said. "It's a finesse game. Everyone screams for home runs, but I like games when the coaches have to earn their money by outwitting the other coach. By switching pitchers for certain batters, bunting in certain instances, stealing bases, intentional walks, things like that. A game of chess between the coaches."

"That's my Dad's game, too." Jake said.

"What's yours?" Cathy smiled at Jake.

Her question caught him off guard. He looked at her and said something that turned Teddy's mood from comfortable and content, holding Cathy's hand, to dark and suspicious of Jake. "Swimming, of course. You saw how great I was, the last time I came home."

"I'd beat you in a race like Fritz beats his typewriter." she grinned at him. Teddy let go of her hand and became glum.

Jake noticed the change. "How's that?"

"Without mercy." she laughed, reaching over and slapping Jake on his hand.

Mrs. Bentley noticed Teddy's mood change also. She decided to change the subject to something she thought was a happy subject, yet would hinder Jake and Cathy from joyfully interacting, which came naturally to them. She felt a chill run up her spine seeing Teddy fall into deep depression over Jake's comment. She looked at Fritz. "Tell them."

Fritz lit up like a night game at Forbes Field. He put his arm around Mrs. Bentley. "We're getting married."

The rest of them weren't as stunned as Cathy's mother and Fritz thought they'd be.

"When?" Cathy asked.

"We haven't set a date yet." Fritz said. "The sooner the better, as far as I'm concerned."

After everyone gave congratulations, Teddy dropped a bomb. "Maybe we could have a double wedding?"

Mrs. Bentley saved the day and let Cathy off of the hook by replying to Teddy without hurting his feelings and sending him into an even darker mood. "I'm not sharing my wedding day with another bride, especially a bride as beautiful as my daughter. She'd steal my show; everyone would think I was her bride's maid."

Jake looked at Teddy. He seemed far away in thought. Cathy took his hand, but he didn't come back to life as he was before Jake mentioned swimming with Cathy. Jake looked at Cathy and started a conversation he didn't want to talk about, Korea. "Whose idea was it to serve me a dinner because I served in Korea?"

"Mine." Cathy said. It was only an excuse to spend an evening with Jake. A patriotic dinner gave her a decoy from saying outright that she wanted to be with Jake and hurt Teddy. She had made up her mind; she would never marry Teddy and would be seeking help from her mother about how to get him treatments for his worsening mental condition.

"Well, thanks. I could only dream of meals like tonight on Hill 122. We called it Bunker Hill. We were repeatedly attacked by herds of charging communists."

Fritz quickly got interested in Jake's experiences and to his surprise, so did Cathy and her mother. But Teddy was gone for the night. He sat slumped, holding Cathy's hand and trying to look less sad than he was. Jake kept answering Fritz's questions about the Marines, life aboard a troop ship, Korea and Koreans, and flying in helicopters. Jake was glad for their interest in his life and tried to stay interested in his own experiences, but was drawn by the love-bug into thinking about Cathy and her plans for the future. He came to believe while watching them holding hands that Cathy would never marry Teddy and she didn't know how to get out of not wedding him without a possible tragedy.

By the end of the night and several pots of coffee, Jake was glad to leave Cathy and Mrs. Bentley's apartment. Wanting to leave the company of the two beautiful women was a feeling he'd never would've guessed ever contemplating. He longed to be holding Cathy's hand, and the desire to touch her only increased as the night went on. It was better to get away from the coveting to caress her. He had also left their table convinced that Teddy had the same stare he saw some fighting men get, a stare into a world of disconnect with reality. He walked to his parent's project home certain that he was in love with Cathy and he believed she loved him too.

His simple life was becoming complicated. Things didn't seem to be changing in his life as far as loving a woman. As a teen, he'd go home to an empty bed thinking of Susan Mallhauser, and now years and a war later, he was going home to an empty bed longing for Cathy Bentley. At least in the Marine Corps he had his M1 rifle to hold at night.

CHAPTER TWENTY EIGHT
Mr. DerRichman

Cathy was giving Colleen milk when the telephone rang. She rushed to answer it, believing it might be Jake. They had been talking by phone at night since he had dined at her apartment before Thanksgiving Day. They had not seen each other since the pork and sauerkraut meal, even though Jake lived only two buildings away. Teddy was the reason they stayed apart and he wasn't aware of their connection developing into a much more serious relationship. Jake only called Cathy after Teddy left for work.

She picked up the receiver. "Hello?"

"Good morning." he said.

"Henry?" her face turned whiter, stunned, as if hit in the face with a bag of flour.

"Guessed right!" he laughed.

She didn't answer, the shock inhibiting her thoughts.

"Still with me, baby?"

She took a deep breath. "What do you want?"

"How's my little girl?"

"Oh, you admit she's your child?"

"Yeah. I'm sorry about that, baby, but you gotta understand. At the time, well, it was a real mess with two girls knocked up at the same time."

"That's over and done," Cathy snapped at him. "I can't believe you're calling now to see how she is. Why are you calling?"

He laughed. "Oh, you're tough."

She didn't respond to his weak attempt at offering praise.

"Okay," he said. "Seriously, I gotta see you."

"I can't believe what I'm hearing. You're crazy."

"It's important, honey. Real important."

"What are you talking about?"

"Your future. Colleen's future."

Cathy turned sarcastic. "Daddy even knows his little girl's name. How sweet."

"Of course I know her name. I like it, too."

"Glad you approve, Dad."

He laughed louder. "Cathy, you've got to meet me this evening."

"You're out of your mind. I'm not meeting you."

"You gotta, baby. It's that important."

"What's so important?"

"I can't talk over the phone, but it's money. Enough for you and Colleen to live more than comfortable."

"I don't understand."

"You will. But you gotta meet me. Alone."

"Oh, no no no."

"Cathy, I know I did you wrong, but this is my chance to make it up to you and Colleen. Don't blow it for me. Please."

"I need more explaining. And what about Susan?"

"I left her."

"I know you did. And you expect me to believe that you've changed."

"You've got some grapevine going. I work for Junior now and I'm going to California with him."

"Doing what?"

"He came into a lot of money with the deaths in his family. I'll be assisting him, something like that."

"Something like that?" she snickered. "Now that's a job worth pursuing. And you're leaving Susan while she's pregnant?"

"She'll be taken care of. We haven't hit it off too well lately. It just didn't work out. I should've married you. I got a glimpse of you at the funeral home. You're a knock out."

"You're rotten. And to think, somewhere a girl is going to go out with you and reward you with sex just for being a scumbag that left his children."

He laughed at her prediction for his future. "I hope you're right many times over."

"I hope you go to Hell." Cathy cussed.

"If I'm as rotten as you think, why would I be giving you a bag of money?"

"Explain how you're getting a lump of Junior's money to help me and Susan. What are your plans? Rob him?"

"No," he chuckled.

"That is why we gotta meet today, so I can explain."

"Why can't you explain now, over the phone?"

"Junior got me a lawyer. There's papers for you to sign. We gotta do this now. I'm flying with Junior to California tonight. Our flight is booked."

Cathy didn't know if she should agree to meet him. She didn't trust him, but she wanted to do right by Colleen.

"Do you want me to bring the papers to your apartment?"

"Yikes no! That's all I need, for Susan or others to get word I was alone with you. In my apartment of all places."

"Afraid people will think you're running after me?" he laughed. "Just kidding, baby. I know I've caused you enough stares from people. That's why I want you to meet me, here at the Century, it won't take long."

"The Century Hotel?"

"Yeah, what other Century is there?"

"What about Susan? Is she coming?"

"It's a little different with Susan. She retained a lawyer. She squealed to him about you and Colleen too. She was hoping to further destroy my character, so I expect no mercy from her side of the fence, or the court. Junior's lawyer is talking to her lawyer and they'll come to an agreement. She'll be getting more than you, I'm sorry."

"She should. I just want monthly support and back payments, whatever they'll be."

"That's nice of you, Cathy. Please, give me this chance. How are you going to explain to Colleen that you wouldn't give me this chance to help her?"

She was thinking and didn't answer.

"So, are you coming?"

"Okay, but this better not be a trick. I'm bringing somebody along."

"Don't bring anyone. Come alone. Junior's order, he's my boss now."

"Why not?"

"He doesn't want people in his suite. Only me, you, and the lawyer will be here. Junior has changed since becoming a rich man. Between you and me, he's a little odd. He doesn't want people around him and he's over protective of his money, he treats it like it's his children. He pays me good and he's willing to help with my child support problems before Susan's lawyer rakes me over the coals. I can't complain."

"How much money does he have?"

"Hold on to something. Over a quarter million dollars." Henry chuckled. "It's hard to believe, isn't it?"

"Is it ever? Is he going to be there?"

"No, only his lawyer. He's with some money-men, bankers, arranging for his dough to be transferred to a California bank."

"How much is Colleen getting?"

"I don't know, honey. Junior's lawyer is setting the payment amounts and arrangements. I'll know when the lawyer gets here. I'll call him as soon as we hang up. When are you leaving?"

"As soon as I can get a babysitter. Or, should I bring Colleen?"

"No, we'll be busy. And to be honest, I'd feel bad if I see her. Spare me the guilt, please."

"I'll be honest, too. I don't want her to meet you."

"Quit with the insults, Cathy. Let's get this over with. When you get to the Century, ask the desk clerk for Mr. DerRichman's suite and just come up. The lawyer will be here by then. If not, I'll leave the door open." he laughed.

"DerRichman?"

"Yeah, its Junior's way of being unnoticed. Plus, he thinks it's funny."

"It's stupid, too."

"Hurry," he said. And hung up.

Cathy quickly telephoned Jake.

"Strussberger's."

"Mr. Strussberger." Cathy said. "Is Jake there?"

"He's not at home, out on a job interview."

"Thank you, I'll call him later."

Cathy wanted Jake to come with her, watch Colleen in the lobby until she completed the legalities. Her mother was working. She'd have to watch Colleen at the reception desk.

If Henry was on the level about the cash, it would be the break she needed to move out of the projects and help Teddy with his problems. With her Mom getting married, it was time for her to go her own way. She rushed about preparing herself to meet the enemy.

She had doubts deciding what to wear. She would've preferred to wear slacks as protection against Henry, should he get funny and make some play toward her, but instead chose to appear more dressed up going to the classy hotel. She put on a light brown skirt and a pastel green blouse. She didn't wear any jewelry or put on any makeup. She borrowed her mother's tan imitation leather coat for protection against the cold December air.

* * *

At the hotel, Cathy caught a break. Fritz was hanging around the lobby looking for a sport story to write about. The New York Giants were in town to play the Steelers. She left Colleen with him, stopped by her mother's reception station and told her of the developments.

Mrs. Bentley told her that she saw Junior in the lobby, but avoided him by going to the restroom to hide out for awhile. Seeing him at her work would be uncomfortable. It would bring up bad memories for them both so she sat on a toilet and hid. They made a plan. If Cathy wasn't back in the lobby in one hour, she'd send Fritz and the House Cops to the suite. They both agreed it would be unlikely that Henry would act stupid by committing a crime in the Century, which had excellent security and in-house cops. Cathy took the elevator to Mr. DerRichman's suite.

She was nervous. Her better judgment warned her to beware. Exiting the elevator on Junior's floor felt like crawling onto a spider web. She tried to compose herself and took a few deep breaths before banging the door knocker. She looked at her watch. Close to five minutes passed since she left the lobby. She pictured a sneaky spider behind the door.

The door opened wide. Henry looked handsome wearing a white shirt and tie under a buttoned up vest. "Thanks for coming, Cathy."

She entered the luxurious room. The furniture was off-white with gold trim. Two king sized beds covered by gold colored quilts flanked opposite walls. The room was quite bright, which helped to diminish her fears of a pending spider bite. Henry took her coat and laid it on the nearest bed and went to the bar. "Want a drink?"

"No. Where's the Mr. DerRichman's lawyer?"

Henry chuckled. "He'll be here any minute. Are you sure you don't want a drink?" he asked, holding up a bottle of wine.

"I'm certain."

"Sit down, please," he said, pouring himself a mixed drink. "I wish you'd have a drink, it would make me feel better. Take the edge off."

She sat on a padded chair. "This isn't a social call, Henry. I want to get this business over with."

"Fine." he said. "I have something to say before the lawyer gets here." He looked at his drink and rolled the glass between the palms of his hands. "Promise me you'll hear me out before answering or making a smart comment."

"I knew there was more to this. Okay, I promise. Get on with it."

"All right. It's a proposition." he stared at her, waiting to see her reaction.

"What?" she said and started to get up. "I knew it was too good to be true."

"You promised." he reminded her.

"Go on." She sat back on the chair.

He took a big swallow from his drink. "I'll put it plain and simple. I want you to sleep with Junior."

"You're both out of your minds. Is there a lawyer coming or not? I've had enough of this nonsense."

"Yes, a lawyer is coming." he lied. "Please, listen before you run back to your poorhouse. It's worth ten thousand dollars in cash."

She laughed at him. "Forget it." then laughed again. "Junior, excuse me. Mr. DerRichman wants to pay ten grand for me?"

"Yeah." Henry laughed with her and shrugged. "Money's no problem."

"Your boss is a lunatic." she said. "I hope you know that."

"I agree with you, honey. I even told him that. But he's, how should I put it, had dreams about you since we hung out at the Owl's."

Cathy turned sarcastic. "That's a long wet dream."

"It surprised me too." he said, going to the bar and pouring himself another drink. "Please, have a drink. It'll relax you."

"No, don't ask me again."

"So, what do you say, five minutes fulfilling Junior's teenage dream and you'll walk away with ten grand to do with what you please."

"No way." she chuckled. "Even if I did, I wouldn't trust either of you to pay off."

"Come on, Cathy. What the hell? I got the cash under the bed," he put his drink on the bar, and kept talking while pulling a suitcase from under the bed. "It's no big deal, let Junior fulfill his fantasies."

"No." she snapped. "Where's the lawyer?"

He flipped open the suitcase. Cathy saw a bundle of cash inside of an opened Christmas wrapped package. "Here's the money and its all for you, count it if you want." He handed the bundle to her. She refused to take it. He sat on the bed.

"Does the lawyer know about this proposition?" she asked.

"Of course not." Henry grinned.

"If he's not here in five minutes, Henry, I'm gone." She looked at her watch. Thirty minutes had passed since the lobby plan.

"Why?" he yelped and threw his hands into the air in disgust. "You slept with me for a smile and you sleep with creepy Teddy. Why not Junior? Because he's fat?"

"Teddy lives with me and my mother."

"Don't hand me crap. This is Henry, remember?"

"I don't know why I'm even explaining. I don't care what you think."

"Ten thousand." Henry cried out walking in circles and throwing his arms in the air.

"Is this your new job?" she was angry. "Pimping for Mr. DerRichman?"

"What if it is?" he said and then quickly started pleading. "Please, Cathy. I can't go back in time. I quit my job. Junior's expecting me to get certain things done for him. I need him and his money now. Susan moved in with her parents. I have nowhere else to go but to California with Junior."

"Boo-hoo-hoo. I'm leaving." She started to get up when the door knocker sounded. She looked at her watch again. Thirty three minutes had passed since the lobby plan. She was relieved, thinking it was the lawyer.

Henry stopped his pacing and went and opened the door.

Cathy was wrong. It was the big spider.

Junior entered the room in a black tailor made suit and sunglasses. "It doesn't look like it's going very well." he said. "You must be slipping, lover-boy. Maybe I won't need you in California." Junior removed his sunglasses and put them in his coat pocket.

"Oh, come on, Junior. You know I can help you out there."

"Relax, Henry." Junior grinned. "I'm toying with you. Get used to it."

"No lawyer is coming!" Cathy snapped. "I'm leaving."

Junior stood in her way. "You couldn't use ten grand?" he asked her. "You must like it in the projects, living with the niggers."

Suddenly, the look on Junior's face told her she was in a bad situation. "Get out of my way, Junior. My mother and her fiancée are in the lobby waiting for me."

"Make me a drink, Henry." Junior ordered. "Your mother's in the lobby? Yeah, I believe that." he chuckled. "I was just in the lobby. Don't you think I'd recognized the bitch that killed my father?"

"She works here. Go down and see for yourself."

Henry brought him his drink. "Nice try, Cathy. My father had cravings for your mother and now you're going to treat my cravings." He looked around the room. "No steps here to push me over a cliff." he smiled. "Yet, I'll be nice and pay you for your services. Name your price."

She turned furious and warned him again. "I told you that my mother is downstairs! She knows I came here. Let me leave!"

"How much?" he grinned at her.

"Nothing! Get out of my way!"

"That's even better." Junior quipped. "Thank you."

"I didn't mean it that way!" Cathy shouted. "I meant you don't have enough money!"

"We'll see about that," he said and swallowed all of his drink. "Put her on the bed."

Cathy managed to get a peek at her watch before Henry's hand clamped over her mouth and his arm went around her waist. Forty minutes had passed since she left her mother. Henry pulled her toward the bed. Cathy dropped to the floor, kicking and twisting.

"She's tough." Henry said.

"Why didn't you give her the mickey?" Junior scolded.

"She wouldn't take a drink."

"That was your job, lover boy. To charm her into a mickey."

Henry finally got her onto the bed, but was unable to keep her from kicking and twisting. The package of money broke open further after Cathy's foot sent it flying across the room.

Junior walked to the bed and looked down on the two of them still wrestling on the mattress. Henry was becoming exhausted.

"This will never do." Junior said and took a small bottle and handkerchief from his pocket. He soaked the cloth with the bottle contents and covered Cathy's nose and mouth. In moments, Cathy when limp. Junior started undressing.

"What am I paying you for, Henry? Undress her. Don't rip her clothes. I want her walking out of here as pretty as she walked in." Henry began carefully undressing Cathy.

Junior placed his suit neatly on the opposite bed, walked to the bar naked and made himself a drink. "Call when you have her ready for me."

"We could get in big trouble, kidnapping and rape." Henry worried.

Junior sipped his drink. "Don't worry about it. Who's going to believe her? Everyone we know remembers she screwed you, and then practically secluded herself for years at home after you dumped her for Susan. It she squeals on us, say she came running after you left Susan. Also, she's unmarried and living with Teddy-boy, that'll do wonders for her character. Plus, everyone knows her slut for a mother killed my father. Quit worrying, it's her word and reputation against my word and reputation. And expensive lawyers if need be."

"She's ready." Henry said, getting off of the bed.

Junior looked down on Cathy's nude body. "Damn, she's beautiful. Get yourself a drink, Henry."

After Junior satisfied his lust, he sat on the edge of the bed depleted, unable to speak. He motioned for his employee. Henry hustled to his side. "Yeah, Junior?"

"Batters up." Junior gasped.

"Naw, that's okay." Henry said, looking down upon Cathy's crumpled body.

"Do it." Junior commanded him with difficulty, still breathing hard. "It's time you learned to take seconds."

Henry dropped his pants and climbed on the bed. Junior stayed sitting on the edge of the bed. No sooner had Henry started carrying out Junior's command, the door knocker sounded. They froze.

"Who is it?" Junior asked turning as white as an albino rhinoceros.

"The house cops and Fritz Der Lip. Open up."

Junior and Henry ran around like the Keystone Kops trying to dress.

The knocker kept pounding with shouts to unlock the door.

Henry looked around. Hundred dollar bills were scattered over the carpet. Cathy was unconscious, exposed on the bed with the handkerchief and small bottle of chloroform on the floor. Junior was bending over his suit, trying to put on his tailor-made pants, without much success. The voice on the other side of the door was becoming harsher. Henry knew his Playboy days were over when hearing the unthinkable. A key opening the door and the house cop shouting "the police are on the way."

Henry started sobbing, making convulsive sounds, and Mr. DerRichman, breathing in rapid gasps and standing on one leg had a bowel movement putting a fat limb into a pant leg.

* * *

When Cathy was released from the emergency room, she asked her mother to call Jake and tell him what occurred. Jake met them at their apartment. Mrs. Bentley and Fritz left the young couple to themselves and sat in the kitchen drinking coffee.

Jake and Cathy cuddled on the couch, the same low and long sofa he sat on the night Otto Wernher died. Only this time he was touching Cathy instead of her mother.

She whispered. "I wish you could hold me forever."

"That's my plan," he said. "And soon. But right now, I'm worried about you. Are you going to be okay? Your system's been shocked, traumatized."

She sobbed. "After the chloroform, I don't remember a thing."

"I love you, Cathy. When you're well, I want to elope. I'll find a job, and then we'll do it."

"But we've got to keep it a secret until I speak with Teddy. I'll speak with him soon after the holidays, and when the police complete their investigation."

"That sounds like a plan," he tried to add some humor. "I better go, the sun is coming up and Teddy will be coming home. How is he going to take what happened? Will he get dark and moody?"

"I don't know. And right now, I don't care. He needs help, Jake. I don't know what he'll do when I tell him that I love you."

"We'll tell him together. I feel sorry for him, but he's got to go for help. And soon. We'll talk about getting married and getting Teddy out of your life as soon as you feel better. I love you, Cathy."

"Okay." she whispered. "They kissed and kissed and kissed again in the doorway and out into the corridor before he left for home. His little vacation was over. He needed a job and soon.

Walking the project grounds at Christmastime wasn't the same as when Jake walked the cobblestone roads. The old row houses, decorated in an almost celestial way had colorfully lit windows, doors, porches, and even the framed outline of some of the houses themselves. It just wasn't the same. The project building windows had a wreath and a string of lights here and there, but Jake was unable to see a single lit Christmas tree on the inside of a window.

When Jake left Cathy's side, the first rays of sunshine came through the glass block windows along the corridor wall. The lovers didn't see Teddy in the shadowy hallway coming from the opposite end of the corridor but Teddy saw them. He turned around and left the building.

CHAPTER TWENTY NINE
Point Bridge

A week passed since Cathy had been drugged and raped and Teddy hadn't been seen or heard from. Mrs. Bentley called his workplace and he hadn't been to his job in as long a time. They concluded that he saw, heard, or imagined something hurtful and as always, it put him into a spin and he fell victim to the darker side of his troubled mind.

The arrest of Junior and Henry was in the newspapers, but protocol had been followed and the victim's name wasn't disclosed. The women, as well as Jake and Fritz, concluded that Teddy must've found out that Cathy was the victim at the Century. In some strange way this blew his mind from a functional mental state into a dysfunctional condition.

Cathy was worried about him, yet in a selfish way, was glad their strange romantic ties were going to conclude once and for all. With Jake at her side, Teddy would be told to get help and afterwards, prepare to be on his own. If he agreed to seek help for his mental problems, they'd all stand behind him.

Fritz had already arranged for him to be treated at a state institution outside of Pittsburgh for as long as needed. They would all promise to visit him and often. It would be his choice because he would have to volunteer to be institutionalized. Unless when found, he was dysfunctional and unable to earn a wage and live on his own.

When all of the evidence was gathered against Junior and Henry, the County District Attorney became aware of Junior's wealth, and their flight tickets to California. He considered them flight risks and asked for bail to be denied at their arraignment. The Judge concurred and they would face trial for rape, kidnapping, and assault and battery. Cathy expected their trial to be a trial for her also, but with Jake at her side, she'd endure. Their trial would be sorrowful in another way also. Rightfully testifying against Colleen's father would still be a sad moment and as Mrs. Krombach used to say, "vot a luff."

Before Mrs. Bentley left for work, she agreed with Cathy that she should file a missing person report. In that way, should the police come across Teddy under any sort of circumstances, they'd be notified and know he was alive. When Jake came from his home to help her put up a Christmas tree, they sat in the living room and Cathy telephoned the Deutschtown Police Station. She was nervous, fidgeting with the big white buttons that ran down the front of her light grey dress. Jake took her hand and laid their clenched hands on her lap.

"Deutschtown Station, Desk Sergeant." the male voice said.

"I want to file a missing person report."

"Your name?"

"Cathy Bentley."

"Spell it."

She spelled her name.

"Address and telephone number?"

She gave the additional information.

"Now, what's the complaint?"

"It's not a complaint. It's about a missing person. Teddy Vonovich."

"Spell it."

She did.

"What about Vonovich?"

"He's missing. For a week. I'm worried he may be suicidal."

"Did he try to kill himself before?" he asked.

"No."

"Did he ever run away before?"

"Once, years ago." she recalled.

"Where did they find him then?" he asked.

"Deutschtown City Park. He was sleeping on a bench." she answered.

"Well. He'd freeze to death if he did that now." he commented.

There was silence between them for awhile.

"Does he drink?" The Desk Sergeant questioned.

"No, he never touches alcohol. He hates it. His mother was an alcoholic." she reported.

"Why do you think he might commit suicide?" he asked.

"He's depressed about a lot of things. His life has been difficult." she answered.

"Did he ever mention he was going to kill himself?"

"Once, he mentioned jumping off the Point Bridge." Cathy remembered.

"Which one? There's two. The Allegheny and the Monongahela?" he reminded her.

"I know," she paused. "But I don't know."

The Desk Sarge groaned.

"That sounds dumb." she murmured. "I mean, I know there are two Point Bridges, but I don't know which bridge Teddy was talking about jumping off."

"Where does he live?" he asked.

"With me and my mother." Cathy said still murmuring.

"Well." the Sergeant paused. "I'll dispatch a squad car over to the bridges to keep on the lookout. There's a bunch of bums hanging out under the bridges in the winter, huddling around bonfires. We'll check, if we make contact, I'll call you."

"Thank you," Cathy said, hanging up the receiver.

"Teddy mentioned suicide before?" Jake asked.

"I remember him saying it." she said.

Colleen woke up and began crying. "I'll get her." Jake said.

Cathy watched Jake leave the room. He was wearing his Marine Corps boots, blue jeans, and a heavy plaid shirt and wished to be his wife at that moment. She turned her eyes to the box of Christmas decorations on the floor and something new in a box. A small artificial Christmas tree made in occupied Japan. It wouldn't be a merry holiday season with so many troubles. The pending trial, Teddy's craziness, her father and brother ignoring her, even after she'd been raped and brutalized. Skipping the decorations was out of the question. She started opening the box with the fake tree inside and looked around the project apartment wondering where in the hell could Colleen's stocking be hung for Saint Nick to stuff in rooms without fireplaces and mantels.

* * *

Just as they sat down for a leftover supper, Fritz lied to Cathy about how swell the decorated apartment and artificial tree looked. Then the telephone rang before she could thank him for perverting the truth. Cathy answered, "Hello?"

"Miss Bentley?"

"Speaking."

"Desk Sergeant, Deutschtown Station. We've located Teddy Vonovich. He was under the Point Bridge, on the north riverbank with the bums. I think we made the situation worse. We had no intention of arresting him, only to inform him that people were concerned about his whereabouts. Well, he took off running, got up on the bridge, climbed out on an overhanging steel beam, and swore he'd jump."

"Oh, my God." Cathy moaned. The others at the supper table listened intently.

"My officers talked to the bums under the bridge and they said he had joined them about a week ago. They think he's a nut. He keeps mumbling to himself, 'I knew it, I knew it.' When the bums ask what he knew, he'd shut up, then after while, start mumbling again. My problem now is that I can't have my officers walk away because he needs help. Could you come down to the bridge, try to talk him off the overhang and then we'll take him for help?"

"I'll be there."

"A squad car is on the bridge. They'll be expecting you. Thanks, Miss Bentley."

"Oh, my God!" Cathy cried replacing the receiver. She told the others about Teddy's situation. Fritz said he'd drive her and Jake to the bridge. Mrs. Bentley would stay home with Colleen. Fritz kissed Cathy's mom and they bundled up in heavy winter garments, and then rushed to Fritz's automobile. They rode to the bridge in silence.

Fritz drove onto the bridge. The squad car lights were flashing near the middle of the span. Fritz pulled behind the police car. Other reporters were there. Fritz knew them all, including the cops. Cathy rushed to a waving cop beckoning for her to join him at the bridge rail. "Cathy?" he asked.

"Yes."

"Over here." he said.

She went to the bridge railing. The cop pointed to a bundled up Teddy in the dim bridge light, perched on a steel beam. Jake stood beside her. Fritz huddled with the other reporters.

Cathy screamed. "Teddy! Get up here, please. I'm begging you!"

"Well, well, well." Teddy sang. "Look who's here. Mirror, mirror on the wall, who's the prettiest of them all? Cathy Bentley, of course!"

"Teddy, stop it! Come up here, and then we'll talk."

"I feel honored! The prettiest of them all has come to watch Humpty Dumpty take his great fall."

"Please, Teddy. Please come back up here." she pleaded.

"Why?" he asked.

"So we can talk to you." she cried out.

"We can talk? We? Is Prince Charming with you? What am I thinking? Of course he is. Hello, Jacob!"

"I'm here Buddy." Jake answered.

"Buddy? Did I hear Buddy? Is that like Pal? Or best friend? I need help everyone, what's the definition of a buddy? Or buddy-boy? I got it! The new definition is Fool!"

The cop whispered to Cathy. "Keep talking to him. Sometimes after they get all of their anger out with insults, they mellow and choose to live and get help."

"I knew it. I knew it. I knew it." Teddy was mumbling more to himself then Cathy.

"What did you know?" Cathy called down to him. "Please tell me, Teddy?"

"Remember when we fought in the kitchen of the old row house? I got mad that Jake wrote to you from North Carolina. Remember?"

"I remember." Cathy said.

"Remember what I told you?" he asked.

She was thinking, trying to bring up their fight in her mind's eye. "I remember fighting, but we made up quickly."

"I said I saw something. And you said, 'Teddy, that's silly, you can't see a...' Come on Cathy, you can recall."

"A feeling."

"Bingo! Now do you believe you can see a feeling?"

"Yes." she answered softly. "Then this bridge sitting is about me and Jake and not something else?"

"Bingo, give the lady a prize! And the prize is, not a Teddy-bear, but a Jobless Jake!" Then he added in a softer tone. "What do you mean, something else?"

She looked at Jake and whispered. "He doesn't know about the Century?"

"I guess not." Jake whispered back.

"You're a swimmer, Cathy. If I jump, float on my back, passing the Point, go down the Ohio and into the Mississippi, how long will it take me to reach New Orleans, and...?"

Teddy kept rambling. Cathy and Jake huddled. They were lost as to how Teddy had found out how serious their relationship had gotten unless he knew they were telephoning one another, which seemed unlikely. If she told him they were in love and going to marry, he'd jump they were certain. She answered his nonsense. "You're not a log, Teddy."

He laughed. "I love you, Cathy. I will not live without you in my life. Marry me. And I'll come up."

She didn't know what to say. Jake whispered an answer to her. She nodded and answered Teddy.

"That's emotional blackmail, Teddy. I want to be the bride of a man that knows I love him and wasn't forced into the marriage. You know I love you, but not..."

"Stop lying!" he screamed. "About loving me! Haven't you ever read *Alice in Wonderland*? What she said to the White Queen?"

"You didn't let me finish saying..."

"Stop it! Stop it! Stop it! Stop this nonsense of loving me! *Alice* was right. *You can't believe impossible things.*"

"Okay, Teddy. Please calm down, please."

"Answer me, Cathy. What broke the camel's back and brought me to this deadly perch?"

"I don't know, Teddy. Please come up and we'll talk about it."

"Take a guess and maybe I'll come up. Guess, Cathy."

She looked at Jake, and shrugged.

"The Century Hotel?"

"The Century!" Teddy snarled. "What's the Century have to do with us?"

"I'll tell you why I said 'the Century' when you climb up here."

"Great, now there's more behind my back stuff that I don't know about. Guess again!"

Cathy grabbed Jake's hand. She was feeling certain that he was going to jump.

"I'm waiting, Cathy. Jobless Jake, give her a clue."

"It could only be our behind his back telephone calls," Jake told Cathy.

"Telephone calls to Jake." Cathy shouted down to Teddy.

He laughed. "Telephone calls, you'd think I'd kill myself for telephone calls? I expected telephone calls between the two of you. I knew it; I knew that you had the right feeling for each other. I told you I saw the feeling. But no, no, no, you said. Silly Teddy, you can't see a feeling. Wrong answer. Guess again, Prettiest of them all."

"I don't know." she answered. "Please come to me, Teddy and we'll talk this out. Me, you, and Jake. Please."

"Talk this out. We'll talk this out when Jobless Jake changes half as many poopy diapers on Colleen as I have. Or cuddled her when she was cutting baby teeth. Or finger tasting mush and baby formula, until I now like its flavor. Or watching a million hours of Howdy Doody, freeing the Prettiest to do her household chores without a worry or care because her child was in the good and loving hands of her Fool. I know them all, Buffalo Bob, Clarabelle, Princess..."

"Teddy, stop it, please!" she was sobbing. "Please come up, for Colleen's sake!"

"Guess again, Cathy, if you want me to come up."

"Please, Teddy, you're killing me. There are things you don't know that has happened to me since you haven't been home. Nasty things, please..."

He stopped her. "Nasty things? Nasty for me!"

"What on earth are you talking about?" she pleaded. "Please tell me."

"I saw you and Jobless Jake all over one another outside of our apartment in the corridor, when I was coming home from my job. At sunrise, no less! Did you serve him breakfast after his graveyard shift at loving you before he went home? Seeing the two of you was my nasty breakfast after a hard night at work. Seeing a girl that is supposed to be keeping her desires stored up for me but was releasing them on Jobless. He had a kissing motor mouth and you were glued onto him so tight, I thought he was dressed in flypaper. How long has that been going on? Any wonder Jobless doesn't work. He's too exhausted after you're done with him."

The cop came to Cathy. "Hang in there; he's going to simmer down. I've seen it before."

"Well, aren't you going to lie? Tell me I was sleepwalking or some other crazy answer."

Cathy couldn't keep the truth from him any longer and he knew the truth anyway.

"Teddy, you're right. I do love Jake."

"I knew it."

Everyone was quiet for quite awhile. Everyone was afraid to speak.

Finally Teddy spoke, asking softly. "Are you and Jake getting married?"

Cathy answered and she was crying. "Yes, Teddy. But I do love you, too."

"I know." he said. "When?"

"Soon." she tried to humor him. "After Jobless gets a job."

Teddy laughed. "By then you'll be on Social Security."

"Please come up, Teddy." Cathy pleaded. "Colleen loves you."

Everyone went silent again.

"Well, I'll get out of your hair and give you my wedding present now." he said and stood up on the beam.

The weather was changing, getting cooler and windy.

"Teddy, please come..."

He cut her off. He was crying, sobbing loudly. "Get me help, Cathy, please. My wedding gift is that I'm coming up. I'd never ruin your wedding, I love you too much."

"Oh, thank you, God," Cathy screamed.

Teddy started walking along the overhanging beam. He was cold and stiff and his eyes bleary with tears. A gust of wind blew up from under the bridge. He staggered, lost his balance and fell.

Before they heard the splash, Cathy had her shoes off and started climbing over the rail yelling. "He can't swim!"

Jake grabbed her, yanking her away from the rail. "Cathy, the water is too cold, honey." She quit struggling and collapsed into Jake's arms like a helpless child. Then she heard the cop.

"They got him."

"Cathy perked up. "What? Who?"

"The River Patrol." the policeman said. "The Desk Sergeant alerted them earlier. They drifted under the bridge a while ago with their motor off and lights out. Sometimes it's best for them to hide and wait. It worked out good tonight."

They all gathered around the squad car, awaiting the radio transmission from the boat. The broadcast came.

"Somewhat dazed and cold, but he'll be fine. Transporting to shore for further transport to a hospital. Over and out."

Cathy leaped on Fritz, gave him a kiss. Then she did the same to every cop and reporter on the bridge, while yelling "Merry Christmas."

PART THREE
Summertime 1955

"We are tomorrow's past."
Mary Shelley, British Novelist of Frankenstein

CHAPTER THIRTY
Ouch

When the homes lining both sides of Brookhurst Road, including the Owl's Mart, were demolished, the road was widened. The cobblestones and trolley tracks were asphalted over to the end of the trolley line at the loop and into the heart of the North Slope. The North Slope homeowners bitterly protested to City Hall, claiming the politicians had broken their promise by expanding construction into their side of Pigeon Hill.

City Hall dismissed their concern, claiming the entire Pigeon Hill community was now served by bus. When the Mayor's representative addressed the homeowners at a meeting with what they surmised a fifth-grade explanation of the obvious, that cobblestone roads were fine for trolleys that rode on tracks, but are bumpy for bus riders, the North Slope citizens lost faith. Property values started dropping, and *for sale* signs littered the lawns. Displaced Pigeon Hill citizens living in the projects began buying the homes using their relocation money given by the government as down payments.

The Republicans were being driven into the hinterland and Pigeon Hill's North Slope was expected to be solidly Democratic by the next mayoral election. Jake secured a job at the steel mill where Susan's father worked and using his GI benefit, purchased a grand old three story house on the North Slope with enough room for him and his family, Struss and his mother. Jake, Cathy, and Colleen moved in after Easter week and Struss and Jake's mother would be moving in soon after.

Cathy's mother moved into Fritz's bachelor pad located on Pittsburgh's Mount Washington. It had a panorama view of the Steel City from the bedroom window. Her mother decided to move in with FritzDerLip before their planned June wedding after Cathy eloped and moved away. She was concerned about living alone in the projects when, from time to time, Fritz needed to leave town for a special sporting event. They often went to the Century together in the morning, and came home together at night.

She'd never been so happy. The only disagreement that came between them was their wedding. She wanted a small wedding service with a small celebration after uniting. Fritz and his big German family wanted a huge event. The family, for traditional reasons. Fritz, on the other hand, for selfish reasons. He longed to invite his friends from the GermanAmerikaner, the Pittsburgh main media and newspapers, and quite a few professional ball-players from Pittsburgh and other cities. It was going to be much more than a wedding. It was going to be a Sports-A-Rama, but she agreed to allow it to occur.

She loved Fritz, she loved her family, she loved her job, and she loved God and her life. Her only sorrow was Carl. But he was young, and in time, perhaps he'd come around and once again become her son. She could only petition God in her prayers. To enlighten Carl to see the truth, that his mother and sister aren't the harlots as his father had tagged them.

Jake and his wife lay on their bed, enjoying their love for each other and talking over the normal concerns of a working-man's family. They also discussed Teddy's progress at the mental facility and the ugly subject of Henry and Junior's crime.

A morning sunray pierced the high ceiling bedroom through the window; the kind of big window Cathy loved and missed in the projects. As they did since eloping, weekend mornings were passed ticktocking time away in each others arms and for as long as they could before Colleen awakened. She now called Jake, "Daddy."

Jake ran his finger softly over Cathy's lips as he often did before kissing her. He gently kissed her. Cathy responded as always, by murmuring her love for him. After satisfying their love and lust for one another, they discussed Teddy's surprising interest in another woman and the latest news about Henry and Junior's trial.

"Your Mom said that?" Jake asked. "Teddy and a part time nurse at the institute got caught in a compromising situation?"

"Yes." Cathy giggled. "You've seen her. The tall nurse we'd see tending to him like a mother hen on our visits."

"She looks a few years older than him." he said.

"They fired her, but Teddy told Mom she already got hired at the veteran's hospital. She's a former army nurse, served in Korea, and according to Teddy, they love each other, and as soon as he is released, he's moving in with her."

"Good for Teddy!" Jake said.

"Fritz checked around. Apparently she's quite a nurse. Works part time and is continuing her medical education under the GI bill at Pitt's medical school."

"Good." Jake said. "Teddy's smart and can be very funny, outside of his dark side. I still consider him my best childhood friend."

"I know." Cathy said. "I think everything is going to turn out okay for him and life will deal him a better hand at last."

"We'll find out more when we visit him." Jake said

"Enough talk about Teddy." Cathy grinned and wiggled up against Jake. The telephone rang.

Jake reached to the bed stand and answered. It was Susan. She sounded excited and wanted to speak with Cathy. Jake played with Cathy's hair while she spoke with Susan. By Cathy's answers and questions to Susan, it was obvious something big occurred regarding Henry and Junior's trial. He heard Colleen crying from her bedroom. He leaned into Cathy and kissed her on the cheek. Playtime was over for him. He went for Colleen to bring her back to their bed.

When he came back with his daughter and climbed back into bed beside Cathy, Jake was brought up to date on the saga of Henry and Junior. The District Attorney scared the farts out of Henry with life in prison, unless he'd turn on Junior and rat him out for a lighter sentence. Henry went for it and would be given twenty years without a chance of parole.

When Junior heard Henry was ratting him out and with all the other evidence against him, he pleaded for a deal. The District Attorney offered a life sentence with a chance of parole after thirty years if he would plead guilty. Junior accepted. Sentencing would be only a matter of the Judge accepting their plea and ordering their sentence. Cathy would have to attend, but not have to take the stand. She was ecstatic and buried her face into Jake's chest.

Jake hugged her and Colleen. "What a break!" she said. "Thank God."

"There's more news." Cathy mumbled into his skin. "Susan's lawyer wants to file civil charges against Junior on my behalf. Sue him for any money he still has, which could be very much since there will be no trial. Her lawyer said it will be a slam-dunk."

Jake took her by the chin and looked into her face. "What did you tell Susan?"

"I said on one condition. After the lawyer gets his cut, we split the rest of the money, fifty-fifty."

Jake chuckled. "What did Susan say?"

"That she loves me."

Cathy took Colleen from Jake and pulled the covers up over all of their heads. "God, I love you both," she murmured. And then bit her husband on his shoulder, as a way to release some of the desire that she had for him at that moment.

"Ouch!" Jake complained.

"Get used to it, Marine'!" Cathy warned and bit him again.

CHAPTER THIRTY ONE
Over the Hill

After Jake and some friends loaded the rented truck with the last of his parent's belongings from the project apartment, he climbed into the cab behind the steering wheel. Struss sat in the passenger seat beside his son. As the truck moved through the projects, Struss sat quietly observing the new broad concrete streets and wide sidewalks. Struss was glad to put the projects behind him when Jake turned the truck up the steep slope toward the top of Pigeon Hill.

Up the newly paved and widened street they rode. With fewer winding turns on the new, but still steep road, they got to the Resurrection Cemetery entrance gate soon. Struss hadn't been to the crest of Pigeon Hill since he'd moved into the projects. Where the Owl's Mart once stood was a playground and basketball court. They rode over the top of the hill and down into the North Slope.

"Brookhurst doesn't seem the same without twists and turns." Struss said. "The road curves gave the hillside character."

"It's not Brookhurst any longer." Jake said. "The official name is Pyramid Pike."

"Yuk! Who's the camel head at city hall that came up with that name?" Struss growled. "I've never seen a humping camel, let alone an Egyptian in Deutschtown."

Jake slowed the truck. "Dad, see that truck coming up the road? That's the new Owl's Mart. He drives around the projects selling basic necessities like bread, toilet paper, mostly nonperishable stuff. It's a convenience for those people without a car and that's how he promotes his business. Owl's convenient mobile store."

Jake slowed down as they passed the truck with a big owl painted on its side. Struss stretched his neck to get a good look at the truck. "Old Lady Miller would spin in her grave if she saw her General Store on wheels."

"I saw the Jew last week." Jake said. "I told him you were moving in with me. He said he's retiring soon, but he'll stop and visit you before he hangs up his homburg for good. He doesn't go into the projects. Said it's too confusing, hard to keep track of who lives where and he doesn't like the buildings with those long corridors."

"They're all gone, the iceman, coalman, knife sharpener, peddlers, horse and wagon hucksters. All gone, and now the Jew." Struss sighed and mimicked Mrs. Krombach. "Vot a luff."

The truck rolled down into the heart of the North Slope, passing the paved over trolley loop tracks. Reaching Herman the German's Saloon, Struss started feeling less down in the dumps. The entrance door was open and he could hear music, familiar German polkas coming from inside the crowded barroom. Herman's would be an easy way, and nice place to mourn his lost life, and in the company of tribal kin. A place where losers like him and the Jew could feel right at home. He'd invite the Jew to Herman the German's to celebrate his soon retirement.

The truck turned onto the street where Jake lives. The old homes lifted Struss' heart further and it felt a bit like home inside the outsider's territory. Struss looked out the door window. He scanned the skies. No pigeon flocks were flying.

EPILOGUE
Love

Friends of Fritz were already calling her Lady FritzDerLip with the wedding only two weeks away. The wedding service would be held at the majestic Heinz Chapel near the University of Pittsburgh, with the reception at the Great Hall in Deutschtown.

She lost count at how many people were attending, but was assured by Fritz's parents and family, that there would be plenty of food and drink for however many showed. Fritz had many friends and she worried if they all showed from across the country, the Great Hall and its beer garden wouldn't be enough to contain the crowd. Fritz's answer to her concerns were always the same. A kiss, a smile, and reassurance not to worry, because everything would be grand.

She wore a knee length terrycloth bathrobe and around her neck hung Fritz's army field glasses that he used at sporting events. Through the elongated windowpane of their apartment on Mount Washington's bluff, she had a panoramic view of downtown Pittsburgh. Using the binoculars, she could see across Pittsburgh's Golden Triangle to Deutschtown and Pigeon Hill.

From afar, the elimination and replacement of the Pigeon Hill community appeared to be done in a small and orderly confined area. When she resided on Pigeon Hill, throughout its demolition and rebirth as a government developed community, destruction seemed widespread and hectic.

She viewed the new Pigeon Hill through Fritz's binoculars to verify what she had been told by Cathy, that the wooden public steps were being torn down and rebuilt with concrete. The old steps were kept in place until the hilly winding streets were eliminated or widened, leaving the walking citizens with still a means to get up and down the hillside. She could see the men, working like ants, tearing the steps apart and toting the old lumber down the hillside to awaiting trucks. She was glad that speck of a place would be taken from her sight.

She heard Fritz pounding away on his typewriter. He was writing his last article for the GermanAmerikaner. The paper was shutting its printing presses down forever. There wasn't enough German reading customers to keep it profitable. The competition from Pittsburgh newspapers issuing morning, noon, and late afternoon editions, was too overwhelming for the English edition of the GermanAmerikaner to make a profit. Fritz was immediately hired by the Pittsburgh Sun-Telegraph.

The typewriter went silent and she heard the paper being pulled from the roller. He had finished writing his last article in both German and English for the GermanAmerikaner. She knew Fritz would miss writing German for publication, but times change and for her, the changing was good.

She removed the binoculars and packed them inside of Fritz's traveling bag. She poured a cup of coffee she had made earlier for her Sport Reporter, who needed black coffee while composing his witty writings. She sat at the kitchen table and waited for him to bring the English copy for her to read. He loved when she would laugh at his comic descriptions about life and sports and she loved being made to laugh by his funny writings. She wasn't expecting many laughs in his final article.

He entered the kitchen in his underwear and handed her the English written article, then went to shower and shave. His eyes were slightly bloodshot. He'd been crying. She said nothing to him, nor tried to comfort him, letting him keep the sad moment for himself. She swallowed some hot coffee and began reading the GermanAmerikaner's obituary.

After the first sentence, she saw teardrop stains on the margin. She quit reading and dropped the paper onto the table. She changed her mind, deciding to comfort him after seeing his tears on the paper. She'd finish reading his last article later.

She went into the steamy bathroom, dropped her robe onto the floor, and slithered into the warm shower and caressed him. They embraced and kissed. Fritz put his sadness aside, stroked her wet, red hair and murmured, "I love you, Arlene."

The End
&
Aufwiedersehen

Addendum #1

Back in the 1930's, the United States was struggling through the Great Depression. During the late 1940's, the country was recovering from World War II and rationing. By the 1950's, America was at war once again in Korea against the universal spread of communism. It was during those decades, when baseball was the king of sports in America that sandlot football thrived in urban communities.

On barren dirt neighborhood fields, lads faced off with a football, often poorly protected from the brutal hits and crushing blows they would experience for no other reason than they believed it to be fun. They never expected to be written about or even known outside of the streets where they played and lived. In the novel, *Deutschtown's Pigeon Hill*, the newspaper clip on *The Pigeon Hill Arrows* is fashioned after an authentic Pittsburgh sandlot football team, *The Spring Hill Arrows*. Below is a roster of the 1954/55 *Spring Hill Arrows*, *No Glory League* coaches and players.

Coaches	Players	
Eddie Stebler	Don Adametz	B. Klein
Syl Heller	Bill Barie	Frank Klein
Jack Schanbacher	Bob Bauer	Ernie Konecny
Don Willy	Bill Benzer	Ambrose Korn
John Herzer	Joe Borza	Richie Krist

Pete Hoffman	Chuck Bummer	Tom Lyons
Joe Schrott	Joe Frankovich	Ray Massey
Ambrose Bummer	Bob Galley	Ron Moore
	Al Greco	Lou Pail
	Rich Graf	Don Peshek
	Jim Harvey	Bob Pryor
	Charlie Herrmann	Ray Short
	Richie Hirt	Jimmy Stebler
	Jim Huckstein	Ed Werner
	Don Hein	John Wilson
	Bill Johnson	Sam Winghart

Addendum #2

The Pittsburgh Press article mentioned in the Deutschtown's Pigeon Hill novel, whereas Pittsburgh lays claim to being the birthplace of the Republican Party is authentic, as printed in the Sunday Edition dated June 10th, 1928, page 17 of the editorial section. The birthplace title for the Grand Old Party is also claimed by the cities of Ripon, Wisconsin and Jackson, Michigan. However, the first GOP National Convention was held in Pittsburgh in 1856. Abraham Lincoln attended as a delegate from Illinois.

About the Author

Enlisting as a Private in the Marine Corps only days after his seventeenth birthday, Ambrose remained a Marine for twenty years, serving in the United Sates, the Caribbean, Asia and on the high seas. He retired a Captain and lives in Western Pennsylvania with his wife, Doris.

Made in the USA
Lexington, KY
21 March 2012